The Boss

CAZ FINLAY

KILLER
~~**READS**~~

A division of HarperCollins*Publishers*
www.harpercollins.co.uk

KillerReads
an imprint of HarperCollins*Publishers* Ltd
1 London Bridge Street
London SE1 9GF

www.harpercollins.co.uk

This paperback edition 2019

First published in Great Britain in ebook format by HarperCollins*Publishers* 2019

A catalogue record for this book
is available from the British Library

ISBN: 978-0-00-834068-1

This novel is entirely a work of fiction.
The names, characters and incidents portrayed in it are
the work of the author's imagination. Any resemblance to
actual persons, living or dead, events or localities is
entirely coincidental.

Set in Minion by
Palimpsest Book Production Limited, Falkirk, Stirlingshire

Printed and bound in the UK

For Jude, Fin and James.
You inspire me every single day

CHAPTER ONE

Present Day

Grace Sumner steeled herself against the bar, her fingers splayed against the cool, polished wood as though it could ground her somehow. It was the moment she'd been expecting for a long time and finally there he was – Nathan Conlon, or Nate as she'd once affectionately called him. The pub was as busy as usual for a Friday night in Liverpool; but from the moment she saw his face, it was as though there was no one else in the room but the two of them. The constant chatter, the laughter – the incessant din of the place – faded into the background, until she could hear nothing but the blood rushing in her ears. She knew he'd make his way back into her life one day. His arrival was no surprise. She'd thought about nothing else for days.

But nothing could have prepared her for seeing that man's face again.

He scanned the room quickly as he entered. Was he looking for her? For a moment, she thought their eyes met, but perhaps she'd imagined it? There was no recognition from him if they did. She took a moment to appraise him; he still had those incredible blue eyes and that smile that could make you forget your own name. He had a beard now too, and not one of those ridiculous hipster ones which seemed to be in fashion, but a neat one, which framed his strong jawline. It looked good on him. The dark grey suit he was wearing fitted him perfectly. He'd always looked good in a suit. He was bigger than she remembered. No doubt all that free time he'd had to work out in the gym.

It had been a long time since she'd seen him, but the image of him was burned into her retinas like the negative of a photograph. He was still the best-looking man she had ever seen. Gliding through the crowded bar effortlessly, he smiled at everyone. Friends, acquaintances or strangers – it didn't matter to Nathan, who was always equally comfortable in anyone's presence. He was one of those people that everybody loved to be around – well almost everybody.

He was the first man she'd ever loved, the first man she'd ever made love to. The irony of that didn't escape her. Because he was also the man who'd given her nightmares for the past nineteen years, the man she feared more than anyone or anything else in the world: her ex-husband, and the father of her only child. A shudder ran down the length of Grace's spine as she remembered what he was capable of and what he would do if he ever found out about the things she'd done.

'Another pint please, Grace,' one of the regulars piped up, and the world around her came back into focus. She poured the drink as if on autopilot and smiled as the next customer signalled for some service, but her thoughts returned to Nathan. Released on licence from prison the week before, he was there to see their son, Jake. Eighteen years old and practically his father's doppelganger. She hoped that Nathan had changed; after all, she had – a lot could happen in twelve years. His new girlfriend, Kayleigh, was with him. Grace assumed it was her at least. It didn't escape her attention how young Kayleigh was. Beautiful too, and much more suited to Nathan in Grace's opinion, with her long blonde hair, tiny waist and perfect figure.

Grace watched Jake as he fiddled with the collar of his shirt; so anxious for his father's approval, it terrified her. What would their son do if he knew the truth about the man he idolized?

'Dad!' Jake beamed, his face full of adulation, as Nathan approached him and wrapped him in a bear hug. He tousled his son's hair as though he were still a small child. They began talking animatedly, although Grace was too far away to hear their conversation. But she could see Jake visibly relax and the two of them were laughing. Kayleigh was smiling proudly as she took hold of Nathan's arm, clinging onto him like a limpet.

Try as she might, Grace couldn't seem to focus on any one task for too long. Shifting constantly from one job to another, clearing glasses, wiping spillages, serving customers. Stopping to chat from time to time, she found herself unable to hold even a simple conversation. She was about to ask one of the regulars, Crazy Len, just why he was wearing a flower in his lapel when the crowd parted, creating a direct path to the bar. Grace had only ever seen one man have that sort of effect on a crowded pub and he was making his way over towards her. She wanted to walk away and pretend she hadn't seen them, but her legs were rooted to the spot. Feeling the once-familiar knot in her stomach, she swallowed the bile rising in her throat. Her face frozen in some sort of non-expression, as though it was waiting to be told what the appropriate reaction should be.

'Grace,' Nathan smiled, all charm and perfect teeth. Taking her hand, he leaned in towards her. 'You've let yourself go, haven't you, love?' he said quietly, before giving her a brief kiss on the cheek. He laughed; a sound she'd once mistaken for being warm and friendly, she now recognized as cruel and mocking.

She forced a smile in return. God, he was such an arrogant prick!

Grace noticed Kayleigh looking her up and down before extending her hand. Obviously, Kayleigh had decided that she was no threat to her. If only she knew.

3

Grace made some drinks for them; she didn't usually drink when she was working, but she had a brandy. Pretended that she too was drinking to celebrate Nathan's triumphant return, but it was a futile attempt to steady her nerves. For all intents and purposes they looked like any family, making polite conversation and laughing at each other's jokes. Kayleigh and Nathan seemed happy and in love. But outward appearances could be deceiving. Grace, of all people, knew that. However, there was no reason to believe that Nathan wanted anything from her – not anymore. As far as he was concerned, she had nothing left to offer him. So, she went back to serving her customers, thankful that their first encounter in twelve years was as uneventful as she'd hoped. Nathan had moved on, and she was simply a footnote in his past.

As closing time approached, the pub was empty, except for Jake, Nathan and Kayleigh, who were huddled around a table in the corner. Grace wanted them to leave too so she could go upstairs and finish cashing up. She'd moved out of the flat above the pub two years earlier because living in such a small place with a stroppy teenager who enjoyed playing his music so loud it made the windows rattle, sometimes made her feel like the walls were closing in. But if Grace was honest, she'd always dreamed of owning a nice house with a garden, and a proper kitchen. Once Jake was old enough to look after himself in the evenings, she'd bought them a beautiful little detached house just outside Liverpool. She still used the flat for storage and as an office, and she stayed there occasionally when she was too tired to face the drive back home.

Approaching their table, she could see Jake grinning inanely. His head rolled around on his shoulders as though it were only held on by a piece of string.

'You need to get yourself to bed and sleep this off,' she told him, pulling him to his feet. 'Nathan, can you make sure he gets home safely?'

'Of course, Grace. I'll look after my boy.' Nathan slurred as he stood up and gave Jake a slap on the back.

Grace arranged a taxi for the three of them and they fell out of the pub into the warm night air.

Twenty minutes later Grace was closing the safe in the office upstairs when she heard the heavy tread of feet on the stairway, making her stop and freeze mid-motion. The doors were all locked, weren't they? She was always so careful about that. Yes, she'd definitely locked the doors and set the alarm for the whole place, except for the back entrance to the flat. Besides, no one would be stupid enough to try and knock off the Rose and Crown. Would they? It must have been Jake coming back. Why had she relied on Nathan to get him home?

But what if it wasn't Jake?

Picking up the golf club she kept in her office as a precaution, she edged away from the safe, fooling herself into believing that the piece of iron would offer some protection from whoever was walking up those stairs. Swearing under her breath, she realized she'd left her mobile phone in her handbag, which was hanging out of reach near the front door.

The door swung open to reveal a grinning Nathan. Jake's keys dangled from his fingers. Her heart almost stopped. In an instant, she was transported back to a time when he would walk through that door, and she would experience that seemingly eternal moment of not knowing what type of mood he'd be in, in constant fear of what would happen next.

Grace's mouth felt so dry she couldn't even swallow, although she tried to anyway. She had to make a conscious effort to stop her hands from shaking, but she was not the same scared young girl he'd once known. The things she'd done, the choices she'd made – they had shaped her into a different person.

'What do you want, Nathan? Where's Jake?'

'Relax, Grace. Kayleigh is taking him home, and I told her I was going to see an old friend. That's true, isn't it? We are old friends, aren't we?' He moved towards her and she bristled. 'I thought you might like some company,' he leered. 'And I don't mind slipping you one for old times' sake.'

'You're drunk, Nathan. Please go home. Kayleigh will be waiting for you.' She sighed, putting down the golf club; it offered her no protection against him.

'Haven't you missed me then?'

She laughed. It was a dangerous move, but she couldn't help it. 'Missed you? The man who made my life hell? No I really haven't.'

He smiled and sat on the desk, before grabbing her by the hips and pulling her to him until she was standing between his legs. Moving his hands to her behind, he pressed her body into his groin until she could feel how hard he was. He smelled good, of soap and expensive aftershave. The heat from his hands penetrated the thin fabric of her skirt. She used to love those hands, the feel of them on her skin, in her hair, on the small of her back. Hands that once knew her so intimately.

Looking into his eyes, she saw they were glassy from the whisky he'd been drinking, and who knew what else. But it seemed like they could still bore right into the deepest part of her. There was a time she truly believed that he could read her mind. So much so, it made her unable to look him in the eye towards the end of their marriage, for fear he would discover some truth she didn't want him to know. But not anymore. She stared at him, confident in the knowledge that he would never know, not unless she wanted him to at least. He would never believe his naive little Grace could be capable of such things. What if she told him though? The look on his face. That would be something worth seeing.

What would have happened if things had been different? Could she have saved him? Would they have had a home full of children? Retired to the country and lived in a big old house, and kept chickens and horses? She smiled fleetingly at that thought before she was pulled sharply back to reality as Nathan tried to kiss her, the smell of whisky on his breath invoking so many contrasting memories. Pushing him away, she managed to wriggle from his grip.

'This is not the welcome I was expecting from you, Grace. I'm disappointed in you. And you know I don't like to be disappointed,' he said, the cold edge creeping into his voice.

It was a threat and she knew it; but maybe she'd forgotten what it felt like to be hurt by him. After all, there was nothing he could do to her that he hadn't already done. So, rather than giving in to him like the old Grace would, she replied with a threat of her own.

'Aren't you on licence now, Nathan? Doesn't that mean you have to behave yourself or you can be carted back off to prison to serve the rest of your sentence? I'm sure a phone call to your probation officer about you beating up your ex-wife would justify hauling you back there pretty quickly, wouldn't it?'

The change in him was instant, his handsome face distorted with rage. He took hold of her face with his hand, his fingers squeezing her cheeks. 'You are playing a dangerous fucking game,' he spat. 'Be careful, Grace.'

And then he was gone.

She sat in the chair before her legs gave way beneath her. How had she once loved that man with every fibre of her being?

But that was a lifetime ago. Grace Sumner was no longer the naive little girl who'd fallen in love with the man of her dreams. She was a woman with a past of her own. Nathan thought he knew her. He had no idea.

CHAPTER TWO

Replaying the events of the previous night over and over in her head, Grace pondered what a fool she'd been thinking Nathan might have changed. He'd made Grace's life hell for the first couple of years he'd been in prison. First it was the constant phone calls, then there were the visits. Always someone sitting at the end of the bar glaring at her, watching her every move. Always someone to deliver a message that she'd better watch her back, because apparently, the only thing that kept her safe was being Mrs Conlon. What a laugh!

John Brennan was okay, though. She'd met him once before when he'd come to their flat one night when Nathan had almost died from an overdose of ketamine. He used to call in on his way home, go through the motions and reiterate the same tired threat. Then Grace would pull him a pint and make him a sandwich.

'Can't you just put up with being his missus, Grace?' he'd ask her. 'Isn't it easier than all this?'

'No, John. It's not,' she'd tell him.

It was a price worth paying for her freedom. After all, she'd endured much worse than the occasional threat and menacing glare.

Then one day it all stopped. No more threatening phone calls.

No more visits from his henchmen to try and scare her. He'd signed the divorce papers she'd sent him and, except for the occasional phone call when he felt lonely, he'd left her in relative peace.

Then shortly before Jake's sixteenth birthday, she asked him what he'd like for a present, thinking he'd ask for a new computer or some sort of gadget. Her head had almost popped off her shoulders when Jake had revealed that what he wanted more than anything was to visit his dad in prison. She couldn't have been more shocked if he'd asked for a trip to the moon.

Of course, she'd told him no. It was then that Jake revealed he'd been in almost daily phone contact with his father for nearly two years. How had she not noticed? How had Jake been able to lie to her all that time? He said he was sorry, that he hadn't wanted to hide it from her, but he knew she'd go crazy and try to put a stop to it. And how could Grace argue with that? He was right.

Grace had always tried to prevent Jake from discovering the full extent of Nathan's violent temper. He'd been so young when Nathan had been sent to prison and, given Nathan's propensity to remain on the missing list for a lot of the time, the two of them had never developed a close bond.

After Nathan had been sent to prison, Grace had never told Jake much about him. She thought the less he knew, the better. She certainly didn't want him to know what a monster his father truly was. In hindsight, she realized that pretending Nathan never existed was a huge mistake. With no other information to go on, Nathan became some enigmatic, mythical figure in Jake's mind. By the time Grace learned of their contact, Nathan had cemented himself in Jake's life as the most incredible father in the world; a legend, who was only doing time because he was trying to provide for his family.

Despite having to endure a year of Jake's moody teenage stroppiness and his constant declarations that his father was a changed man, Grace would never agree to let him visit Nathan in prison.

She confiscated his mobile phone, but Nathan procured him another one and then another. Jake told her there was nothing she could do to prevent him from contacting his dad, and as much as that aggravated and, if she was honest, scared the hell out of her, she knew he was right. So, in the end she'd relented. She realized that he'd only keep speaking with Nathan in secret and if she at least pretended to accept their communication he could be open with her about it. She thought that would allow her at least some insight into their relationship, and thereby give her some modicum of control.

For Nathan's part, he seemed to adore Jake and appeared to have accepted that he and Grace were long over. According to Jake, he only ever asked if Grace was doing okay and nothing more.

Shortly after Jake turned seventeen, Nathan was transferred to an open prison and started having home leave. *Release on temporary licence* they called it. Jake would sneak off to meet him, much to Grace's annoyance. But short of locking her son in his room, she could see no way of preventing the two of them meeting up. Thankfully, Nathan always stayed away from the pub, and well away from her, and from what Jake told her, his dad seemed to have become an entirely different person.

Jake almost had her convinced for a while, but Grace didn't buy it. Nathan was incapable of behaving like a decent human being for any length of time. He could be the most charming man on the planet when he wanted to be, but it never lasted. He was a master manipulator, earning himself super-dad status from the confines of a prison cell. God knew what kind of influence he could exert now that he was out. If Jake followed in his father's footsteps, she didn't know what she would do. It pained her to even think about it, making her stomach contract and her throat feel like it was closing over. She would never let Nathan taint him. Not her sweet, precious boy.

Jake looked so much like his father, from the smile to the same blue eyes. He had the same confidence, too. Fortunately, that was where the similarities ended. Jake had always been a sweet and caring child. There was many a time he would come home from school with some stray or injured animal he'd found, and he would plead with his mum to keep it. The flat, and then the house, sometimes resembled a menagerie.

Providing he passed all of his exams, Jake would be off to university in a few months to study business and economics. Grace had worked hard to provide him with the best opportunities in life; sent him to the best private schools, made sure he always had everything he wanted. She would have been proud of him no matter what path he chose, but she was so pleased that he'd decided to go to university. Her heart could almost burst with pride whenever she looked at him. He was the most precious thing in the world to her.

Despite her hatred for Nathan, he had at least given her Jake, and because of that a part of her would always be connected to him. Grace knew that she would never escape him entirely, so she'd had to figure out a way to protect herself from him instead. And she had, making sure that she would never again be at the mercy of the monster she'd married.

Grace had no doubt that Nathan believed he'd made the decision to stop harassing her entirely on his own. He would never have done so otherwise. She knew him too well; knew exactly how to play him. Smiling to herself, she recalled the night she'd met a man named Patrick Carter. An encounter that would change her life beyond all recognition and lead to the realization that she could play Nathan Conlon at his own game – and win.

CHAPTER THREE

Ten Years Earlier

Grace watched as the attractive man in the suit threaded his way through the crowd towards the bar. He looked vaguely familiar to her, and she was sure she'd met him before but couldn't place him.

'Pint of Stella please, love,' he said.

'Coming right up,' she smiled as she set about pulling his pint.

'Grace Sumner, isn't it?' he asked.

She nodded, surprised that he knew her maiden name. Most people knew her as Conlon now, much to her annoyance. 'Do I know you?' she asked.

'You used to,' he smiled. 'But I've not seen you since you were a dot.'

'I thought I knew your face.'

'Patrick Carter.' He extended his hand to shake. 'You can call me Pat. I knew your dad. We went way back.'

Grace knew his name. Patrick Carter was a Liverpool legend. He'd worked for Nathan's old boss, Tommy McNulty, and she wondered briefly if he'd worked for Nathan too. Carter had a reputation for being as hard as nails. Rumour had it he'd once been jumped by a rival firm. Six of them had taken him on and all six had ended up in intensive care, while Patrick had escaped with nothing more than a cut lip.

'Oh, you were one of *those* friends, were you?' she teased him.

'What's that supposed to mean?' he laughed.

'I know all about my dad's colourful past, Pat. And no offence, but you look just the type.'

'I wasn't aware we all looked the same,' he chuckled.

'Yes.' She nodded as she passed him his drink. 'Trust me. I used to be married to one of you lot.'

Patrick nodded. 'Yeah, I know. Nathan Conlon.'

Grace bristled. Mentally checking that her mobile phone was in her trouser pocket should she need to call someone to escort Mr Carter from the premises. Nathan's former colleagues, John or Ben would do that for her if she asked.

'Look, if you're here to settle old scores with Nathan then you'd better think again. I have nothing to do with him anymore. This place is sod all to do with him.'

Patrick shook his head. 'Not at all. I've just got out after a long stretch. Only got out a couple of months ago. I was sorry to hear about your dad,' he said. 'I just wanted to pay my respects and see what the old place looked like. I spent a lot of my early twenties in here.' Taking a sip of his pint, he looked around him. 'It looks exactly the same.'

Grace smiled. She'd worked hard over the past two years to ensure that the pub was restored to its former glory. Nathan had almost ruined the place. Milking it for every penny, allowing the place to become run down and letting his mates have free rein. As a result, they had lost all of their regular custom.

'I appreciate your condolences, Pat.'

Grace watched him drinking his pint for a moment. He looked a little younger than her dad would have been. He was tall, with dark hair, greying at the temples and brown eyes. He must have been a hit with the ladies in his younger days. Probably still was.

13

'So what are you up to now that you're out?' she asked him. By the looks of his suit, he was doing well for himself.

'This and that.' He shrugged. 'And how about you? Is that husband of yours behaving himself in the nick?'

Grace laughed. 'I doubt that. And I told you, I have no idea what he's doing in there. I have nothing to do with him now. At least I try not to. If only he would bloody leave me alone.'

'Oh?' Patrick raised an eyebrow at her. 'Giving you a hard time, is he?'

'That would be an understatement. I'm sure that man lives to torment me.'

'Well maybe there's something we can do about that, Grace?'

'I can handle him,' Grace replied. She didn't want to be in Patrick's debt, as nice as he seemed, she really didn't know him at all.

'Look, Grace,' he said with concern in his eyes. 'Your dad was a good friend of mine. He helped me out of a few sticky situations. I know he left this life behind, but I always respected him for that. If there is a way I can help his daughter out, then it would be my privilege to do so. Besides, my lads were given hefty sentences because of Nathan Conlon's inability to keep his trap shut, so any chance to give that greedy bastard his comeuppance would be a bonus for me.'

'I'll think about it,' she said to him.

He nodded. 'You should. You seem like a woman with her head screwed on and I bet you know what makes that fucker tick better than anyone. I'm sure you could fix your problem all by yourself, but sometimes it's good to have a little help.'

Grace smiled at him. She couldn't deny there was some truth in what he said. She knew her ex-husband better than anyone alive. His insecurities; his weaknesses. Maybe she really would think about it.

Five weeks later, Grace and Patrick were sitting in her living room drinking tea. He'd become a regular visitor to the pub. On the

14

nights she wasn't working, he was invited upstairs to the flat once Jake was tucked up in bed and they'd talk long into the night.

'So, you, my dad and Tommy were the best of friends then?' Grace asked.

She'd learned about her dad's connection to Nathan's former boss, Tommy, a couple of years earlier. It had come as a massive shock at the time. Her dad, the gangster. She'd only ever known him as a funny, loving, if overprotective, father. She'd wished she'd known before Tommy's death. Among other reasons, it would have been nice to talk to someone who'd known her dad back then.

'Yeah. Thick as thieves we were. Funny really when you think about it. We were thieves and we were pretty thick too,' Patrick laughed.

'I suppose Tommy was always the ringleader? He seemed the type to always want to be in charge.'

'No.' Patrick shook his head. 'Your dad was the boss. Ever since we were kids. He was just a natural leader, you know. Me and Tommy followed him around like a pair of stray dogs until he finally gave in and let us join his gang.' Patrick laughed again at the memory.

'What? No?' Grace could hardly believe Patrick was talking about her dad.

'Yeah. Well he was a couple of years older than us. And the girls loved him; he always had loads of dough, so me and Tommy thought he was the dog's bollocks. He had quite the little empire built by the time he left it all behind.'

'And he gave it all up, just like that?'

'Just like that. When you were born, your mum told him she wasn't having anymore of his nonsense. So, he walked away and he concentrated on this place.'

Grace shook her head in disbelief at the life her father had once lived. The life she'd known nothing of until after he'd died. She felt immensely proud of her mum though, standing up to her dad like that. 'If only I could have given Nathan that kind of ultimatum,' she sighed.

'Wouldn't have made any difference to him, love. Your dad gave it all up because he loved you and your mum too much not to. All the unpleasant stuff was a means to an end for your dad. But that's what Nathan lives for.'

'You worked for Nathan for a while, didn't you?'

'Yeah, I'd just come out after doing a few years for armed robbery and went back to work for Tommy. It was a few months before he was killed. After Nathan took over the firm I just kept doing what I was told to. Until I got lifted for bloody drug supply anyway.' He shook his head. 'Managed to get to the grand old age of thirty-eight before setting foot inside a nick and then got two long stretches almost back to back.'

Grace swallowed the last remnants of her tea, needing to regain her composure before continuing the conversation. Any mention of Tommy McNulty's murder always brought her out in a cold sweat. The memories of that day were burned into her brain as though someone had branded them there with a hot poker. When she was sure she could speak without a tremor in her voice, she asked him. 'You've never thought of striking out on your own then? You must have a lot of contacts in the business?'

'Nah.' Patrick shook his head and chuckled. 'I'm just the hired muscle, me. Never had the brains, or the inclination to be the boss. That's for people like Nathan, who are born for it, or people like you who've got the brains. You know how people work. You could go far in my world, Grace. You get that from your dad.'

'Me?' Grace laughed. Surely he was joking. 'That's the daftest thing I've ever heard, Pat.'

'Not daft at all. You've got all that money sitting there doing nothing. And everyone likes you, they respect you. And the way you've handled Nathan is brilliant. I was ready to have my lad go in there all guns blazing, but your idea about the fake buyer for the pub was genius.'

16

Placing her empty mug onto the coffee table, Grace considered what Patrick had said. She thought about the million pounds she had stashed away in bank accounts in various company names, tied up in numerous business ventures. Money she'd stolen from Nathan before he was locked up. Money, he believed the police had nicked from him, when it had been his quiet, unassuming wife who'd taken it from right under his nose. He'd never suspected a thing. Maybe Patrick was right.

'I wouldn't say it was genius, Pat. I just know how Nathan thinks, that's all. He needs to believe he's making the decision to leave me alone. It couldn't have worked out better, him being on a wing with your Michael. Being told I'm about to do a moonlight flit with his son, is the surest way to get Nathan to leave me in peace.'

Grace smiled. Who was she kidding? It was a stroke of genius. When Patrick had told her that his son, Michael, was on the same wing as Nathan in Walton, she realized it was the perfect opportunity to beat her soon-to-be ex-husband at his own game. Suddenly, she had someone on the inside who could feed Nathan false information. Information that she wanted him to know.

She had thought about selling the pub soon after Nathan went to prison, but a lot of soul-searching had made her decide against it. The Rose and Crown was her parent's legacy, and more importantly, it was her sanctuary. But it had given her an idea. As much as Nathan was a monster, he was also a scared little boy. He was terrified of losing the only people he'd ever loved – her and Jake. If Nathan believed she was about to sell her pub, and move abroad, he'd panic. Terrified that she would take their son and never return, he'd back off. It played on every single one of his insecurities – his fear of being abandoned by the only people he loved. The old Grace might have said it was cruel, but it was certainly effective.

'You must have thought about doing a runner though?' Patrick said, snapping Grace from her train of thought.

'Yeah, of course. Many times, But, why should I? This is my pub. My home. I've lived here for my whole life. It's the only place I've ever really belonged. The only thing in my life that has ever been entirely mine. My dad entrusted it to me. And these people are my friends. I've made this place a success again, all on my own. Jake is happy and settled here. Why should I give that all up for my scumbag ex-husband?'

Patrick laughed. 'Well you shouldn't. And like I said, you're a strong woman, Grace. You should really think about what you want to do with your life.'

Grace picked the empty mugs from the coffee table. 'Another one?' she asked.

He looked at his watch. It was just after midnight. 'Yeah, go on. Why not?'

Patrick walked into the kitchen as Grace was boiling the kettle. 'I meant to thank you for your help with my other situation, Grace,' he said sheepishly.

'Not a problem, Pat. You and Michael have really helped me out with Nathan. I'm happy to reciprocate.'

When two heavy-set cockneys, with more scars than teeth, had come looking for Patrick in the Rose and Crown the previous week, Grace had known he was in some serious trouble. She'd denied all knowledge of him, but they'd told her to pass on a message in any case. If they didn't get the hundred grand he owed by the end of the week, he'd be taking a dip in the Mersey with some lead in his head and his pockets.

A poor choice of business associate had left Patrick on the wrong side of a dangerous moneylender in the East End. A twenty-five grand debt had quadrupled in the eight weeks since he'd left London. Grace had offered him the money and he'd gratefully accepted. His cockney counterparts had left Liverpool a lot happier and richer than when they'd arrived.

'I'll pay you back with interest, of course,' Patrick said.

'I know you will.'

18

'And I'm forever in your debt, Grace. I'd hate to think what would have happened if I hadn't been able to get that money together. Anything you ever need, just call me.'

'Thanks, Pat,' she said, hopeful she would never need anything from him but his companionship.

As she continued making the tea she thought about Patrick's comments earlier. Imagine her the boss of some criminal empire? Dressing in power suits and barking orders at her minions. A small laugh escaped her lips as she contemplated the absurdity of the notion. But what if? She'd have her own, personal army at her disposal. Nathan would never be able to get to her again. She'd be untouchable. It was certainly something worth fantasizing about at least.

CHAPTER FOUR

Glancing at the entrance to the pub, Grace checked her watch. It was a little after nine, and Patrick was usually always there by eight on a Monday. She had grown used to his presence in the bar most nights, but particularly on Mondays when she finished early and they would share a takeaway and a bottle of wine after hours. She enjoyed talking to him. He could regale her for hours with his tales.

Grace was beginning to feel anxious. What if something had happened to him? It reminded her of all the nights she'd sat waiting for Nathan to come home, worrying about what he was up to. At least that was until she could no longer bear the sight of him. Why did she invest so much of her time in men who were clearly up to no good?

Just as she was contemplating phoning Patrick's mobile, he came bounding through the double doors. Despite her annoyance at him for making her worry, she felt herself instantly relax. The tension in her shoulders and chest slipping away as he made his way over.

'Grace,' he said excitedly. 'I've got a very interesting business opportunity for you.'

'Oh?'

'Can't talk in here. But I'll tell you all about it. Shall I nip out and get us an Indian?'

'Yeah, okay.' She nodded. Intrigued and bemused. What possible business proposition could he have that might involve her?

Once the pub was locked up and Grace had checked on Jake, she and Patrick sat down with their curries while he poured two glasses of wine.

'So, what's this about a business opportunity, Pat?'

'Well,' he cleared his throat and smoothed back his hair – looking very pleased with himself, 'do you remember that guy in Manchester I told you about? The one I used to work for? Solomon Shepherd?'

'Yeah.'

'Well, he told me he'd been hearing whispers of a massive upset with the dealers in Liverpool and he asked me to look into it. It's not good for his business either. Well, it turns out that they've all been under surveillance for a massive police operation. The biggest in Liverpool for years, Grace. Even bigger than when Nathan and my lads went down. So, there is basically a massive gap in the market for someone to take control of things and everyone who's anyone, is or has been, under surveillance, so none of them can fill it.'

'Yet?'

Patrick nodded. 'Exactly. So, we have to move fast.'

'What?' Grace laughed. 'Us? Are you serious? What the hell do I know about drugs?'

'I can teach you the basics. And you don't need to know everything straight away. That's what you've got me for. You can learn the business as you go. You'd have to provide the capital, obviously, but this will make you a very rich woman. You'd make more in a week than this place takes in a year. I'll take all the risks, Grace. You won't have to get your hands dirty if you don't want to. And with Sol's backing we're already off to a great start.'

Grace shook her head. 'You're talking crazy, Pat. Me and you drug kingpins? You're almost a pensioner and I'm a pub landlady!'

'Hey, you cheeky mare,' he laughed. 'There's still life in this old fella, you know. And don't sell yourself short either. You might not realize it, but you've picked up a hell of a lot from Nathan about this business. Mostly, how not to do things. The lads that come in here all listen to you. They respect you. Partly because you're your dad's daughter and Nathan's ex-wife, but mostly because there's something about you, Grace. People trust you.'

Grace took a sip of her wine. 'How would I sleep at night, Pat? Besides the obvious fact that drugs are a mugs game, and are responsible for far too much misery in this world, it's just too dangerous. I have Jake to think about?'

'If we don't step in, Grace, someone else will. Besides, we won't be at the coal face doing the grunt work. That's the beauty of being the boss, you can pay other people to do that for you. And what better way to be able to protect Jake? You would be one of the most powerful players in Liverpool. Come on, Grace. What do you say?'

Grace considered his proposal. Was there a better way to protect Jake? Or herself? Particularly from Nathan. Was the only way to defeat the monster to become one yourself?

'I'll think about it, Pat,' she said. 'About funding you, at least. I wouldn't want any part in the actual day-to-day operations.'

'That's all I ask, boss.' He grinned at her.

CHAPTER FIVE

Present Day

It was midday when Grace heard Jake emerge from the crypt that was his bedroom.

'Do you want anything to eat, son?' she shouted up the stairs.

'A fry-up, Mum. The full works,' he called back jovially.

She envied him his cast-iron constitution, and his body's ability to burn off all that alcohol and avoid a hangover. She supposed that was what came from being eighteen. She remembered her life as an eighteen-year-old and how different it was to Jake's. She'd had so much responsibility, yet so little experience of the world. It had been a dangerous combination. One that had left her open to the likes of Nathan – who'd seen her as the perfect target.

How easily she had allowed herself to be taken in by him. How quickly she had given up everything to him. He'd moved in within two months of their first meeting, had his name above the door within six, and they'd married just three months later. At the time, she'd thought it was true love – a whirlwind romance, just like Baby in her favourite film, *Dirty Dancing*. What a naive little girl she'd been. Now that she saw it for what it truly was, it made her cheeks burn with shame and anger.

Jake tucked into his breakfast with the voracity of a man who hadn't been fed for weeks.

'This is gorgeous, Mum,' he mumbled, his mouth full of toast.

Kissing him on the top of his head, she sat at the table with him. 'So, any plans for today?'

'Dad's going to show me his club and then we'll probably grab something to eat,' he replied, and her heart sank.

'Is he coming here?' she asked, trying to hide her uneasiness with that arrangement.

'Yeah, he'll be here in a bit.'

Grace got up from the table, telling Jake she needed to start getting ready for work. She hoped that she could be out of the house before Nathan arrived.

Nathan's timing was as inconvenient as ever and he was ringing the doorbell as Grace was changing into her work clothes. She heard Jake let him in and the two of them fell into an easy banter. She wondered what reception she'd get from Nathan and whether he would still be annoyed about her rejecting his advances the night before. She hoped that they could put it behind them and at least maintain a degree of civility, if only for Jake's sake; although knowing Nathan she didn't hold up much hope for that.

Grace walked into the kitchen to find Nathan helping himself to some toast and coffee. He was dressed in a suit again and she marvelled at how fresh he looked given the state he'd been in the previous night. How typical of him that he'd been there less than ten minutes and was already making himself at home.

'Grace!' he said with a smile on his face. 'You look lovely today.'

'Thanks,' she replied, not buying his nice-guy act for even a second. 'You look very smart. Off anywhere interesting?'

'Just some business to sort out. I'm taking Jake to The Blue Rooms. Got to show the boy the ropes, haven't I?'

'Sharon McNulty's place?' Grace asked.

'No, my place,' he snapped. 'In all but name anyway. I've ran it since Tommy died, haven't I? Besides, I'm buying it off her. I'm just waiting on my solicitor to draw up the paperwork and then it will all be official.'

Jake looked up at him with pure admiration in his eyes, and she had to physically stop herself from shaking some sense into him. She tried to appear indifferent in front of her son, but her stomach was churning. Jake would be off to university in a few months and then he'd be far away from his father's grasp, but knowing Nathan, a lot of damage could be done during that time. There was no way Grace was going to allow Jake to get sucked into his father's nefarious dealings.

Jake's chair scraped across the kitchen floor as he stood up, interrupting Grace's train of thought. 'I'll go and get ready, Dad. Be back down in a bit.'

And then there was just the two of them. Nathan's presence in the room was, as ever, pervasive and suffocating. Every fibre of her being was aware of him and on edge. The incident from the previous night remained unmentioned, and she wondered how his anger might manifest itself.

Striding across the kitchen, head held high, Grace was not shaken by his presence; this was her house, her territory, and he was the intruder. Picking up the cafetière, she poured the remaining contents into a travel mug before spinning around on her heel, careful not to have her back to him for too long. He was up off his chair and standing in front of her before she could move another inch. He was so close that she could smell the expensive soap he'd used that morning. She glared at him. What the hell was he up to?

'Anymore of that coffee?' he asked, his voice low and calm. Reaching behind her to lift the pot; he almost pinned her to the kitchen counter as he did so.

'No, all gone.' she said, placing her free hand on his chest to create some distance between them.

'No worries. I'll make a cup of tea instead,' he said before moving to the sink to fill the kettle.

'You do realize Jake's going to uni in a couple of months, don't you?' she said.

'So?' Nathan shrugged.

'He doesn't need you filling his head full of crap about how wonderful your life is in the meantime,' she snapped.

'I can't help it if the kid idolizes me, Grace,' he smirked. 'I have that effect on people. You should know.' He winked.

'Ha,' she snorted. 'You haven't had that effect on me for a very long time, Nathan.'

He lit a cigarette and sat back down at the kitchen table as he waited for the kettle to boil. She didn't bother to tell him she didn't allow smoking in her house; deciding she had a bigger axe to grind with him.

'If he gets into any trouble because of you, Nathan, I'll—'

'You'll what, Grace?' He smirked, but she could see the anger flash momentarily across his face.

'Just remember he's an eighteen-year-old kid, with his whole life ahead of him, Nathan. Do *not* do anything to screw that up for him.'

He shrugged. 'Whatever you say.'

Grace watched him as he blew smoke rings across the kitchen.

'This is a nice place you've got yourself here,' he said, changing the subject, his eyes twinkling as he talked. 'The pub must be doing well?'

'Yes, the pub does okay. It keeps me and Jake anyway.' She almost told him that it had taken her two years to make the place viable again, after he had almost run it into the ground. But that was old news. All that would have done was start an argument, and she was in no mood for one with him today. Besides, he appeared to be in a very affable mood and she wondered if the previous night's antics had been forgotten. Or at least written off as some drunken lunacy, brought on by his nostalgia at being

26

back in their old home. Maybe her warning had actually worked, and he realized she was not a woman to be messed with anymore. Whatever the reason, she was grateful that he hadn't brought it up and appeared to hold no ill feelings about it.

'How is Kayleigh?' Grace asked, trying to steer the conversation away from her financial affairs.

'She's good, got a terrible hangover this morning though,' he laughed.

'She seems like a nice girl.'

'Yes, she is. She's a star, my Kayleigh. The way she waited for me to get out of prison. Not many women would do that, it seems.'

'Well not many women would put up with you, full stop,' she smiled. 'Personally, I think I deserve the George Cross for sticking it out as long as I did.'

He shook his head. 'You've developed a sense of humour while I've been away, Grace. You never used to be this funny.' He smiled as he said it, but Grace knew he was rankled by the way he momentarily clenched his jaw.

'Well, I'd better get to work. You and Jake have a good day,' she said breezily.

He stood up as she started to leave and kissed her softly on the cheek. 'You too, Grace.'

As she left the house, Grace undid the top buttons of her blouse to allow some air at her skin, which burned red hot. Nathan was being so nice it was unnerving. Even when she'd tried to push his buttons, he'd kept a lid on his temper. That was Nathan, she supposed, always keeping her on her toes. Or maybe he really had changed? She laughed out loud at that last thought. She was willing to play along with his little charade for now. It was easier for her, after all. But she knew it wouldn't be long before the charming facade slipped – it always did.

CHAPTER SIX

Grace walked into the almost empty bar area of the Rose and Crown. Her bar manager, Marcus Holden, was placing menus on the tables in preparation for the usual lunchtime crowd. He usually opened up so she could have a lie in – a perk of being the boss. Marcus was her longest serving and most reliable employee, as well as a good friend.

He'd worked at the bar since Grace was seventeen, and at just two years older than her, they'd clicked from the very beginning. When her dad died a year later he helped her to navigate the running of the place and had been by her side ever since, apart from a brief hiatus when Nathan had sacked him without Grace's knowledge. The first thing she'd done after taking control of her pub again was to phone Marcus and beg him to come back. He'd accepted before she'd even finished the question. He often joked that Grace could never fire him because he knew where the bodies were buried, and Grace always smiled politely when he did, because Marcus had no idea. He was a great pub manager, but she did her best to keep him far away from her other business activities. They both preferred it that way.

Patrick Carter was sitting at the bar on a stool, reading a newspaper and eating a bacon sandwich, which he'd no doubt talked the chef into making him, even though the kitchen wasn't officially open.

'Morning, Pat.' She smiled as she greeted him. 'What brings you here so early?'

'Just wanted to make sure you were okay.' He smiled back.

'I'm fine. I can look after myself.'

'I know that, boss. Just here in case you need me,' he said before returning to his newspaper and sandwich.

It still sounded odd to hear the legendary Patrick Carter calling her Boss. He'd given her that moniker shortly after they'd met ten years ago, and he'd worked for her ever since. But not in the same way Marcus did. No, Patrick undertook more specialized work. He did the type of jobs that you couldn't advertise in the local newspaper. Running a pub in Liverpool could be a dangerous game after all. Patrick was what some might call her right-hand man. One of her most trusted confidantes. He gave good counsel, but more importantly he knew when to keep his opinions to himself and do as he was told.

Grace took one of the discarded bread crusts from Patrick's plate. 'You always leave the best bit,' she said before taking a bite.

He grinned at her. 'Leave them for you, don't I?'

Marcus approached her and put an arm around her shoulder, giving her a light peck on the cheek. 'Morning, lovely,' he said. 'You all right?'

'Yes, I'm fine,' she snapped. She hated to be coddled by them.

'Okay, keep your knickers on,' he pouted. 'I'm only asking.'

'We're just worried about you,' Patrick added. Before she could reply he interrupted her. 'Yes, we know you can look after yourself, but that doesn't mean we can't be concerned about you.'

'I know,' she sighed. 'I'm sorry. I'm just on edge, that's all.'

'I'm not surprised,' Marcus said. 'The way he walked in here last night, like he owned the place.'

'Well that's Nathan,' Grace said.

'I don't get what you ever saw in him, Grace,' Patrick said. 'He's such an arrogant prick.'

Grace smiled. He was an arrogant prick, there was no doubt about that. But he hadn't always been that way. Sometimes she allowed herself to think about when they first met and how incredibly happy he'd made her. After losing her dad she'd felt so alone. And then Nathan had bounded into her life, full of energy and confidence. He could make her laugh like no one else ever had. Whenever she was around him the whole world had seemed brighter, and she felt as if she could face anything with Nathan by her side. Dear God, the naiveté of a love-struck teenager, she laughed to herself.

'What's so funny?' Marcus asked, snapping her out of her thoughts.

'Just thinking about old times,' she said. 'Remember when we were young and dumb?'

'Aw yes.' He smiled. 'You used to be so sweet.'

Patrick laughed so hard he spat some of his coffee onto the bar.

Grace ignored them both. She concentrated on picking an imaginary piece of fluff from her skirt so they wouldn't see her eyes brim with tears. This was why she hated thinking about the past. About the person she once was. The person Nathan was. The possibilities of young love and everything that could have been.

CHAPTER SEVEN

Twenty Years Earlier

New Year's Eve

Grace saw him as soon as he walked into the Rose and Crown. She still considered it her dad's place, even though it was now entirely hers. She felt completely out of her depth sometimes but being in the bar made her feel close to him. The familiar smells; the constant hum of chatter; the smooth wood of the bar beneath her fingertips; all of them were comforting in their own way.

Grace continued to stare at the handsome stranger. He was so incredibly gorgeous, that it almost felt like her heart stopped when she saw him. She unconsciously held her breath, afraid that if she dared to breathe the spell might be broken, and he would disappear into thin air. He couldn't be much older than her, but he walked into the room with the confidence of someone who knew exactly who they were, and what they wanted.

As he made his way over to a group of people at the table she was clearing, she noticed the most incredible eyes she had ever seen. Cornflower blue, they sparkled under the bright light of the cheap chandeliers. His dark brown hair stuck to his forehead from the rain. Catching her eye, he smiled, and she almost dropped the tray she was carrying. It was as though someone had hit her knees with a sledgehammer.

'Whoa!' he said as he caught her by the elbow. 'You been drinking on the job? You'll get the sack if you're not careful.' He laughed.

'That'd be difficult,' one of the regulars chuckled. 'It's her pub.'

The good-looking stranger raised an eyebrow at her. 'Really? I'm impressed.'

Scurrying away with a bright red face, Grace's heart pounded in her ears. She hadn't had much experience with boys. Having gone to an all-girls' school, and raised by an overprotective, although well-meaning, father, she never got the chance to.

After taking the tray back to the bar, Grace went into the ladies' toilets in an attempt to compose herself. She wished Marcus didn't have the night off. He was as hopeless with men as she was, but at least he'd have made her laugh about the whole thing. Splashing her face with some cold water, she tried to cool her flushed cheeks. What an idiot, running off like that. What would he think? She looked herself over in the mirror. Was she plain looking? Well she was never the type of girl who got noticed at any rate. Fashionable? God no. Judging by the teasing she'd got from the other girls at school. *Do your make-up in the dark, Grace? Go clothes shopping with your nan, Grace?*

Her figure wasn't bad though. Tucking the loose-fitting T-shirt she was wearing into her jeans, she smoothed the fabric over her flat stomach. Marcus was always telling her not to hide herself away in baggy clothes and to make more of an effort. Oh, God! How she wished she'd made an effort tonight. He must have a girlfriend anyway, and if he didn't, he'd never be interested in someone like her. After drying her face, she left the sanctuary of the ladies' room and made her way back out into the crowd, deciding to avoid him for the rest of the night before she got the chance to make an even bigger fool of herself.

'You managed to break any glasses yet?' A voice interrupted Grace's thoughts as she sat on a stool at the side of the bar, nursing a Diet Coke. 'I'm Nathan,' he said and smiled.

He looked right into her eyes until she thought she might pass out from fear and excitement. She looked at him blankly for what felt like minutes, until he laughed. If it were possible, his laugh was better than his smile.

'I'm Grace,' she finally whispered, all the while chastising herself for being such an idiot.

'Nice to meet you, Grace,' he said as he extended his hand.

His hand was warm, and it engulfed hers. The roughness from his calloused fingertips juxtaposed against the soft skin of her palm. She held onto it just a little longer than could be considered polite, not wanting to let him go. When he pulled his hand away she missed the feel of his skin immediately, as though she had always known his touch.

'So, is this really your pub then?' he asked.

Grace explained about her mum passing away when she was just a toddler, and how she was an only child. She told him that her dad died a few months earlier, and left the place to her, lock, stock and quite literally, barrel. She told him all about how close she and her dad were and how lost she'd felt without him. Her only remaining relative was her beloved aunt. She was helping out with the pub over the festive period but had moved to Leeds a few years earlier when she met her husband. Before long, the handsome, intimidating stranger, had her jabbering about herself in a way she wouldn't have thought possible only fifteen minutes before.

'Grace! I hate to interrupt your social life, but your break finished ten minutes ago and unless it escaped your notice, we're a bit busy,' her Aunt Helen shouted from across the bar.

'I'm sorry. I've got to get back to work.'

He took hold of her arm as she climbed off the stool. 'So who is the lucky fella who gets to kiss you at midnight then?'

33

'There is no lucky fella,' she said as she felt the heat creep up her neck. 'Why?'

'Well we can't have that now, can we? Everyone has to kiss someone at midnight on New Year's Eve.'

Grace's stomach started to perform all kinds of unexpected gymnastics. What did he mean by that? Surely not?

'I'll come find you at twelve,' he said, before winking at her and disappearing into the crowd.

The rest of the night passed in a blur. Grace kept replaying the conversation with Nathan over in her head. Did he really mean he wanted to kiss her? Surely he was joking? Or drunk? Or both? What if he left before midnight?

As the night went on she became a bundle of awkwardness. Unable to concentrate on anything, she passed the same table three times before remembering she was supposed to be clearing it of empty glasses. She'd never kissed a boy before, at least nothing you could call a proper kiss. There was that one time when she was fifteen, with Jason Miller, the cool sixth former from the local boys' school who all the girls fancied. Shuddering, she recalled that encounter. Although he claimed to be St Michael's High School's very own answer to Brad Pitt, he appeared to have no idea what he was doing. His tongue felt like a slimy fish, and he just stuck it in there. She'd almost choked. It had not been a pleasant experience. Grace had a feeling that kissing Nathan would be entirely different, and she couldn't wait.

It was just before midnight and Nathan continued laughing and drinking with his friends. Grace began to wonder again whether the elusive kiss would happen. Why hadn't he come over to her yet? Was it all a joke? Shifting from one foot to the other as the ten second countdown started, she was still alone in the crowd when she was suddenly grabbed by the waist. Turning around, there he was, that handsome face and those amazing eyes, looking right at her.

'You're fucking beautiful, do you know that?' he said.

Before she could respond, he kissed her, and it was everything that she'd hoped it would be. She could taste the whisky he'd been drinking, and she wondered if it was that which was making her head spin and legs wobble. She swore, even if she never saw him again, she would remember that kiss for the rest of her life.

CHAPTER EIGHT

Present Day

Nathan stretched his muscular body across the cool cotton sheets as he admired the naked body of his girlfriend, Kayleigh, while she was deciding what to wear.

He'd met her six years ago, while he was still inside. She was the younger sister of one of his many pad mates, Tony Gallagher. He'd first seen her when she was visiting her brother and within a few weeks she was visiting Nathan instead.

At twenty-seven, she was fourteen years younger than him. She had the body of a page three model. She didn't have much else about her, but she certainly looked the part, and she gave some of the best head he'd ever had in his life. She told people she was an underwear model, but now her only ambition in life was to look good on Nathan's arm, and let him keep her in the lifestyle to which she'd recently become accustomed.

'What do you think about this one, Nathan?' she asked, holding up a hideous pink dress that wouldn't look out of place in a knocking shop on the dock road.

'How about you come here instead and remind me how much

you've missed me?' he grinned as he patted the empty space on the bed beside him.

'Behave yourself!' she squealed. 'I've got to get a shower or we'll be late.'

Sighing, Nathan lay back down on the bed. Kayleigh was gorgeous. She did what she was told, when she was told. Everywhere they went, men stared at her and he liked having what other people wanted. She was perfect for him. So why the hell couldn't he stop thinking about Grace? She occupied his every waking thought.

He'd thought he could just walk back into her life and she'd be waiting for him. Time had a way of standing still in prison. It was easy to forget that the world outside moved on without you. He'd spent years imagining the look on her face when he introduced her to Kayleigh and told her he was no longer inter-ested in middle-aged women nearing their forties. He was going to break her heart – just like she'd broken his when she'd sent him those divorce papers. It had almost killed him to sign them, but he'd had no choice. It had been the only way to stop her running away with Jake.

Walking back into the Rose and Crown had felt like travelling back in time. Despite not setting foot in the place for over twelve years, it still looked, and felt, the same to him. Even the smell was the same – real ale, and people. The mixture of perfume, aftershave, sweat, the cigarette smoke that lingered on the clothes. It was funny how your senses could trick you into believing you were in another time and place. The same faces were still sitting at the bar or doing business at the same vinyl topped tables. He was greeted by everyone. He was a well-known face, and even if people didn't know him, they liked to tell people that they did.

The only thing that had changed was her. She still looked like his Grace. Still had her long dark hair and curves in exactly the right places. But she wasn't looking up at the doors, waiting for

37

him to come home anymore. She didn't smile at him like she used to or look at him like he was the most incredible person she'd ever known. She held herself differently too, full of confidence – and class. She was the type of woman men would look at and think was out of their league. And she'd grown a backbone too. He admired the new Grace. It was hard not to. Not that he would admit that to anyone, especially her.

He felt exactly the same way about her as he always had. As though he'd only left yesterday. He'd spent years convincing himself that she meant nothing to him anymore and it had only taken a few seconds in her presence to undo it all.

He'd seen her as soon as he'd walked into the pub. His eyes drawn to her like she possessed some kind of magnetic field. His chest had tightened, as though someone was squeezing his heart and lungs from the inside, making his breath catch in his throat. How could she still do that to him? He'd looked away before she'd seen him. When they came face to face again, it would be on his terms. There had been no reason to let her believe she had any power over him.

She was still the most beautiful woman he'd ever seen. And God, she could still make his dick twitch. Maybe it was muscle memory, he smiled in spite of himself; the memory of all the things they'd done, right there in that pub, on that bar, on those chairs and tables.

It had seemed like fate when Jake dropped his keys just as Nathan was thinking about going to visit some old friends. Seeing the key to the flat above the pub on Jake's key ring, made him decide just which old friend he'd like to visit. He smiled as he remembered Grace standing there wielding a golf club and how it took all his strength not to burst out laughing. But what happened next was entirely unexpected.

He'd expected her to be the same Grace she'd always been – compliant. But she was tougher now. Not the same gullible girl she was when he left. Even in his drunken state, he could see that.

She might just be capable of carrying out her little threat to phone his probation officer. Maybe he would have to tread carefully – for now. But Nathan had a plan. He always had a plan.

Grace thought he'd let her go. He'd thought that he could too, but now he realized she was as essential to him as breathing. She was the only person who really knew him; the only one who knew his secrets – and she'd loved him anyway. Grace was his. She belonged to him. She always had, and she always would. The sooner she remembered that, the better.

CHAPTER NINE

Twenty Years Earlier

New Year's Day

Nathan woke with a jolt, his heart pounding in his ears, his body covered in a thin film of sweat. The ghosts of the nightmare that woke him began to fade as the sun filtered through the gap in the curtains. Waiting for his heart rate to slow to a normal pace, he went through his usual morning ritual and scanned the small bedsit, taking note of the various flaws which ground him down on a daily basis. The paint that peeled from the top of the walls exposing the damp beneath, despite the numerous fresh coats of paint he'd painstakingly applied. The myriad of brown and yellow stains on the small kitchen cupboards which no amount of scrubbing could remove.

On any other morning, he'd be filled with a crushing sense of despair at the realization that he'd spent another day, another night, in the shithole he'd called home for the past year. But the memory of the previous night reminded him of the opportunities which were about to come his way. No more grotty bedsits. No more scratching around for bits and pieces of money. He was about to start earning some serious dough after his meeting with Tommy McNulty, which had gone better than he could have ever expected.

Tommy was the owner of The Blue Rooms, a lucrative lap-dancing club on the dock road. But that was just his respectable front. He also controlled the bulk of the huge quantities of drugs that came in and out of the docks. No one dared breathe without Tommy's say-so. He was one of the most feared and respected men in Liverpool. In his late forties, he'd been at the top of his game for almost twenty years. Ruling with brutality, he was considered fair to those who were straight with him. But cross him, and you'd be likely to never walk again at the very least, or more likely you'd disappear and never be found. And he guaranteed his employees a good earn, ensuring they remained loyal soldiers.

Nathan could hardly believe it when the big man had asked for a meet with him. The fact that Tommy even knew his name made him nervous. He wondered if he'd stepped on some toes he shouldn't have. But no one turned down a meet with Tommy McNulty, not if they wanted to live to tell the tale anyway.

As it turned out, Tommy was looking for some new muscle, and he'd heard about Nathan's growing reputation. His job offer came at just the right time for Nathan. Bored taxing petty drug dealers, he was keen to find employment more befitting his particular expertise. He was smart enough to realize that an offer of work from Tommy was a ticket to the premier league and just the opportunity he'd been waiting for.

Nathan knew he'd impressed Tommy. Well, why wouldn't he? He was good at what he did. Tommy said he was a cocky little bastard but then he offered him the job on the spot. If Nathan could prove himself, he could move up the ranks quickly, and one day maybe even run things himself. It was the opportunity he'd been waiting for. His whole life had been in preparation for this. The thought that he was destined for greater things was the only thing that got him out of bed every morning. Working for someone like Tommy was what he was born for. Nathan Conlon was well aware that he was only good at one thing – hurting people. After all, he'd learned from the best.

Then there was that bird – Grace. There was something about her. She was gorgeous, but she seemed to have absolutely no idea of that. He closed his eyes and pictured her. Big brown eyes and long dark hair. She'd been wearing a baggy T-shirt and jeans, but he'd still been able to see her big tits and slim waist beneath. She was shy too, and different from the girls he usually fucked about with. He smiled as he remembered how she blushed and almost ran away when he spoke to her. And then of course there was the fact that she owned that pub. The place was a gold mine. Eighteen years old and it was all hers. The things he could do with that kind of capital behind him.

He was looking forward to seeing her again later. If he played his cards right, she'd probably let him spend the night. Sitting up in bed, he took a cigarette from the packet on the bedside table, lit it and took a long drag.

Yes, this was going to be a good year for him.

CHAPTER TEN

Present Day

Grace could see Ivan waving frantically through the coffee shop window, trying to get her attention. She ordered a latte from the young barista and joined him at his table.

'Thanks for meeting me here, Grace,' he said. 'I didn't fancy the prospect of your Nathan turning up and giving me another grilling.'

'Not a problem,' she said. 'But he's not my Nathan.'

She had other plans that required her being out of the way for the day anyway, now that Nathan was calling into the pub almost every day, as he had done for the past two weeks. Always under the pretence he was there to see Jake, of course. Jake, who neither worked or lived there. It was infuriating. Knowing that he could turn up at any moment made her feel like she always had to be on her guard. It was bloody exhausting.

Ivan Golding had been Grace's accountant for almost twelve years. He handled all her money and investments and he was very good at what he did. He had become a dear friend and she trusted him implicitly.

'What did Nathan say to you, then?' she asked Ivan.

'He came to my office and asked me why I was visiting you at home and what business we had together. He started getting a bit aggressive, Grace. So, I had to tell him I'm your accountant, just to get him to stop glaring at me like that.' Then in a voice that was barely a whisper, he said, 'I think he thought we were, well – you know.'

She stifled a laugh. Ivan was a lovely man but he was over twenty years older than her and a few inches shorter too. Not Grace's type at all. Not to mention he was as camp as they come. She was sure Nathan didn't think that anything was going on between them, it was just one example of his many intimidation tactics.

'So, then what did he say?' she asked, anxious to find out just what exactly Nathan was up to.

'He kept asking me why you needed an accountant and what pies you had your fingers in, or something like that. He really is quite vulgar, Grace; I truly don't understand what you ever saw in him. Well, aside from the obvious,' he said, raising his eyebrows in a gesture so comical it almost made her spit her coffee at him.

'Whatever do you mean, Ivan?' she asked him with a smirk, feigning her ignorance.

He let out a short laugh. 'You know exactly what I mean. You cheeky mare; he looks like he just walked out of a photo shoot for *GQ* magazine.'

She nodded then. 'Ah yes, that, and there's also the fact that he's hung like a donkey.'

Ivan looked at her in mock horror, his mouth agape, until they both started laughing so loud they started to draw attention to themselves.

'Anyway,' Ivan continued, 'I told him you just like to keep the pub books in order, and that was that. I was quite firm with him, and I think he got the message. I told him nothing of the restaurants. And certainly, nothing of your other investments and activities,' he said quietly. 'And obviously, I never would.'

'Thank you, Ivan. I appreciate your discretion,' she told him, giving his hand a squeeze. She had no doubt that Nathan would keep digging and find out about her involvement in what had once been his domain soon enough. But the longer she could keep it from him, the better. While he still thought she was nothing more than a pub landlady, he'd be more likely to divulge information about his own business dealings – and that could prove very useful.

Ivan and Grace discussed her finances over another cup of coffee and a pastry.

'So, everything has been sorted and is in order, Grace, just like you asked. I've moved what money I needed to, so everything in your new place will be entirely above board. Well, it will be as far as the taxman is concerned anyway.'

'Thanks, Ivan. You are a legend,' she told him, before giving him a kiss on the cheek as she got up to leave.

He took hold of her hand as she started to walk away. 'Be careful, Grace. That Nathan seems like a real nasty piece of work. If he ever finds out what you did …'

'Don't worry. He won't. Not unless I want him to anyway.' She smiled at the irony of Ivan warning her about Nathan's character. As if she didn't know better than anyone else in the world just exactly what type of man Nathan was. It was that knowledge which sometimes kept her awake at night, but also what made her certain that she could take him down if she needed to.

Stepping outside into the street, Grace cursed as she felt the drops of rain falling onto her bare arms. She'd forgotten her umbrella and was supposed to be meeting someone on the other side of the city centre. She'd get soaked to the skin if she walked there. Taking her phone out of her handbag, she dialled his number.

'Can you pick me up? I've forgotten my coat and my umbrella.'

'I hope you've forgotten your underwear too,' he laughed.

'Behave yourself,' she said, feigning her indignation.

'Be there in five, babe,' he said, and she could imagine his smile as he said it; that lovely relaxed grin of his that made her want to kiss him all over his face. She smiled too, thinking of the wonderful afternoon they were about to spend together. For a few hours at least, she would forget that Nathan Conlon even existed.

CHAPTER ELEVEN

Grace had just finished serving one of her regulars as she heard the doors of the Rose and Crown burst open. The sun rushed in behind him, illuminating his silhouette against the doorway. She groaned inwardly as he approached her. It had been almost four weeks since he'd walked back into her life and she'd had to endure seeing him almost every day since.

'What are you doing here, Nathan?'

'Is that any way to greet the love of your life, Grace?' he smirked.

'Jake's not here,' she snapped.

'That's okay,' he said as he took a seat at the bar. 'I'm here to meet a friend of mine. I'll have a whisky while I wait.'

She poured his Scotch and placed it on the bar in front of him. 'That'll be £2.80,' she said.

'Piss off,' he spat. 'I can't believe you're still making me pay for my drinks. Are you serious?'

'Yes.' She held out her hand until he reluctantly placed a £10 note in it.

'I've been hearing some interesting rumours about you, Grace,' Nathan said as she was handing him his change.

'Have you?' She sighed, in no mood for conversation with him.

'Yes. Very interesting,' he persisted.

'Okay, Nathan. I'll bite, What sort of rumours?'

'That you're not quite as lily-white as you used to be.'

'Well you'll know I'm not the same idiotic girl who used to think the sun shone out of your arse then? You can't push me around anymore.'

He started laughing. 'Is that so?'

'God, you're such a prick,' she replied.

'Aw come on, you know you still love me really.' He grinned before he took a sip of his whisky. 'Anyway, tell me, why is Patrick Carter always hanging around here? Every time I come in here, he's skulking around.'

'He is not skulking around. He's a paying customer. He's very welcome here. Unlike you.'

'You're not fucking him, are you?' he asked, his face contorted in disgust.

'Not that it's any of your business,' she hissed. 'But no, I am not fucking him. He's a friend of mine, and besides, he's old enough to be my dad.' She glared at him. If he registered the veiled insult about his relationship with Kayleigh, then he didn't show it.

'Who are you fucking then?' he asked, his tone suddenly serious.

She stared at him. Who the hell did he think he was? 'None of your damn business, that's who,' she snapped.

'It will always be my business, Grace. You're my wife.'

'I'm your ex-wife, Nathan.'

He ignored her correcting him. 'So, there is someone then?'

She leaned in close to him and said quietly in his ear: 'You were enough to put me off men for life, sunshine.'

Turning her back on him, Grace went to serve another customer. She smiled and made polite conversation, but her stomach churned and her heart pounded in her ears. Nathan knew exactly how to push her buttons. The way he treated her like she was his property made her skin crawl. There was a time, when she was an idiotic, love-struck teenager, that she'd thought

48

his possessiveness was quite endearing and his jealousy simply an outward display that he loved her just as much as she loved him. What a fool she'd been.

CHAPTER TWELVE

Twenty Years Earlier

Nathan brought out the heavy tray of freshly washed glasses from the kitchen and placed them on the bar. He'd decided to work at the pub for the night. He liked to keep an eye on the place sometimes and make sure no one was taking the piss. It gave him a chance to keep an eye on Grace too, and he was glad he'd decided to tonight. There was a young lad who'd been sitting at the bar for a while. He'd been fucking about with the same beer for about half an hour and the cheeky prick had spent most of his time staring at Grace's arse. Nathan looked at her. Wearing trousers and a shirt, her usual pub attire, nothing was on show as per his instructions. But there was no hiding her figure. She just had something about her.

He started to get hard thinking about what he was going to do to her later, and the way she was always so eager to please him. For her part, Grace seemed oblivious to the lad drooling over her. But that meant she was as friendly to him as she was any other customer, and that just encouraged the poor bastard. Fortunately, for them both, Nathan was in a good mood. He saw the lad signal to Grace to serve him. As she reached him,

Nathan came up beside her and slipped an arm around her waist.

'I'll get this, babe,' he said against her ear.

Nathan pulled the young lad's pint. 'Not seen you here before, mate, what's the name?'

'Liam. I've been coming here the past couple of weeks.'

'Yes, I bet you have,' he mumbled. Handing him his pint, Nathan leaned down, his elbows on the bar and his face just a few inches from Liam's. He smiled for appearance's sake, but he knew with certainty, that it did not disguise the menace in his voice. 'You do know that's my girlfriend whose arse you've been staring at all night, don't you?'

Liam swallowed hard. 'I wasn't staring, mate. Honest,' he stuttered.

'If I ever catch you looking at her again, I will rip your fucking nuts off, and stuff them down your throat. Do you hear me?'

Liam nodded and scuttled off out of the pub. Nathan laughed to himself, sure that would be the last they'd see of him.

The pub had been so busy; Grace had barely had time to think. It always seemed busier when Nathan was there. So many people stopped in to see him, to discuss something or other. He was so at ease behind the bar and the customers loved him too. He always kept them all in good humour, with his constant jokes and easy charm, making sure that they stayed all night to spend their hard-earned money. She, on the other hand, always felt a bit uneasy when he was there, like he was always watching her, waiting for her to say or do the wrong thing, to laugh a little too much at one of the customer's awful jokes. It was probably just her imagination, but it was a feeling she couldn't shake. Liam had left after Nathan spoke to him. Grace hoped he hadn't scared him off; Liam had become a regular and he was harmless.

Once they had seen the last punter out and locked the doors, Grace started to climb the stairs to the flat, with Nathan at her heels. If he were any closer, she would have fallen over his feet.

As always, she felt his presence so acutely and wondered what sort of mood he was in. He'd been in good spirits all night, but she knew better than most how quickly his moods could change. As soon as they were inside the flat he grabbed her by the waist and pushed her up against the wall, the full weight of his body pressing into hers, his erection pressing into her hip. He put one hand on her throat, just holding it there.

'I saw the way that Liam kid was looking at you tonight, Grace. He wants you.'

'Don't be daft, Nate. He's just a kid.'

Nathan shook his head. 'Trust me, he wants you. I can tell by the way he looks at you, wondering at what lies beneath,' he said as he started to unbutton her trousers with his free hand. 'Do you know how hard it makes me when I see other men looking at you, Grace?' He growled as he pushed his groin into hers as if to prove his point. 'When I know they're thinking about fucking you, about touching you the way I do.'

Conscious of his fingers on her throat, she flinched, but his grip didn't tighten, and he began to caress her neck with his thumb.

'But I'm yours, Nathan, only yours,' she said, her voice barely more than a whisper. Hoping that he would stop talking about other men wanting her, as it was a subject which was sure to enrage him sooner or later.

He laughed. 'Oh, I know you are, and don't you ever forget it!'

Pushing his tongue into her mouth, he kissed her in that way that made her forget her own name before making love to her right there in the hallway.

CHAPTER THIRTEEN

Present Day

Nathan sat at his usual table in a quiet corner of the Rose and Crown, waiting for his best mate, Ben McKinley, to talk over a business proposition Nathan had for him. Ben had been semi-legit for a long time, and owned his own garage, but he could still be persuaded to get his hands dirty when the occasion called for it. And Nathan was about to pull off a big takeover; he needed people he trusted around him – and there was no one he trusted more than Ben.

Jake had turned up and was sitting at the bar watching Everton getting slaughtered, as usual. Grace pottered about around him. Nathan watched them both from his vantage point. The closeness they shared was clear enough for a blind man to see. The way Jake looked at his mum every time someone scored – either to convey his joy or dismay. And the way Grace smiled at him, reassuring him everything would always be okay. Nathan had always been envious of their bond. He'd sometimes felt like a voyeur intruding on their happiness. Always standing on the side-lines and never truly one of them. He'd wanted to be. He'd tried to be one of them. Especially after Jake was born; he'd really tried to change. But the pull of his other life had always been too strong. He missed the adulation, the respect, the look in someone's eyes when they knew they were beaten.

He loved them both more than he'd ever loved anyone. They were the only family he'd ever known. At the age of thirteen, he'd promised himself he'd never let anyone have that sort of power over him again. But ever since he'd met Grace, he'd been besotted by her. He loved her so much, sometimes it felt like he couldn't breathe without her, and he'd gone and forgotten his most important rule.

Then Grace fell pregnant and it was game over. He'd never wanted kids. That was until she'd told him they were going to have one anyway. If there was anyone he would have chosen to have a baby with, it was her. She was everything a mum should be: warm, caring, and fortunately for him, forgiving. She was an amazing mum, he could never deny that. She had given their son the best home a child could ask for. Not like his own slut of a mother who had never given him any of those things. She'd left him to fend for himself most of the time and was more interested in the various men that drifted in and out of her life than she ever was in Nathan. He was never a priority, never first choice. He always felt like he was in the way. *Her greatest regret* – that's what she always told him anyway.

Social services took him away from her when he was eight and she didn't even try and stop them. Nathan told everyone, even Grace, that she'd died. The truth was, he had absolutely no idea where she was. She probably was dead anyway, her body ruined by years of alcohol and drug abuse.

Nathan never knew his father and, apparently, he didn't even know his son existed. His mother would never tell Nathan who he was, and claimed she didn't know, but he never believed her. He always fantasized that his dad would find out about him one day and would rescue him from his miserable life. But of course, his father never came, and Nathan learned that the only person who could rescue him was himself. Only he could pull himself out of the stench and the ugliness he was born into. Shake off the dirt and the shame that were the shackles of his childhood and become something better.

What was it about Grace? He'd always been able to have any woman he wanted. Why could she get to him the way no one else ever could? He used to ask himself those questions all the time. But now he knew. It was the way she made him feel. The way she looked at him like he was the most incredible person in the world. She saw through his suit of armour to the monster beneath and she'd still loved him. She made him feel safe. She was home.

Seeing her and Jake together gave him a hollow feeling in his chest. It didn't matter how many people were around him, or claimed to be loyal to him, to love him even. When he saw Grace and Jake together, it made him feel more alone than he ever had in his life. It reminded him of the nights he'd spent at home, abandoned, as a small child, waiting for his mother to return. Sometimes it was hours, sometimes days before she came back to him.

Grace and Jake were his family. He belonged with them. He already had Jake believing he was the best dad in the world. His next step was to convince Grace to take him back again. He would make it happen if it was the last thing he did. Whether she wanted to or not. After all, it was her fault that he'd ended up on the path he had. There was a time he was so close to a different life. He had it all planned out. It was just within his grasp. Then he gave it all up – for her. Everything was always for her. Even if she didn't know it.

CHAPTER FOURTEEN

Twenty Years Earlier

Nathan lay awake staring at the ceiling, listening to the soothing rhythm of Grace's steady breathing. Despite putting a twelve-hour shift in earlier, which made all of his limbs ache in a way they never had before, he couldn't sleep. He could never switch off like Grace did. Within minutes of her head hitting the pillow she was out like a light, but he lay awake for hours. He'd never been a great sleeper; the constant nightmares had seen to that. But this was something else. A nervous energy that kept his mind racing.

He smiled as he remembered a tale he'd told a few of the regulars in the pub earlier, which had ended in Morris the handbag laughing so hard he almost choked, bitter running out of his nose, and old Mick having to run to the gents before he pissed himself. Nathan always had a gag or a funny story to amuse them with, and they lapped it up. They said he was the best thing to have happened to the place in a long time. Now that his name was above the door, people looked at him differently. He was someone. He could refuse to serve any one of them simply because he wanted to. He could throw any of them out on their arse if they even looked at him the wrong way.

Working for Tommy McNulty wasn't panning out quite as he'd expected. He hated being the new kid. Some days he felt like a glorified errand boy and he was tired of it. Maybe that was why he'd always preferred to work alone? No need to impress anyone. No requirement to 'fit in'. Of course, he was always needed when something was about to kick off, but he knew he wasn't being let anywhere near the real danger – or the real money. He was never invited to the quiet little meetings at Tommy's club, or the after-hours drinking sessions when the good whisky came out.

Of course, there was a certain kudos that came with being associated with someone like Tommy, but he couldn't shake the feeling that his boss was either waiting for him to prove himself – or to fuck up, and Nathan didn't have the patience to wait and see which one happened first.

Maybe he'd just keep managing the bar? Tell Tommy that Grace needed him there and he just didn't have time for anything else. Could he do that? Just walk away from Tommy McNulty? Surely the fact that it was to manage the Rose and Crown and look after Grace would make Tommy more amenable to the situation, given Tommy's connection to Grace's dad. A connection that Grace was entirely unaware of and one that Tommy insisted she would never find out about.

Yes, his mind was made up. Tomorrow he was going to talk to Tommy. Thank him for the opportunity he'd given him but tell him that he couldn't do it anymore. He was going to concentrate on being the landlord of the pub. He had loads of ideas to bring in more business. Live bands. Maybe some food? Quiz nights. He laughed quietly as he turned to bury his head in the pillow. Nathan Conlon going legit. Who'd have thought it?

Tommy McNulty handed Kenny the glass of Scotch he'd just poured. Kenny Lennox had been his right-hand man since his best mate, Patrick Carter, had got sent down for a twelve stretch. Kenny had been with him since the beginning, but the sad truth was that, at the age of forty, Kenny was already past it. One too many run-ins with a fist or a baseball bat, and on one occasion a crow-bar, had left him with a dodgy knee and a bad shoulder. He'd never been the brightest bulb in any case, but the repeated blows to the head had left him with little in the way of the old grey matter. It was only a matter of time before Kenny was replaced by a younger, stronger model. And Tommy knew exactly who that man would be. He'd been grooming the lad ever since he'd met him.

'So he's gone to sort the daft prick out on his own then. Boss?' Kenny asked as he took a seat on the chair opposite Tommy's desk.

Tommy nodded. 'Yeah. He'll be fine. Have you seen the lad in a scrap? He can look after himself, Ken. Plus, he's got balls of solid iron.'

'I know that, it's just …'

'Just what?' Tommy snapped.

Kenny swallowed. 'Well, Terry's no mug. And Nathan's just a kid. I could have gone with him, that's all.'

'Listen, Kenny. Nathan is more than capable of handling Terry fucking Barnes. The lad is an animal. And he wanted to sort this himself. He won't have anyone threatening Grace, or her pub.'

Kenny frowned. 'But Terry would never threaten Grace. He's not *that* stupid. He knows the score.'

'Yeah. But Nathan doesn't need to know that. So, Terry never *actually* threatened her. I embellished a little.'

'But …' Kenny started but one look from his boss obviously made him think again and he stopped mid-sentence.

'Look, this is the perfect opportunity for the kid. Give him a chance to show us what he's made of. And if Terry Barnes should be wiped off the face of the earth as a result – then all the better. He's been getting right on my tits lately. Save me topping him myself. He's been taking far too many liberties and I can't have it, Ken.'

'You think Nathan will finish him off then?' Kenny raised an eyebrow.

Tommy shrugged. 'Possibly. There's no saying what that crazy bastard will do. Especially if he thinks Grace is in trouble.'

'Well I suppose it makes sense, boss.'

'Of course it makes fucking sense. In a few hours, my Terry problem will be sorted, and I'll have the true measure of Nathan Conlon.' Tommy smiled as he downed the last of his Scotch.

CHAPTER FIFTEEN

Nathan slid down the wall of Terry Barnes's flat as if in slow motion, until he was seated on the floor, legs outstretched in front of him. His heart pounded so hard he thought it might burst through his ribcage. Holding out his hands in front of him, he blinked as he surveyed the damage. The skin of his knuckles so broken and red he couldn't tell which blood was his and which was Terry's. The blood. It was everywhere. Covering his hands. His forearms. A glance down at his clothes confirmed his suspicion that it didn't stop there – his T-shirt and jeans streaked with violent splashes of red.

Three feet to the left of him lay Terry's lifeless body. His face unrecognizable from the man who'd opened the door less than half an hour ago. Nathan hadn't meant to kill him. Things had just got out of control.

Tommy had phoned him earlier; told him it was urgent. Like the dutiful soldier, Nathan had obeyed, thinking it would be his chance to tell Tommy about his plans to manage the Rose and Crown full-time. But then Tommy had told him about Terry.

Terry Barnes was a low-life coke dealer who liked to shout his mouth off and make threats to anyone who'd listen when he'd had a few too many. The fact that he was the nephew of a well-connected city councillor made him think he had a free pass to piss off anyone he fancied, although he was usually smart enough not to mess with people like Tommy – people who didn't give a flying fuck about his uncle, because they had far more important people in their pockets. But anyone who'd ever had cause to have any dealings with Terry would happily toss him into the Mersey with a pair of concrete wellies if they thought they could get away with it.

He'd been in the pub a few nights earlier, pissed as a fart, making threats to anyone who'd listen and giving Grace a hard time. Nathan had thrown him out and given him a slap for his trouble and thought no more of it, but Terry had other ideas. According to Tommy, he'd been telling anyone who'd listen that the Rose and Crown and its owner were in big trouble. Specifically, he would give that *stuck-up bitch* who owned the place a good hiding. That revelation had made Nathan's head almost explode. The thought of Terry fucking Barnes with his hands on Grace – his Grace.

Tommy told Nathan to 'have a word' and make sure that Terry never darkened the door of the Rose and Crown again. Threatening Grace was personal as far as Tommy was concerned, and he was trusting Nathan to deal with it.

So, Nathan had gone around there straight away, with the intention of giving Terry a good kicking. Maybe breaking some bones. And he would have done just that. But Terry made a fatal mistake. He laughed at him. Called Nathan a nobody. Then he offered to show Grace what a 'real man' was.

Nathan had felt a rage like he hadn't experienced in a long time. He punched a still laughing Terry full force in the face. There was a sickening crunch before Terry dropped to the floor like a sack of spanners. Nathan kept punching him. Over and over. Pummelling the unconscious Terry's head and face. Releasing all of his pent-up rage. He didn't stop until his arms ached.

Terry hadn't stood a chance. No one would underestimate Nathan Conlon ever again.

Wiping his hands on his jeans to remove some of the sticky, congealing liquid, Nathan took the mobile phone from his back pocket and dialled Tommy's number. His boss answered after three rings.

'Yeah, kid?'

Nathan didn't answer. What could he say? He'd fucked up big time. He was supposed to warn Terry off, not turn his face into a plate of chilli con carne. Terry was connected. How the hell was he going to get away with this?

'Nathan,' Tommy snapped.

'I've killed him, boss,' Nathan said quietly.

There was a moment's silence that felt like it lasted for hours before Tommy laughed. 'Fucking hell, lad. You don't mess about, do you?'

'Sorry.'

'Don't worry, kid. You did good. Stay put and I'll send some people to sort it out.'

'Thanks, Tommy. I owe you.'

'You certainly fucking do.' Tommy laughed again and hung up the phone.

Nathan sat in the hallway of Terry's flat. He was no stranger to violence. He'd been around it all of his life. But he'd never killed anyone before. He supposed he should have felt bad somehow. Should have been begging whatever God there was out there for forgiveness. But he didn't. He felt relief. He'd just beaten a man to death with his bare hands and it felt good. At that moment, he knew he'd never be satisfied just being the manager of a pub. A normal job would never be enough for him. He had a gift. He'd been told that before but now he believed it. And he would use it to make sure no one would dare laugh at him ever again.

CHAPTER SIXTEEN

Present Day

Grace could see the blonde head bobbing up and down in the crowd as Sandra Redman, one-time barmaid of the Rose and Crown, made her way towards her. Sandra was late as usual and she was almost running. Her face broke into a smile when she spotted Grace through the crowd.

'Grace,' she beamed and pulled her into a hug. 'You look lovely – as always.'

'As do you, Sandra. Married life must suit you.'

Sandra shrugged her shoulders and the two women went inside the busy restaurant. As they were seated by their waiter, Grace could see him eyeing Sandra's legs as she slid into the booth. Sandra had always been fond of her short skirts. She certainly had the legs for them.

'How's Jake?' Sandra asked.

Grace told her all about his plans for university and how she was hoping he'd get the exam results he needed. 'And how's Eddie?'

Sandra rolled her eyes. 'Oh, his usual charming self. I despair with him, Grace, I really do. He's nineteen going on forty. He won't get a job. Treats me like his skivvy. I swear he becomes angrier every day.'

Grace shook her head in sympathy. 'I'm sure he'll sort himself out soon, Sandra,' she tried to reassure her. 'He's probably just trying to figure out what he wants to do with his life. And at least now he has Richie to look up to.'

Sandra shook her head. 'Eddie and Richie don't seem to be getting on at all. They rub each other up the wrong way. Richie just wants a quiet life, but Eddie seems to want to cause World War Three every time he comes through the door. You're so lucky Jake has his head screwed on.'

'Jake has just found something he likes to do. I'm sure Eddie will soon, and then he's bound to settle down a bit.'

'I'm sure you're right,' she sighed. 'I'm just afraid of what he will discover he likes doing!'

Jake and Eddie had met a few times when they were younger, but they didn't get on at all; they were as different as day and night. Sandra and Grace, on the other hand, had a lot in common and were good friends.

They made small talk and caught up on what had been going on in each other's lives, but Grace knew there was something else on Sandra's mind. There was a nervousness about her; she fidgeted more than usual and constantly looked at the door.

'Have you seen him then?' she asked Grace eventually.

Grace nodded in response. She'd seen him almost every bloody day for the past six weeks. It was maddening, never knowing when he was going to turn up. No doubt it was part of his ploy to remind her exactly who was boss. He had no bloody idea! It would be funny if it wasn't so annoying.

'How did it go?' Sandra asked.

'Fine,' she replied nonchalantly. 'He's got a new girlfriend now. She seems nice.' Grace knew Sandra wouldn't ask her what she really wanted to know, so she told her. 'Don't worry, Sandra. I would never tell him about you and Eddie. He doesn't know. I swear.'

Sandra blushed. 'I know you wouldn't tell him. Thanks, Grace, it's just that he terrifies me.'

Grace smiled at her. 'Well I know that feeling,' and they both laughed.

After they ordered their meal from the waiter, Sandra slipped a small envelope across the table to Grace. 'Here's that information you asked for,' she said quietly.

Placing the envelope in her handbag, Grace smiled at her companion. 'Thanks, Sandra. I really appreciate it.'

'Any time, Grace. I'm glad I can help.'

'I wish you'd let me pay you for your trouble.'

'It's no trouble, honestly. I'm happy to help you out. I told you, no one questions anything I do. I've been there longer than everyone else so I'm pretty much given free rein. And our IT systems are so antiquated there's no way to tell what information is accessed.'

'Well at least let me treat you to dinner,' Grace said.

'Deal,' Sandra smiled.

Grace watched her friend as she tucked into her prawn linguine and felt a brief pang of guilt. She knew Sandra would do anything for her. Their history was a complicated one and it was one which allowed Grace to call in a favour whenever she needed to. It made Grace wonder at the woman she'd become. Manipulating her friendship with Sandra for her own ends. There was a time she'd never have even contemplated such a thing. But that was before Nathan. Before he'd taught her how to be just like him.

Sandra was a receptionist in a doctor's office and had access to a wealth of NHS data. She'd provided Grace with information before and she was under the impression Grace used it to thoroughly vet her employees. But in fact, Grace used it as a means to gain an advantage over her rivals – whether it be an address to trace someone who'd gone on the missing list or finding out someone's health or personal issues, to manipulate a weak spot. The possibilities were endless once you knew what to look for.

The envelope in Grace's handbag was going to help Patrick negotiate a new business deal with an old rival of Nathan's, Kevin Mitchell. Kevin was as arrogant and as ruthless as Nathan, but he'd never quite been able to reach the top of his game like Nathan had. With Nathan sniffing around wanting to know who had the monopoly on supplying drugs to the vast majority of clubs in Liverpool, Grace had realized it might be helpful to bring in a business partner. Someone who could be the face of the operation. If Nathan wanted to go to war over it, then he could go to war with Kevin, who had a small army of hired thugs at his disposal. The outcome of which wouldn't matter much to Grace. Kevin's and Nathan's firms could battle it out to the death as far as she was concerned. But she'd get the lion's share of the profits with none of the aggravation.

Grace didn't like to use the term blackmail, but the fact she had evidence that Kevin's mistress had recently aborted his child, would certainly make the negotiations with Kevin much smoother. If his wife, Mel, ever found out about his extramarital dalliances, she'd string him up in Liverpool city centre by his balls, for the whole world to see.

CHAPTER SEVENTEEN

Squinting in the evening sunlight, Nathan pulled his sunglasses from the glovebox of his car. He was parked on a side road, with a clear view of Antonelli's restaurant on the high street, hoping to catch Grace when she came out. He'd called at the Rose and Crown to look for her earlier and had tried his best to hide his disappointment when Jake told him where she'd gone. She was meeting a friend apparently. With nothing else to do, Nathan decided it wouldn't hurt to find out just who this *friend* was.

He'd never been to Antonelli's. It was a new Italian, owned by Sean Carter of all people. Nathan frowned as he realized it was probably no coincidence Grace was choosing to eat at Sean's place. She seemed to have some connection to the Carter family that he couldn't quite get to the bottom of.

It looked like a nice place. All chrome and glass and fancy signage. Apparently, it was a new Liverpool hotspot. Nathan had no idea how Sean had managed to walk away from his former life and open a string of restaurants, but he was seemingly squeaky clean these days. Where had he found the capital for his business venture? He must have had a backer, but who?

Sean and his brother Michael had been arrested as part of the operation that saw Nathan doing twelve years inside. He knew that the brothers had lost everything, just as he had. Their houses, cars, money. Proceeds of crime, apparently. Not that Nathan's losses could be explained away so easily. Over a million he'd had stashed in his lock-up from the job they'd been working on, had mysteriously disappeared – apparently. Nathan knew exactly who'd taken it. The thieving, scumbag, bizzies. There was no way they couldn't have found that in his lock-up. They put on a good show though. For all outward appearances, they appeared to be scratching their heads looking for it, and he could hardly say anything, could he? The money he'd paid that shower of cunts over the years and they still saw fit to rob him blind.

Nathan had never found out who grassed him up all those years ago. It had to have been a set-up. There was no way the plod were that clever, or that lucky. They'd burst into the place when him and two of the lads were inside, up to their necks in drugs. If that wasn't bad enough, Nathan had two shotguns and a Baikal handgun in there as well. His prints were all over the handgun too, on account of the fact he had it in his hand when the door was bust open. They'd only been moving them through though, and had only been inside the place for ten minutes before it was raided.

As much as he'd hated prison, Nathan knew that doing that long stretch had probably saved his life. He'd been out of control and doing so much Charlie that he didn't care about anything or anyone. He was reckless. That's how he ended up inside; and if he hadn't, he was sure he'd have ended up with a bullet in his head instead.

He'd had it pretty good inside. As far as anyone could anyway. There were plenty of people who wanted to be associated with him and follow his orders. He still managed to run things from inside. He spent his first year in the seg because he couldn't swallow his pride, and he fought with anyone and everyone who crossed his path. But being in there for so long gave him the opportunity to get clean for the first time in his adult life. His mind became sharper than it had ever been. Even the nightmares stopped after the first rough couple of months. And as he'd been stuck in a cell on his own, he'd been able to scream and shout without someone looking at him like he'd grown an extra head.

He'd forgotten how smart he was, always one step ahead of everyone else. He'd thought the drugs had made him quicker, stronger, but he realized they had actually dulled his senses. So, thanks to his reputation, his skill for business, and his loyal workforce, he built himself a solid empire to come out to. No longer frittering his money away on a flash lifestyle, he'd netted himself a small fortune. He was fucking loaded. He had it all. The fancy waterfront pad. The nice car. Tailored suits. Attractive young blonde on his arm. He was a respectable club manager – soon-to-be owner. No one could touch him.

There was no way he was going back to prison though. He realized why people like his old mate, Tommy McNulty, had other people doing the grunt work for them. It was so they never ended up inside. And, if you did things right, people were too scared, or too loyal, to ever grass you up. He had learned that was how to do business; maintain the presentation of a respected businessman, and let other people get their hands dirty on your behalf.

Nathan had his own army of loyal foot soldiers; people who would do what he told them to without question. People who would allow him to remain at a safe distance from the scene of the crime, which was a shame in some ways because that was the stuff he loved. He'd much rather have been smashing someone's head open than shaking hands and negotiating deals. He missed the adrenaline; the thrill of hurting someone; that unmistakeable noise of a bone snapping. Although he still got to give someone a good slap or kicking when the occasion called for it, it wasn't the same as being right in the middle of it, all day, every day.

Nathan's thoughts returned to the present as he noticed the huge glass doors of Antonelli's opening. Grace stepped outside into the street. She was laughing as she held the door for the blonde who walked out behind her. Nathan recognized the other woman. It had been a long time since he'd seen her, but he'd never forget that face. What the hell was she doing with Grace? Did Grace know about Sandra's little bastard? What was his name? Eddie? Yes, Eddie. That was it.

No. Grace couldn't know. She'd have given him hell for it and would have definitely used it in the divorce against him. Besides, Jake would have told him if he'd discovered he had a half-brother. That lad couldn't hold his own water. The slightest bit of pressure and he folded like a wet *Echo*.

Nathan continued to watch as the two women hugged each other and went their separate ways. Grace climbed into her Mercedes, and Sandra walked off down the high street towards the train station. Nathan thought about following her and asking her what the bloody hell she was playing at. Hadn't he warned her to stay away from his family? Fortunately for Sandra, his phone rang and he saw John Brennan's name flashing on the screen.

'What?' he snapped.

'Trouble at the mill, boss,' John answered.

'For fuck's sake,' he spat. 'I'll be there in ten minutes.'

Nathan started the engine of his car and pulled away from the kerb. He thought about Sandra, and what possible connection she could have to Grace, all the way to the club.

CHAPTER EIGHTEEN

Eighteen Years Earlier

The fan in Tommy's office blew warm air onto Nathan's face. A trickle of sweat ran down his brow, and onto the notebook he was writing in. Tommy was in Spain with Sharon for a couple of weeks, and he'd left Nathan in charge. He was waiting for someone to bring him a cold drink when he heard the door open.

'About fucking time,' he growled, but when he looked up it wasn't someone with a drink. Instead, some young blonde walked in, pushing a pram. She looked vaguely familiar to him.

'Can I help you?' he snapped.

She started laughing. 'Well I fucking hope so. Remember me, Nathan?'

He looked at her face, trying to place her. He'd definitely seen her before, but he couldn't recall where.

'I worked in your pub for a couple of weeks last year.' She scowled at him.

He remembered her then. 'Emma?' he said, just to piss her off.

'Sandra!' she spat.

'Well, what the fuck do you want?' Although already, he had

71

a sinking feeling it was something to do with the baby in that pram. About eighteen months earlier, he'd given Sandra a lift home one night after her shift had finished. He'd been unable to resist her. Eighteen years old, with legs up to her armpits, pigtails, and a tiny, tight miniskirt. He hadn't used a condom. He usually kept a stash in his car. He hated them, but he used them most of the time, especially with some of his regular girls who'd had more cock than a farmyard hen. But he'd been as horny as hell, and she was too young to have slept around much.

Nathan remembered their encounter. Running his hands over the soft, taut skin of Sandra's hips, her perfectly shaped tits bouncing up and down as she rode him like her life depended on it. She was clearly inexperienced, but that just made her more eager to please him.

'I'll see you at work tomorrow then?' she'd said expectantly as Nathan had zipped up his trousers.

'No, I don't think so. I don't think you're going to work out. Here's your wages for the rest of the week,' he'd said coolly, as he threw her two £20 notes.

'You fucking bastard. Don't think you can treat me like some cheap slut,' she'd snarled at him.

He'd laughed and told her to get out of his car. She took the money though. It always amazed him, these women who threw themselves at him, and then acted surprised when he treated them like the whores that they were. What did they expect? That he would leave his wife and run off into the sunset with them? As if he would. None of them could compare to Grace.

'I'd like you to meet Eddie,' she said sarcastically, snapping him from his thoughts. 'He's your son!'

Nathan started to laugh. 'Fuck off! You expect me to believe that. He could be anyone's.'

'Believe me, I hoped he wasn't yours. But my ex took a DNA test and he's not his. He's nine months old. The only other man I was with was you. So obviously, he's yours. You can get a DNA

72

test too if you like, but he is yours, Nathan, and you will pay for him. It's only fair.'

'What the fuck is that supposed to mean?' he barked, barely able to control his anger.

'It means, you prick, that I expect you to contribute to his upkeep. Babies are expensive, you know.'

Suddenly, he felt sorry for the little bastard, having a mother like that, who saw him as nothing more than a means to make some easy money.

'And if I don't?'

She laughed again. 'Then I'll ask your wife for the money instead. I'm sure she'll pay up. She seems decent like that.'

She stood there, hand on her hip, grinning at him, like she'd just won a raffle and he was first prize. She was clearly taking great delight in holding something over him. Who did this bitch think she was? Coming into his place of work and threatening him. Did she have any idea who she was fucking with?

'Write down your address. I'll call round later, and we'll sort something out.' He almost spat the words at her.

'Don't you want to see him?' she smirked.

'Later!' he growled, his tone betraying the calm facade he was trying to present.

'I won't be home until seven,' she told him with a smirk, swaying her hips as she walked out of the sweltering office.

Nathan threw his pen through the open office door. 'Where is my fucking drink?' he shouted into the now-empty hallway.

CHAPTER NINETEEN

Sandra cursed under her breath as she pulled the heavy pram up the stairs to the fifth floor of the block of flats. The lift was broken again. She hated living in this dump, but hopefully soon she wouldn't have to. Nathan was obviously raking it in and it wouldn't be any hardship for him to support her and little Eddie too. His wife was pregnant and from what she'd heard, Nathan was over the moon about it. She was sure as soon as he got to know Eddie, he'd fall in love with him too, just like she had. Sandra had enjoyed seeing the look of shock on Nathan's face when she told him. It served him right after the way he'd treated her. Karma was a bitch.

Eddie was fast asleep, so she'd have time for a quick freshen up before Nathan arrived. She wanted to look her best and remind him just what he was missing. Despite her best intentions to despise him, and regardless of the way he treated her, she thought that maybe having his baby would make him see her differently. She hoped they could come to some sort of mutual agreement, something that would benefit them both.

Opening the door to the tiny flat, Sandra left Eddie asleep in his pram in the hall. She walked into the living room and almost fainted when she saw Nathan in there, waiting for her.

He was reading a newspaper and sitting there like he owned the place.

'How the hell did you get in here? You cheeky fucker!' she yelled at him, her heart pounding in her chest.

'Sit down, Sandra!' he growled.

'Don't tell me what to do. This is my home,' she shrieked. Who the fuck did he think he was? But she regretted the words as soon as they were out of her mouth. He moved so fast she didn't have a chance to react. Grabbing her by the hair, he dragged her to her knees until all she could feel was the searing pain in her scalp. She was kneeling in front of him then, her face level with his crotch. Heart hammering in her ribcage, her breathing fast and shallow, she swallowed. What was he going to do to her next? How the fuck would she get out of this? Before she could think of anything else, he grabbed her by the throat and started to squeeze her neck as he pulled her back to a standing position until her face was level with his. The look in his eyes made every hair on her body stand on end. He was enjoying himself. She was struggling to breathe, and just as she was about to lose consciousness, he released his grip.

He smiled at her. 'Are you going to sit down now?'

Nodding, she sat down in the nearby armchair as quickly as she could.

'There's ten grand in there, Sandra.' He nodded towards a carrier bag on the coffee table. 'You can take that today on the understanding that you never, ever, bring that little bastard anywhere near me or my family again. You tell no one that he is my son, and that includes him. I don't want to see either of you ever again. I don't even want to hear your names. Do you understand me?'

'Yes,' she whispered.

'Should you decide to change your mind,' he went on, his voice low and full of menace, 'remember how easily I let myself in here tonight. You have no idea of the things I am capable of. I could kill you in your bed while you sleep and not even break a sweat. And who would look after your little bastard then? And should my wife ever find out about your little offspring, then you really will wish that you'd never laid eyes on me.'

She believed every word he said, and suddenly she felt sorry for his wife having to spend her life with that animal. The woman she had envied for so long, she now felt nothing but pity for. One thing Sandra did know was Nathan would never be a part of Eddie's life – that she would make sure of.

CHAPTER TWENTY

Present Day

Glancing at her mobile phone, Grace sat in the endless snake of city-centre rush-hour traffic. Leaning her face against the driver's window, she enjoyed its pleasant momentary coolness on her flushed cheeks. Her thoughts drifted to Sandra and how worried she'd been that Nathan would find out about their friendship. Fortunately for both of them, Nathan had no idea.

She remembered the day when Sandra had walked, or crashed, back into her life. Grace had just been to a meeting with her accountant and was making her way through town to catch the train back to the pub. 'It was raining and she was in such a rush she didn't see the woman with the young boy rounding the corner. As their umbrellas collided she was almost knocked to the ground.

'I'm so sorry,' the woman said as she reached her hand out to steady the stumbling Grace. 'I wasn't looking.'

Grace looked at her. She looked tired and drawn, pale skin, her eyes red, maybe from crying, Grace thought. The blond boy beside her was probably only a little older than Jake. He wore a coat that was too thin for the wintry weather and Grace noticed the bottom of his trousers were soaked through. The other woman attempted a feeble smile and it was then that Grace recognized the young lady standing before her. 'Sandra Redman? Is that you?'

It took Sandra a few seconds to recognize her too. 'Grace,' she replied sheepishly. 'How are you?'

'I'm hungry, Mum,' the boy's voice interrupted. 'Can we have McDonald's?'

'Not now, Eddie,' Sandra said quietly, and Grace got the impression this woman couldn't afford such a luxury.

'Well, what a coincidence,' Grace said leaning down so she could see the boy's face. 'I was just going to McDonald's myself. But I hate eating on my own. Would you like to join me? My treat,' she added, directing this to Sandra now.

'Can we, Mum? Can we? Please?' The young Eddie pleaded, his cheeky smile hard to resist.

Twenty minutes later Grace and Sandra were enjoying a coffee while Eddie tucked into his Happy Meal.

'Does Nathan know about Eddie?' Grace asked matter-of-factly. She knew as soon as she saw the boy's smile that he was Nathan's. He had the same blue eyes too.

Sandra stared back open-mouthed, no doubt waiting for the reprimand or the accusations which were about to follow. But Grace wasn't concerned with any of that. She knew her ex-husband well enough to know he would have used this woman as he used all of them. And right then, it appeared that Sandra and her son, were in need of a little compassion.

'He is Nathan's, isn't he, Sandra? I can tell by looking at him. Does Nathan know?' She asked, her tone softer now, trying to convey to the other woman that she wasn't angry – not with her at least.

Sandra nodded, tears pricking her eyes. 'He doesn't want anything to do with him though. With either of us. I'm so sorry, Grace. I was a kid. I was stupid. I don't know what else to say.'

Grace placed her hand over the younger woman's. 'I don't blame you. He saw lots of other women. Got at least one other pregnant,' she added, recalling the mouthy blonde who'd come to the pub on Christmas Eve all those years ago. Screeching like a banshee and demanding to know why Nathan hadn't left his frigid bitch of a wife after she'd aborted their baby like he'd asked. It had led to an almighty row and the worst hiding Nathan had ever inflicted on her. She'd thought she was going to die. But thankfully it had been the last too. It was the proverbial straw that had broken the camel's back.

At Grace's words, Sandra broke down in tears and told her everything. How Nathan had threatened her. How he'd paid her off and how ashamed she was that she'd taken his money. Grace listened intently, wondering if her ex-husband had any idea of the destruction he left in his wake. Sandra told her she was struggling to find work. She'd used the money Nathan gave her to move out of the flat she was in and was in a nicer area, but that money had long gone and she was struggling on benefits.

'I really want to work, Grace. It's just so hard to find something to fit around school hours.'

Grace's heart almost broke looking at this young woman and her son. She remembered how bubbly and vivacious Sandra had been. How confident she once was. Yes, she had made a play for a married man, but it was Nathan who had vowed to be faithful, not the women he screwed around with.

'Well a friend of mine is looking for someone to answer the phones for a few hours a day. You could do that, couldn't you?'

'Yes. Yes, of course.' Sandra nodded furiously.

That's how Sandra ended up working for Grace's accountant, Ivan. Five hours a day while Eddie was in school. A few years later she'd left and her experience from that job had enabled her to get her current one as a doctor's receptionist, which she loved, and which was where she met her husband, Richie.

Grace and Sandra became good friends after that day. Grace would always remember Eddie and often sent a little gift or a new item of clothing in the post for him. She offered to help

Sandra out with money a few times too, but the younger woman would never take it from her. She said that she didn't deserve anything from her.

Sandra often asked Grace if she knew just how much her kindness had changed her life. Grace always laughed it off and told her it was nothing, but Sandra always said the same thing – that it was everything to her. Because of that she was happy to help Grace out in any way she could. So, searching the NHS system for information occasionally really was no hardship at all. The way Sandra told it, Grace saved her that day, and saved Eddie too. And Grace knew that Sandra would do absolutely anything for her.

CHAPTER TWENTY-ONE

Kayleigh started to complain as Nathan was buttoning his shirt.

'I can't believe you're going out again. It's Monday – who goes out on a Monday, Nathan? You've only been home for a few weeks and I hardly see you anymore,' she whined.

'Look, I've got some business to sort out. You're not moaning when I'm giving you money every ten fucking minutes, are you? So, get off my case and let me get to work.'

She sat on the bed pouting like a child and he wondered again why he put up with her.

'I'm sorry. I just miss you,' she whimpered.

He might feel some pity for her if he didn't know it was all an act. She was a manipulative bitch and she was trying to make him change his plans just because she was bored.

As he was taking no notice of her, she changed tack.

'I'll make it worth your while,' she purred as she started to unzip his fly and dropped to her knees in front of him, reminding him exactly why he put up with her.

Half an hour later and Nathan was climbing into his car to drive to Grace's. Jake played football on Monday nights and Nathan knew that meant Grace would be home alone. He had been on his best behaviour for weeks, smiling and laughing at all the right moments. Making her feel at ease. Making her trust him again, until he had her exactly where he wanted her. He was still pissed off over her threat to him, but he knew that the best way to get to her was to remind her why she'd fallen in love with him in the first place. It was only a matter of time before she was putty in his hands again – the way it was meant to be. He would get his own back, in his own way, when the time was right.

She would learn that she could not threaten him and get away with it.

Grace loved Monday evenings. She usually took the night off and had a whole evening of peace and quiet to herself. She would read a book or watch a film – something light and easy. It was her little slice of heaven.

She was just settling down when there was a knock at the door. Swearing under her breath, she got up to answer it. Who the hell was that ruining her peace and quiet?

She answered the door to Nathan's smiling face. 'Jake in?' he asked, brushing past her and into the house.

'No. He plays football on Mondays. I'm surprised he didn't tell you. You two seem to be inseparable lately.'

'He never mentioned it.' He shrugged. 'I might as well stay for a brew now that I'm here.'

She wanted to tell him to sod off, and that she was enjoying some peace and quiet. But she knew it would be useful to her to keep Nathan onside – for the time being at least. It would also be sensible to find out how he was keeping himself occupied now that he was out. So, she invited him into the kitchen and put the kettle on.

'I see more of you now than when we were married, Nathan,' she said, and he laughed in response.

82

'So, Jake said you've bought the club?' Grace asked while they drank their tea.

'Yeah. It's all mine now.'

'Sharon sold it to you then?'

'Yeah. I got it for a steal as well,' he grinned. 'Old cow thought it was losing money, but it's a fucking gold mine.'

'I don't suppose you have anything to do with her believing that it's on the skids though?'

'Me? Never,' he laughed. 'It's a good job I didn't buy the place years ago like I was supposed to. Them robbing coppers would have taken it along with everything else.'

'Oh yeah, proceeds of crime, that's what they call it, isn't it? The NCA looked into the pub after you were locked up. Thankfully, it's always been in my name.'

'Hmm.' He nodded. 'Robbing bastards never declared my money as proceeds of crime though, did they?'

Grace shook her head as she tried not to smile. 'Thieving scumbags.'

One cup of tea turned into two and then before long they were sitting on the sofa in Grace's living room, reminiscing about their misspent youth, until they were both laughing about the first time Grace tried to cook a jar of baby food in the microwave. She'd left the lid on and it exploded everywhere. Both of them had stood there, looking at each other with spaghetti bolognaise running down their faces.

'I can't believe you remember that, Nathan,' she said through tears of laughter.

'Of course I do,' he laughed. 'We were good together, Grace, and we did have our good times, didn't we?'

And it was true, they'd had lots of good times. So many times, when they would laugh until their faces hurt, so many times he would make her feel like the most important person in the whole world.

'Yes we did, didn't we?' She nodded.

'It would be our anniversary in a few months. Twenty years – if you hadn't divorced me, obviously,' he said as he took a sip of brandy. 'So why did you divorce me, Grace?'

'Are you serious?'

He nodded.

'You know why, Nathan.'

He just stared at her. Why wasn't it enough for him that they were getting along? Why did he have to keep dragging the past up?

'Because, Nathan, you were a monster. A bully and you shagged anything with a pulse. Does that answer your question?'

He shrugged. 'Fair enough.'

As far as she could tell, he seemed to genuinely look back on their relationship as some wonderful time in their lives, when nothing could be further from the truth. She thought about that day she'd mustered the courage to see a solicitor about divorcing him. She was terrified and excited at the same time. She remembered her hands shaking when she signed the papers and the relief she felt when he finally agreed to sign them too.

'I could hardly believe it when you signed the divorce papers,' she said.

'I thought about refusing, but I knew I had no grounds to appeal when I was doing twelve years.' His laugh was tinged with sarcasm. 'Unreasonable behaviour, wasn't it?' he said with a wry smile.

She tried to change the subject as this was a road she didn't want to go down with him. She could have kicked herself for agreeing to wander down memory lane with him, especially when his memories seemed to be of the halcyon days of their youth, rather than the horror of it.

'Well you have Kayleigh now,' she said jovially. 'And she's lovely.'

'I still love you though, Grace,' he said, his voice thick with emotion.

She swallowed the drink she was taking and just stared at him.

She knew that he wanted her to tell him that she loved him too, but she couldn't. She didn't. Her instinct was still to want to make him feel better; she knew that little boy inside him always felt he'd never be quite good enough. Even after all that time, after everything he had done, she still had that reflex to comfort him. But she would never give him even a glimmer of hope.

'That's just the brandy talking,' she said instead.

He didn't reply. He moved towards her and started to kiss her, pushing her down to lie on the couch at the same time. The weight of his body crushing hers. She pushed at his chest.

'Nathan, stop,' she said, assuming he would listen. Because he'd changed, hadn't he? But he didn't stop. He continued trying to kiss her, his hands grasping at her clothes.

'You know you want this, Grace,' he groaned. 'I know you still want me.'

'Nathan, stop,' she shouted. 'I don't want this. I don't want you!'

So many familiar feelings of terror and disgust flooded her body as though they had been held back by a dam for too long and had finally broken free of their barriers. She had almost forgotten what it truly felt like to be afraid of him. As though she'd blocked it all out for her own sanity.

As if by divine intervention, Jake arrived home. Fortunately, he was drunk and made a racket coming in, so they both heard him. Nathan jumped up and they both straightened their clothes.

'Am I interrupting something?' Jake asked, raising an eyebrow at both of them as he entered the living room.

'No,' they both said – a little too quickly and firmly.

'Don't be soft,' Grace added, feeling the colour rush to her face.

'I'm off to bed, anyway,' Jake smirked, and she wasn't entirely sure he didn't suspect something had gone on, although thankfully he had no idea what.

'I'll show myself out.' Nathan said as he stood up to leave.

Grace sat on her sofa nursing the remains of her brandy. So, Nathan hadn't changed at all. She'd suspected it was all an act and now she had proof. Still, it had been a worthwhile evening. He'd been surprisingly open about his business dealings, bragging about the big plans he had, which was very helpful indeed. Almost worth having to put up with his unwanted advances – almost.

CHAPTER TWENTY-TWO

'Jake, will you please stop leaving your shoes by the front door?' Grace shouted up the stairs as she almost tripped over her son's size elevens when she went to answer the doorbell. She was expecting Patrick's granddaughter, Steph. They were going into town for the day for some retail therapy. After the previous night, Grace needed something to distract her. And nothing distracted her more than a day out with her favourite girlfriend and spending a boatload of money. Jake would be getting a load of new stuff for university today, whether he needed it or not.

Opening the door, Grace rolled her eyes when she saw Nathan.

'Grace, please let me explain,' he said.

'I have nothing to say to you,' she said quietly so Jake wouldn't hear. 'Now, piss off.'

'I just wanted to say I'm sorry, Grace. I really am.'

Grace didn't think she'd ever heard him apologize for anything in his life before. But it made no difference. He couldn't help himself. There was no being nice with him. He was a sociopath.

'Dad,' Grace heard from behind her and she cursed under her breath. 'What are you doing here?' Jake said chirpily as he came to the door.

'Hiya, son. I wondered if you fancied coming to the match on

Saturday. A mate of mine has got a box and he can get me a couple of tickets.'

Jake's face lit up like a four year old who'd just been told he could have ice cream for breakfast. 'What? Really?'

'Yeah. I might even be able to get you a meet and greet with the players beforehand too.'

'No way,' Jake exclaimed. 'Bloody hell, Dad, you're a legend. Can you believe this, Mum?'

Nathan smiled at Grace and flashed his eyebrows at her. No doubt thinking he was Dad of the fucking year.

'Yeah, it's great, son,' she sighed.

'Wait till I tell the lads,' Jake said, his eyes shining with delight.

'Anything for my boy,' Nathan grinned.

'All right. It's only a football match,' Grace said. 'No need to get overexcited.'

Nathan laughed. 'She's got no idea, has she, son?'

Grace fought the urge to slap the pair of them. How dare Nathan swoop in and start playing super-dad. She had been there every day of Jake's life. Wiping every snotty nose. Every tear. Every cut knee. Nathan thought a couple of tickets to the football could make up for eighteen years of never being there.

'Come on, lad. Let's go and get a pint, eh?' Nathan said.

'If you're paying,' Jake laughed. 'See you later, Mum,' he said as he grabbed his coat.

Nathan climbed into the waiting car with Jake close behind.

'Where to, boss?' John Brennan asked him. John was Nathan's right-hand man. He was one of the few men Nathan trusted. He'd managed The Blue Rooms in Nathan's absence and been the point of contact for most of Nathan's other business ventures while he'd been inside. He wasn't afraid of a bit of hard work and he was loyal to a fault. John was a year younger than Nathan, and almost as wide as he was tall. He was into body-building, and Nathan was sure John could crush a man's skull with one hand. One day, he was determined to find out if it was true. John had one of those faces that put people at ease. He always looked like he was smiling. It could be useful sometimes; it gave him the element of surprise. The Smiling Assassin, Nathan called him.

'The club,' Nathan said.

Jake chatted away excitedly in the back seat, and Nathan did his best to tune him out. Despite his calm exterior, he was seething with rage. Angry with Grace for repeatedly turning him down, and angry with himself for what he'd done the night before. He was supposed to be playing the long game and making Grace believe that he was a changed man. But sometimes he just couldn't think straight around her. He hadn't been able to help himself. He'd misread all the signals. Or had he? Maybe she'd been playing with him? Leading him on? Bitch.

She seemed to have grown a backbone of titanium while he'd been inside. The way she stood up to him. This was the girl who'd once been frightened of her own shadow. Had she forgotten who he was and what he was capable of?

Now she'd be on her guard around him. Gaining her trust would take too long. No, he'd have to think of something else. A change of tactic was in order. He didn't care how he got her back. He just wanted her back. Whether she was happy about it or not.

He'd find a solution to his Grace problem soon enough. He was sure of it.

CHAPTER TWENTY-THREE

The now-familiar sight of Nathan's Audi greeted Grace as she pulled up outside her house.

'What the hell are you doing here now?' she muttered. She could go somewhere else – visit a friend, but she'd been stocktaking with Marcus all day and all she wanted was a hot bath and a cold glass of wine. Besides, this was her home and there was no way she was going to let Nathan bully her into staying away from it.

It had been a few days since the incident when he'd tried to force himself on her and despite her making it clear he wasn't welcome in her home, he just wouldn't bloody stay away. Always claiming he was there to see Jake – obviously! As much as she would miss him, the sooner Jake went to university, the better for everyone. Grace was counting down the days.

The smell of bacon drifted out into the hallway when Grace opened the front door. As she walked into the kitchen she saw Jake and Nathan sitting at the kitchen table, the remnants of bacon sandwiches on the plates in front of them.

'Hiya Mum.' Jake smiled.

'Hey, son,' she replied as she kissed the top of his head.

'Hello Grace,' Nathan said as he looked her up and down, his eyes resting for far too long on her cleavage.

Resisting the urge to fasten the top buttons of her shirt and let him know that he'd got to her, she nodded at him before retrieving the open bottle of wine from the fridge.

'So, what are you two up to?' she asked as she took a clean glass out of the dishwasher.

'Dad called round to see me, so I made us some dinner,' Jake said. 'I'm going to Philly's tonight. It's his brother's birthday so we're going for a few beers. He's picking me up in a minute.'

'Okay.' She nodded, hopeful that Jake's imminent departure would prompt Nathan's too.

Jake's mobile phone vibrated on the table. 'Philly's here. See you tomorrow, Dad. I'll be late back, Mum,' he said as he was disappearing out of the door.

Grace poured herself the remnants of last night's Chardonnay. Swirling the pale liquid around her glass, she stared at her ex-husband. The intruder. Whenever she turned around it seemed he was there. Always two steps behind her. It infuriated her.

'What do you want, Nathan?' she asked as she took a sip of her wine.

He looked at her blankly. 'I came to see Jake.'

'Jake's gone now. Yet you're still sitting here as large as life?'

He shrugged. 'Maybe I thought you might fancy catching up?'

'Catching up? We're not friends, Nathan. We don't *catch-up*. You're my son's father and for that reason alone I tolerate you in my house. But I don't buy this nice-guy act of yours for a minute. I think the incident last week proved that we really can't be anything more than civil to each other.'

He glared at her, his eyes narrowed, jaw clenched shut.

She glared back, arms folded across her chest. 'I'll ask you again. What do you want?'

Rising from his chair at the kitchen table, he walked towards her until he was close enough that she could feel the heat from his breath. No doubt a tactic to intimidate her. But it didn't work. Not anymore.

'Maybe all I want is you,' he growled.

She would have been less shocked if he'd slapped her across the face. 'What?' she laughed. 'Me?' Stepping away from him, she began to shake her head. 'That ship has long since sailed, Nathan. You can't have me. You never will. So please, do us both a favour and give it a rest.'

'I always get what I want,' he said. 'You love me, Grace. You like to pretend that you don't, but you can't help it.'

She stared at him. He was as mad as a box of frogs. 'Are you serious?'

'One day soon, you'll be begging me to give you another chance. Just you wait and see.' He winked at her before grabbing his jacket and walking out of the kitchen.

'You're deluded, Nathan,' she shouted after him.

The sound of the front door slamming behind him reverberated through the house.

Grace leaned against the kitchen counter as she downed the last of her wine in one gulp. Nathan was the most manipulative, slippery bastard she'd ever met in her life. Of course he was up to something. But what? She had no doubt she'd find out soon enough.

CHAPTER TWENTY-FOUR

Looking up from his newspaper, Nathan saw Michael Carter stroll through the door of the Rose and Crown. He'd heard his old business associate frequented the place and hoped it was only a matter of time before they came face to face. He'd been out for almost two months and had been hearing plenty of stories about Michael and Grace and an alleged fling a few years earlier. Nathan was eager to push some of Michael's buttons and find out if there was any truth to them. He wondered if it was because Michael had found out that Nathan had once shagged his wife, Cheryl, back in the day, on their kitchen table of all places. Not that it mattered if Michael knew. It was still no excuse for going after Grace. She wasn't some old slapper like Cheryl.

Nathan also had a suspicion that Michael and his old man, Patrick, were using the pub as their base of operations. If all the rumours were to be believed, the Carters were into everything and anything. Insurance scams, bootleg spirits and ciggies, as well as having their dealers all over Merseyside. They'd always been a family to be reckoned with, but it seemed they'd really got their act together in recent years and were raking it in.

Grace must have been taking a cut from it. She wasn't stupid enough not to. At least not anymore. Nathan would put an end to that soon enough. Once he had Grace back by his side, where she belonged, the Carters would no longer be welcome in the Rose and Crown.

Michael walked straight over to Nathan's table and took a seat on the chair opposite him.

'What are you doing here, Nathan?' Michael said. 'I thought you and Grace were divorced now?'

'Yes we are,' Nathan smiled, not feeling the need to answer the first question. 'And what about you? You and your old fella seem to be hanging around here a lot. What's all that about? Does your missus know you're in here sniffing around?'

Michael glared at him. 'It's fuck all to do with you.'

'You've got a real thing for my wife, haven't you?' Nathan sneered. 'I heard a rumour you two had a bit of a fling a few years back. Are you trying to have another crack at her?'

'She hasn't been your wife for a long time.'

He shrugged. 'I suppose not. So, I tell you what. Grace is all yours if you want her. I'll stand aside,' he lied. 'I have no interest in used goods.' He leaned towards his companion. 'But you just remember, if you're fucking her, that there isn't one part of her where I haven't already been. Not one inch of her body that I haven't already claimed for my own.'

Nathan watched Michael's reaction closely. His clenched fists. Jaw clamped shut. The vein pulsing in his temple. It was obvious to Nathan that he'd touched a nerve and it confirmed what he'd already suspected, that the rumours about him and Grace were true. Michael glared at him, the rage emanating from him like the heat from a furnace.

'I owned her first, mate,' Nathan went on, 'and that will never change.'

Nathan expected a reaction. He hoped that Michael might even take a swing at him. He was always up for a fight, especially with someone who'd been screwing his wife. But instead Michael's

94

shoulders dropped, and to Nathan's confusion and annoyance, he started to laugh.

'What's so fucking funny?' Nathan growled.

'You still don't get it, do you? I don't want to own her. She's not a fucking car.' It was Michael's turn to lean in close to Nathan now. He spoke softly. 'I know that when she's with me it's because she wants to be. Not because she's too terrified of me. Now I know it was a very long time ago, but you must remember what that felt like? To be loved by her?'

Clenching his jaw so hard he feared he might grind his teeth into dust, Nathan thought about his response. His pride wouldn't allow him to admit that Michael could get to him. If he ripped the bastard's head off his shoulders, which was exactly what he wanted to do, then he'd lose face in front of everyone, including Grace. But who did the little prick think he was? Like Michael could possibly know Grace better than he did. Cheeky fucker!

Downing the rest of his pint, Nathan stood up to leave. 'I could have her back in a heartbeat, mate. And don't forget it,' he whispered in Michael's ear before walking away. But Nathan knew it was a lie. As much as he hated to admit it, Grace seemed to be impervious to his many charms. It pissed him off so much he could hardly bear to think about her, but think about her he did. All the fucking time. To think that someone like Michael Carter, might have his hands on her, made him want to gouge his own eyes out – or better still, Carter's heart.

Grace watched the exchange between Michael and Nathan intently. She had no idea what they were talking about but things looked like they were getting heated. Eventually Nathan stood up and stormed out. If only she could have that effect on him.

Michael walked over to her at the bar. 'Can I get a cup of coffee, Grace?'

''Course you can. What was all that about?'

'Your ex-husband is an arrogant twat. That's what. One of

these days, I'm going to wipe that smug grin off his face permanently.'

'Well whatever you said must have worked. I've never seen him walk out of here so fast.'

'Sorry about that. I couldn't help it.'

'Don't apologize. I wish I could get rid of him that quickly.'

He looked at her and shook his head. 'I know, but I said something I probably shouldn't.'

'What did you say to him, Michael?' she snapped.

Before he could answer, Marcus walked up to them. He draped a slender arm over Grace's shoulder. At six foot three, he towered over her.

'Hey Michael,' he said. 'We don't see you around much these days?'

'I've been busy,' Michael replied.

'You used to practically live in this place,' Marcus continued.

'Yeah well, things change, don't they?' He looked at Grace as he said it and she had to stop herself from rolling her eyes.

'Grab us some more filters from the stock room, would you, lovely?' she said to Marcus. 'The one in the coffee machine needs replacing.'

Marcus promptly did as he was asked.

'I have some paperwork that needs your signature, boss,' Michael said. She glared at him. He only called her boss when he was trying to be funny or he wanted to piss her off. She sensed it was the latter.

'Can you leave it on my desk? You remember where that is, don't you?' she sniped.

'Forget the coffee,' he snapped. 'I'll leave the papers upstairs.'

Michael came back down to the bar a few minutes later as Grace was just sitting down with a cup of coffee of her own.

'I'm sorry,' he said. 'Nathan just pushes my buttons.'

'He pushes everyone's buttons. It's like his super-power.' Grace smiled.

'I know I haven't been around much lately. I'll make sure I'm here more often, now that he's back.'

She placed a hand on his arm. 'Don't worry about it. You're here when you're needed. You have other priorities now and that's fine.'

'Don't say it like that, Grace.' He frowned.

'Like what?' she frowned back at him. 'I'm not looking for an argument with you, despite how much you seem to want to start one today.'

He stepped closer to her. Resting his hand on the small of her back, he leaned down and kissed the top of her head. 'I miss you,' he whispered.

She leaned into him. She didn't tell him that she missed him too. She did, just not in the way he wanted her to.

CHAPTER TWENTY-FIVE

Seven Years Earlier

It was a sunny afternoon in July when Grace first met Michael Carter. He'd just been released from prison, after serving five years of a ten-year sentence for drug supply and money laundering. He'd been in prison with Nathan after they were both lifted as part of the same operation. Michael turned up at the bar one day looking for his dad, Patrick.

'I haven't seen him today,' Grace said. 'I think he's taken his new girlfriend off shopping for the day,' she'd lied. She knew exactly where Patrick was, but the fewer people who knew about his whereabouts, the better.

'I'll have a pint then,' he said.

Ten pints later and Michael could barely stand. He'd just found out that his wife, Cheryl, had been having numerous affairs while he'd been inside. She'd been at it for years, apparently, and had cheated on him with some of his mates too. He was a pitiful sight and Grace felt sorry for him.

'Look, sunshine,' she said. 'Let's get you a taxi home.' She and Marcus poured him into a taxi just before closing time and hoped that he remembered where he lived.

The following week, Michael turned up at the pub again with a huge bouquet of flowers – to apologize for being a drunken arsehole, he said. She didn't tell him that she dealt with much worse on an almost nightly basis.

Michael was trying to keep his head down. He was on licence and didn't fancy going back to prison any time soon. But he was struggling to find work; after all his particular expertise didn't lend themselves to the type of jobs that were advertised in the *Liverpool Echo*. He'd come into the pub with Patrick most evenings, looking completely dejected and sorry for himself. Grace wondered how people like him were supposed to be rehabilitated when no one seemed willing to give them a chance. Patrick had warned her about offering him any work that might jeopardize his licence, so Grace offered him some work at the bar and he accepted gratefully.

One Sunday evening, Grace was waiting for Michael to start his shift so she could go upstairs with Jake and finish his homework. It wasn't like him to be late. Half an hour after Michael's shift should have started, Grace heard banging on the back door. She opened it to find him standing there, blood pouring from a cut above his eye.

'Christ, what's happened to you?' she asked him as she helped him inside.

'I need to get cleaned up, Grace. Can I?' he pleaded, indicating the stairs to the flat.

'Of course, wait here for a sec.'

Grace went into the bar. 'Marcus, I know we're short staffed, but I've got to take care of something. Are you okay for half an hour?'

He nodded. 'Yeah. No problem. It's quiet tonight anyway.'

Grace took Michael upstairs and asked Jake to finish his homework in his bedroom.

'What the hell happened to you?' she asked Michael as she handed him a bowl of warm water and a facecloth.

'I was on my way here and two lads jumped me,' he said.

'Did you know them?'

He shook his head. He was shaking like an addict who needed a hit. Grace could see he was a little beaten up, but she'd heard Michael was as hard as nails – just like his father. She was surprised to see him so affected by the attack.

'Are you OK?' she asked as she took the cloth from him and started to clean the wound above his eye.

'I'm fine,' he said. 'But they're not. I left them both lying in the street. They were in a bad way. What am I going to do, Grace? I'll go back to prison once they find out it was me. I'll have to serve my licence and I'll get done for GBH, or wounding. I've got previous for kidnap and wounding. They might life me off this time.'

'Well that's only if they catch you, isn't it?' she said. 'And you were here all afternoon working anyway. Marcus and I can vouch for that. I bet some of the customers could too.'

'Really?' he said. 'You'd be my alibi?'

''Course I would. You're my best worker.' she smiled.

Two days later when the police arrested Michael, Grace, Marcus and six of the regulars from the pub swore that he'd been working in the Rose and Crown that afternoon and therefore couldn't possibly have been involved in any assault. He was released, after twenty-four hours, without charge, pending further enquiries.

The following evening, Grace and Michael were working behind the bar when Detective Sergeant Tony Webster came in. Grace knew him well and the previous year, when a local drug-dealer had been shot outside the pub, they had come to an arrangement that was mutually beneficial.

'Pint of bitter, Tony?' Grace asked.

He nodded in reply.

She handed him his pint.

'Nasty business, that assault on Edge Lane the other day,' he said, pursing his lips and shaking his head.

'Yeah, I heard.' Grace nodded as Michael hung around in the background pretending not to be eavesdropping.

'One of them died this afternoon,' Tony said matter-of-factly.

'Really?' Grace asked, trying to keep her tone as nonchalant as possible. She could see Michael from the corner of her eye. He stopped what he was doing and stood still. 'That's awful.'

'Not really,' Tony said. 'The guy was a scumbag of the highest order. Spent most of his time robbing old ladies and teenagers. The other one wasn't much better either. They obviously picked on the wrong fella this time though, eh?' He looked at Michael as he took a swig of his pint.

'Well, karma's a bitch,' Grace said.

'That's a nasty cut you've got there, mate,' Tony said to Michael.

'It's this stupid till,' Grace interrupted. Pressing a button to open the cash drawer and prove her point as the tray shot out violently. 'He was putting some glasses away and it smacked you right in the eye, didn't it?'

Michael nodded. 'It's a bloody health hazard.'

'Hmm. I'm going to watch the darts. Keep 'em coming, will you?' Tony lifted his pint glass before going to sit at an empty table near the television.

Grace took Tony another pint of bitter and a packet of pork scratchings to his table.

'Here you go, chief.' She smiled.

'Anything else for me?' He raised his eyebrows.

'Of course. The usual?'

'Given the gravity of the situation, I think double my usual fee is appropriate. Don't you?'

Greedy bastard, Grace thought, but didn't say. She owed Michael Carter, even if he didn't know it. She was the reason he'd gone to prison five years earlier.

She smiled sweetly. 'Of course, Detective. I'll have someone drop it off in the usual place tomorrow.'

'Always a pleasure, Grace.' He smiled as he raised his glass to her.

CHAPTER TWENTY-SIX

Present Day

'See you tomorrow, boss.' Marcus smiled as Grace opened the door for him.

'Yep, to do it all over again,' she laughed.

'You wouldn't have it any other way,' he said as he gave her a sideways hug.

'No I wouldn't,' she agreed.

After she bolted the doors behind him, Grace turned and surveyed the empty Rose and Crown – her empire. She loved this time of night. It was so quiet and peaceful. The glow of the streetlights filtered through the long windows, bathing the chairs and tables in a soft amber glow. She knew every shadow. Every corner. Every nook. She loved this place like it was a part of her family. It had always been there for her.

Walking across the room, Grace ran her hand along the freshly polished bar, enjoying the feel of the cool, smooth wood. She remembered the day Nathan had been sentenced. Although he'd been on remand for six months, she couldn't dare to dream that he would actually be convicted and sent down. If she'd believed that, and it hadn't happened, she would have never recovered.

The first thing she'd done after leaving the court room was to come to this pub, her pub, and sack the manager Nathan had insisted on hiring. He was quite possibly the worst pub manager she'd ever encountered, and she was sure he was on the take, too. Then she'd walked behind this very bar, her head held high, and served the next customer as though she'd never been away. It was like putting on an old, comfortable cardigan – all warm and snug, fitting her as perfectly as it always had. She was exactly where she was supposed to be.

Now the pub was thriving. Grace had built up a loyal base of regulars over the years. A combination of her dad's old customers coming back once Nathan and his stooges were no longer running the place, and new clientele who were attracted by the changes Grace made to keep up with the times. The place was always busy. Even when some of the other pubs in the area had struggled, the Rose and Crown had always remained a firm favourite with the locals.

Grace wondered at the ease in which Nathan had taken it all away from her. How she had allowed him to take the only thing, apart from their son, that meant anything to her. Had she really been so afraid of him that she'd given him everything so willingly?

Yes.

Yes, she had.

But she wasn't anymore. Grace would see her beloved pub razed to the ground before she allowed Nathan Conlon to take anything from her ever again. He was a disease. A cancer that consumed and infected everything he touched. The only way to be rid of him was to cut him out of her life entirely. But to do that, she needed to cut him out of Jake's too, and that might prove harder than she'd expected.

CHAPTER TWENTY-SEVEN

The young waitress smiled at Grace as she took her coat. 'Mr Carter is already waiting for you, Ms Sumner,' she said as she led her to a quiet table near the back of the restaurant. The smell of basil, tomatoes, and garlic filled Grace's nostrils as she walked between the occupied tables. Her stomach rumbled and she realized she hadn't eaten since breakfast, almost twelve hours ago.

'Grace.' Sean Carter stood as she approached, and gave her a warm embrace.

'Sean.' She smiled at Michael's brother, and returned his hug.

'You look well,' he said as they sat down. She smiled in appreciation. She'd lost a little weight, no doubt thanks to the stress and anxiety of having to deal with Nathan on a regular basis.

'You too,' she told him. He'd just returned from a few weeks in Italy and the tan looked good on him. He was an attractive man, like his father and brother – tall and dark, grey peppering his hair. Grace wondered, momentarily, whether they looked like any of the other couples who were out for a pleasant dinner that evening. Or perhaps, they might appear like they were on their first date? No – not that. They knew each other too well to look awkward or nervous in each other's company.

'The place looks great,' she said as the waitress returned with some menus.

'It does, doesn't it? I hoped you'd like it. And obviously, our chef is the best in the North West. We're fully booked most nights now,' he beamed, the pride clear to see on his face. The chef, Steph, was Sean's daughter and Grace's closest girlfriend. At twenty-four she was one of the most sought after in the business, having trained at the prestigious Leith's School of food and wine. Sean and Grace were both ecstatic when she'd agreed to take the head chef position at Antonelli's.

'Well, the place is obviously in good hands with you,' Grace said.

He nodded appreciatively. 'Can you believe this is our third restaurant, Grace?'

'No, I can't. I still remember being sceptical that the first one would work out,' she laughed.

'I remember.' He grinned.

Antonelli's was the third Italian restaurant the two of them had opened together. All Grace provided was the capital. Sean ran them all and oversaw most of the decisions. As a courtesy, he consulted her on the major ones, but he knew she was more than happy to remain a silent partner.

After Sean had got out of prison six years earlier, he would hang around the pub with Michael and Patrick a lot. But he wasn't interested in going back to his old life. He'd talk to Grace about his love of cooking and his dream of opening his own restaurant one day. It was him who'd suggested that Grace should start serving food in the pub. He'd said it would attract a whole new kind of clientele, and he'd been right. Grace had given him free rein for twelve months and he'd set up the kitchen and established a basic but tasty menu.

After realizing Sean had significantly undersold his ability to cook and to run a business, Grace had agreed to finance the opening of his first restaurant, Grazia's, in Liverpool city centre.

It remained a well-kept secret between Sean and the Carter family that Grace was his partner, but Sean had proven himself to be an excellent businessman, and like his brother and father before him, a great friend. Together, he and Grace were the respectable faces of Grace's growing empire.

'So, how are you really?' Sean asked, snapping Grace from her thoughts.

'I'm fine.' She frowned at him.

'Come on, it's me you're talking to. I know you have to put on a brave face for the other two, just in case they go rogue and try to feed him his own eyeballs,' he laughed.

Grace wondered momentarily if Sean had ever watched his brother or his father feed anyone their own eyeballs. Given their previous lives as enforcers for some of the most dangerous criminals in Liverpool and Manchester, it wasn't unlikely. Sean had always been the brains of the operation, which is why he'd received a longer sentence than his brother. Rumour had it, he could be the most terrifying of the Carter clan when he wanted to be, but for the most part he'd left the muscle work to others.

'I forgot.' Grace shook her head as she answered Sean's question. 'I forgot how bloody terrifying he is, Sean. He has this way of making me feel helpless. I stand up to him and he laughs at me. I'm worried I'm going to put myself in a vulnerable situation with him, just because of this need to prove myself.'

'I can't ever imagine you as helpless, Grace. I really can't.'

'Yeah, well, I was a very different person when I was married to him.'

'He really did a number on you, didn't he? So, what are you going to do now?'

Grace sighed. 'I honestly don't know. For now, he seems to be behaving himself and he has no idea that I'm involved in anything other than the pub. So, let's hope it all stays that way and we can both get on with our own lives.'

She heard herself saying the words, but she knew that it was all wishful thinking. Nathan was up to something. She could feel it.

'Well I hope so too. I'd hate for you to have to drag me out of retirement,' he laughed as he said it, but Grace sensed the uneasiness in him. It had taken him a long time to put his former life behind him. He had too much to lose to get sucked back in. His wife, Sophia, had already told him she wouldn't stand by him if he got sent down again. She was a fiery, Italian woman with a temper to match, and Sean knew she'd go back to Italy and take their two young children too.

'Of course not,' Grace said as she placed her hand on his. 'Now come on. Let's order.'

Grace watched Sean as he tucked into his carbonara. She knew she only had to say the word and he would deal with Nathan for her. Make him disappear and guarantee the body would never be found. In fact, any of the Carters would. All she had to do was ask. It made her chest hurt to think that one day she might have to. The knowledge that she held the balance of so many lives in her hands sometimes made her feel like she couldn't breathe. She felt like one of the clowns at the travelling circus her dad used to take her to, frantically running around trying to keep all of her plates spinning in the air. One false move could bring everything crashing down around them all.

She had to find out what Nathan was up to, and figure out a way to deal with him that wouldn't put anyone she cared about in danger, least of all Jake. Because if Nathan won, they would all lose.

CHAPTER TWENTY-EIGHT

Nathan sat in the expensive leather chair in his office and poured himself a glass of his favourite fifty-year-old malt. Leaning back, the old leather creaking under the weight of his body, he put his feet on the desk. He sighed as he ran a hand through his hair. He'd been out of prison for over four months and things still weren't working out as he'd hoped. Apart from buying The Blue Rooms from his former boss's widow, Sharon McNulty, he'd struggled to get any of his business plans off the ground.

He still had his main business and was a key player in the supply of drugs across vast parts of Merseyside, but he'd had his sights set on much bigger and more lucrative endeavours. Yet someone seemed to be one step ahead of him all the time. What was even more infuriating was that he couldn't find out who the hell it was. His lads had put feelers out across Liverpool but had been unable to come up with a name. How was he supposed to take down his biggest rival if he didn't know who they were?

Taking a large swig of his whisky, Nathan heard the knock at his office door.

'Come in,' he barked, hoping it was the man he'd been waiting for.

The door opened, and Nathan was pleased to see Eric 'the Echo' Evans. As his nickname suggested, there was little that went on in Liverpool that Eric didn't know about. At first, even Eric hadn't had any information on Nathan's competition. But motivated by a very generous reward, Eric promised to use all of his considerable contacts and resources to find some.

'Anything for me?' Nathan asked as Eric took a seat in the chair opposite him.

Eric nodded. He was grinning from ear to ear. It infuriated Nathan that he always appeared to be so bloody pleased with himself. If he didn't have some worthwhile information he was going to feel the full extent of Nathan's rage.

'Yep. And you will never believe what I found out,' Eric said.

'What?' Nathan snapped, his patience already waning.

'It's the Carters.'

'No.' Nathan shook his head. 'If it was the Carters, I'd know. Sean was always the brains and he's legit now, as hard as that is to believe, it's true.'

'Yeah, that is true. But Sean is no longer the brains behind them. And this is the good part, Nathan. You would never guess in a million years who is.'

'Tell me then,' he barked.

'Grace,' Eric said and sat back in his chair.

Nathan must have misheard. 'Grace?'

'Yep.'

'My Grace?'

'Yep.'

'No fucking way,' he said. 'That's impossible. Grace?' There was no way that could be true. Grace didn't have it in her. She was one of the most naive people he'd ever met. How the hell could she have become a fucking criminal mastermind? It just wasn't possible.

'I didn't believe it myself at first, mate. But it's true. It wasn't easy to find out either. Took me a lot of man hours, and I had to call in a load of favours. People are surprisingly loyal to her. She must be doing something right.'

Nathan shook his head. Surely this was a wind-up?

But then, like a half-completed puzzle, the solution of which had eluded him for so long, pieces of information started to fit neatly together. Grace's connection to the Carters. Her new-found backbone of titanium. The way she stood up to him like she wasn't afraid of him anymore. Her flash car. The designer gear. The big house. Jesus Christ! Eric was right. Grace Conlon was his competitor. No wonder he hadn't been able to find out who it was before now. Never in a million years would he have thought his quiet, mousy little wife had it in her. She'd obviously learned a thing or two from him. The devious little bitch.

Nathan started to laugh while Eric looked on warily. This was going to be easy. He was going to destroy her, and her little empire. He would muscle in on every aspect of her business – every part of her life, and he would enjoy every second of it. She might think she could get one over on him, but he had the most effective weapon anyone could wish for – their son.

CHAPTER TWENTY-NINE

'Mind if I head off a bit early tonight, boss. I've got a hot date,' Marcus asked Grace as he closed the till.

'A hot date? It's almost midnight?' she said.

'I know,' he grinned at her. 'He's a night owl.'

Grace laughed. 'Of course. I can close up here. You get off.'

He checked his watch. 'Now? Are you sure?'

'Yeah, go on. I wouldn't want to stand in the way of true love.'

'True lust.' He winked at her.

The last barmaid had left, and Grace was just about to bolt the heavy double doors when she felt someone push against them. The force propelled her backwards making her stumble.

Her first instinct was to wonder where her phone was, and how quickly could she get to it and phone Michael to get him round there as soon as possible. It was unusual for Patrick not to be there with her at closing time, but she'd encouraged him to have the night off. She could kick herself for that now though.

'Hello Grace,' Nathan said as he walked in and bolted the doors behind him.

She sighed. No need to call Michael then. 'What the hell do you want at this hour?'

'To talk.' He glared at her, making the hairs on her arms stand on end. She'd seen far more of him than she'd have liked these past few months, but there was an edge to his voice tonight that she hadn't heard in a long time. It made her heart race and her breath catch in her throat.

'What about?' she snapped, careful not to show him any weakness.

'I know, Grace,' he growled. 'I know about it all.'

She swallowed. What did he know? He couldn't possibly know everything. If he did then she was a dead woman.

'What are you on about now?' she said, glaring back at him. Looking him straight in the eye, trying to read him.

Brushing past her, he walked behind the bar and started to help himself to a generous measure of her best Scotch.

She followed him. 'Start talking, Nathan.'

'Or what? You'll get one of your heavies to sort me out? Michael Carter, perhaps? You and him used to be fuckbuddies, didn't you?' he laughed.

She rolled her eyes. 'Don't be ridiculous. Are you on something or what?'

'No.' He shook his head. 'Perfectly sober. Well almost,' he said as he downed the whisky in one.

Grace waited for him to talk, fighting the urge to ask him again what he was on about. She needed him to reveal his hand first. If she was going to figure a way out of her current predicament, she needed to know what he knew. It felt like an eternity before he spoke. An eternity in which she imagined every possible worst-case scenario. All the things she'd ever kept from him whizzed through her brain.

'I know all about your business with the Carters,' he said eventually. 'I know all about your shady dealings, Grace. The insurance scams, the bootleg booze and ciggies. Even dabbling in drug dealing now, aren't you? Supplying to half of Merseyside?'

She almost let out a huge sigh of relief. Was that all? It wasn't ideal, but her involvement in what had once been his domain was going to come out sooner or later.

'And what?' she shrugged. 'It's a free country.'

'And what?' he shouted. 'You've been laughing at me all along, haven't you? I've been trying to play nice for our son's sake, and all this time you've been trying to get one over on me. Trying to muscle in on my business.'

She laughed. 'Trying to? I think you'll find I've succeeded, Nathan. I have my fingers in a lot of pies. More than even you. Well, the you from back in your glory days at least. I hear you're not doing quite as well as you once were.'

Slamming his empty glass onto the bar, he walked towards her. She'd taken off her heels a few minutes earlier because they'd been rubbing her feet, so he towered over her five foot four frame. Glaring at her, his body shaking with anger, he snarled. 'I know who every one of your dealers are, and they will all be working for me before the month is out. This is my world, Grace. You're a little girl playing with the big boys. If you're not careful you're going to get yourself hurt.'

Grace could feel the anger radiating from him. Memories of their past forced themselves into her consciousness. The shouting. The beatings. The constant anxiety of living with his rage. Him, always angry. Her, always afraid.

'You asked me what I want, Grace. Well, I'll tell you. I want it all. I will take everything you have until you're on your knees begging me to throw you a fucking bone,' he spat.

Grace reached up her hand and stroked his cheek, noting the shock flicker across his handsome face. Just for an instant, his eyes softened, pupils dilated, his jaw relaxed as he pressed his cheek into her hand. This man was a ruthless bastard, but he loved her. More importantly, he wanted her. And she wasn't afraid of him anymore.

Looking up into his eyes, she smiled sweetly. 'I don't play with the big boys, Nathan, I give them their orders. I think you are

113

the one who needs to be careful, sunshine. This is my world now and you are a guest. You get to do your thing because I allow you to.'

Grabbing her hand, he pushed it away from his face. 'I think you're forgetting who you're dealing with.'

'No.' She shook her head. 'I know exactly who I'm dealing with, but do you?'

'You'll fucking pay, Grace. Soon,' he snapped before pushing past her.

'I already have,' she shouted after him as he let himself out.

Once she had bolted the door after Nathan, Grace poured herself a large brandy and phoned Patrick.

'Nathan knows,' she said. 'About the insurance, the cargo from France, and who most of our dealers are.'

'Is that all?' Patrick asked.

'Yep, but for now that's enough to cause me problems.'

'Hmm, meeting tomorrow then?'

'Yeah, I want everyone there, Pat. It's non-negotiable.'

'I'll get on it, boss.'

'Thanks,' she sighed.

'Try not to worry about him. We'll figure it out. And at least he doesn't know about the deal with Sol, or about Mitchell working for you.'

'Yeah, I know. He could really screw those up for us. Night, Pat.'

'Night, boss.'

Grace smiled as she saw the line of expensive cars parked up outside the Rose and Crown. Everyone had turned up, as instructed. As she let herself in through the side door, she saw Patrick had already assembled the chairs and tables for her meeting. The chef had come in early and was working overtime to keep them all fed and watered. The room, full of powerful men, became quiet as she entered. She smiled at them all as they

114

nodded or mumbled a greeting. They were smartly dressed in suits. She liked to see a man in a suit.

'Thanks for making it at short notice, lads,' she said.

'Thanks for the coffee and sausage butties,' Raving Ronnie shouted.

'Yeah thanks, Grace,' they all chorused.

She took her seat at the head of the table. 'It's the least I could do after dragging you all out of bed at this ungodly hour. Now let's get to work.'

Grace told the assembled men about Nathan's revelations of the previous night and warned them all to be on their guard. 'If you have any aggro with him at all, then let Pat or Michael know,' she said. 'We need to keep on top of him as much as possible. The less he knows about our operations, the better.'

They all nodded their agreement.

After the meeting was over and Grace had seen the last of the lads out, with the exception of Michael and Patrick, she bolted the doors. The pub wasn't due to open for another hour.

The three of them sat at one of the tables with a fresh coffee each.

'Anything else you need me to do, Grace?' Michael asked.

She shook her head. 'Not for now. But I need you with me to meet Sol tomorrow. And are you still okay for the trip to Spain next week? Alejandro is expecting you on the fourteenth. He knows we'll be needing more of his product. Make sure you drive a hard bargain.'

'Of course,' he said as he took a sip of his coffee.

'What about Nathan?' Patrick asked.

'Let me handle Nathan,' Grace said. 'It's what I do best.'

115

CHAPTER THIRTY

Solomon Shepherd smiled as he held open the door of Michael's Range Rover for Grace. Taking her hand as she stepped out, he guided her away from the large muddy puddle precariously close to her feet and her very expensive Louboutin's.

'Sol, so good to see you again,' she said, kissing his cheek.

'You too, Grace. It's been too long.'

Grace linked her arm through his as they walked towards the builder's yard where Sol conducted most of his business. Michael Carter followed close behind.

They were greeted at the door of the old Portakabin, which served as an office, by Sol's right-hand man, Neville Moss, whose large frame almost filled the doorway. He grunted as the three of them made their way into the surprisingly well-furnished room.

'Make us all a brew, Nev,' Sol ordered as he offered Grace and Michael a seat.

'So, how's business, Grace?' Sol asked as Neville made tea behind him.

'Good.' She nodded. 'And you?'

'Just great.' He smiled.

Grace shot Michael a surreptitious glance. She knew Sol was lying. He'd recently lost a boatload of money after a massive police operation had seen his suppliers arrested and receiving hefty sentences. A police informant had been the key to the whole thing. Much to Sol's humiliation and annoyance, the leak had come from within his own workforce. The informant earned himself a bullet to the head and a shallow grave for his betrayal. It was a miracle that Sol himself hadn't been lifted too. Although having a considerable number of Greater Manchester police on his payroll ensured that Sol was rarely in the line of fire.

Never one to miss out on a business opportunity, Grace had offered to become Sol's new supplier. She'd met him years earlier after Patrick had introduced them. Sol was one of the most powerful players in Manchester and Patrick and Michael had once worked as his enforcers. Like most men of his standing, in Grace's experience at least, he thought he was irresistible to women. And despite being married, he'd taken a keen interest in Grace as soon as he'd met her. She'd received dozens of bouquets of roses, jewellery and even a car in his bid to bed her. She returned the gifts to him, but he continued to persist in his efforts.

He was an average-looking guy. Tall, slim build, dark hair, nice smile. But it was his power and status that ensured most women he set his sights on, couldn't, or wouldn't, resist him. He wasn't used to being turned down. Grace knew that it was all about the chase for him. She was simply one in a long line of women who'd turned his head. But men like Sol had very fragile egos and as she was only starting out in the business back then, she'd wanted to keep him sweet. In the end, thanks to her experience of dealing with men just like him, having been married to one for years, they'd parted on good terms and Sol had moved on to his next conquest.

'Sugar?' Neville barked.

'No thanks,' Grace and Michael chorused.

Neville placed the mugs of tea on the small table situated between the four comfortable chairs and took a seat in the empty one.

'Nasty cut you've got there, Neville,' Michael commented on the deep gash above Neville's eye, which was clearly visible now that he was in close proximity. 'Lose a fight, did you?' he smiled.

'No,' he snapped. 'Never lost a fight in my life.'

'Well there's always a first time,' Michael quipped.

'Fuck off, Carter,' he growled.

'In the mood for a fight, are you, Michael?' Sol asked. He'd never quite forgiven Michael for moving on and setting up shop with his brother, Sean.

'Always.' Michael grinned. 'As you well know, Sol.'

Sol laughed. 'Still a cocky bastard, aren't you?'

Grace sighed. She hated these pissing contests. Men were driven by their bloody egos. How much simpler and more efficient would things be if women ruled the world?

'Look, you three,' she snapped. 'Stop waving your dicks at each other and let's agree a deal, shall we? I don't know about you, Sol, but I have somewhere to be.'

Sol turned his attention back to Grace. 'Of course,' he said, barely able to hide his annoyance that she had interrupted his little reunion with his former employee. But Grace didn't care. Sol was no longer the one with the power in their relationship. She was.

'So how much do you need?' she asked.

'How much can you get?' he countered.

'As much as you can sell.'

'I'm not sure you can get me as much as I could sell.' He laughed.

'I'm not sure you could sell as much as we could get you,' Michael interjected, earning him a withering look from Grace.

'How about we start with twenty kilos, Sol. We'll get you more as and when you need it. As much as you can handle.'

Sol nodded. 'That will work for us as a starter. Same price as my other supplier?'

She looked at him and frowned, as though she was considering his offer. 'Okay, but only because I like you, Sol.' She didn't tell him she could offer him a better deal than his previous supplier. She owed him no favours.

Grace fastened her seatbelt as Michael pulled the car away from the kerb. 'I knew you wouldn't behave yourself,' she said.

'What?' he laughed. 'I did.'

'Oh really? Trying to pick a fight with Neville? Winding Sol up?'

He shrugged. 'We've got a lot of history. Anyway, I didn't realize you paid me just to sit there and look pretty.'

Grace laughed out loud. 'Well if that's what I'm paying you for, I think I need a refund.'

He placed his hand on his heart. 'That hurts, Grace,' he joked.

'Just stop antagonizing Sol. We'll be working with him for the foreseeable future.'

'I'll be on my best behaviour from now on. Promise.' He grinned.

'I don't think he's ever forgiven you for abandoning him.'

Michael shook his head. 'Nope. But I don't know why. What was I supposed to do? My dad was inside, and Sean was out setting up on his own. Of course, I was going to back my brother.'

'Well, I don't think Neville has ever quite lived up to his predecessor.'

Michael smiled. 'Well who would?'

Grace closed her eyes and leaned back against the headrest.

'You coming to Nicola's birthday party on Sunday? he asked.

Nicola was Sean's daughter and Michael's five-year-old niece. ''Course I am, she's my goddaughter.'

'I know, she's mine too.'

Grace didn't open her eyes. He always got all melodramatic when the subject of Nicola's christening day came up. They'd been standing near the altar in the church, posing for the profes-sional photographer. Dressed in all their finery and holding a chubby baby Nicola between them, looking every inch the proud Godparents. Grace had seen the look in Michael's eye and realized he wanted much more from her than she was prepared to give him. A couple of drunken snogs had obviously given him ideas that they could ever be more than friends. It had signalled a significant shift in their relationship. Less than twelve months later Michael had met and married his current wife, Hannah. Despite that, he always looked at her like a lost little puppy dog whenever any reference to their relationship that never was arose. She'd broken his heart, she knew that, but she'd had no other choice.

Because Grace was in love with someone else. She had been for a long time. And she could never do that to him. An occasional drunken kiss when she was feeling lonely was one thing. But falling for someone else was an unwritten rule they both followed. They'd been on and off for years. Their relationship always a secret. Because if anyone ever found out, there would be hell to pay.

120

CHAPTER THIRTY-ONE

Relieved to be home at last after being stuck in Manchester rush-hour traffic for the better part of two hours, Grace kicked off her shoes. It had been a long day. Walking down the hall, she noticed the living room light on. Her heart leapt into her throat. After Jake and his mates had received the A Level results they needed, they'd all made plans to go on a massive boozy camping weekend. So, who the hell was in her house?

'Jake? Are you home?' she shouted anyway.

'Yeah, Mum. In here.'

Sighing with relief, Grace walked into the living room to see Jake lying on the sofa.

'What are you doing home, son? Why aren't you in Wales?'

Jake shook his head. 'Philly's car broke down, and then Izzy and Oscar had a massive row and Oscar stormed off and now no one knows where he is. So, we're going down tomorrow instead. Philly's brother's going to take us.'

'Oh, God. Poor Izzy, she must be worried sick,' she said as she moved his feet to sit on the end of the sofa with him.

'It's okay, Philly's looking after her.' He grinned. 'And Siobhan Davies is going to come with us tomorrow now.'

Grace smiled. Jake had had a crush on Siobhan since he was eleven.

As they chatted, Grace noticed a photograph on the coffee table. She recognized its well-thumbed edges immediately. She must have spent hundreds of hours staring at that thing.

'What's this doing out?' she asked, picking it up.

Jake shrugged. 'I found it in the kitchen drawer when I was looking for some new batteries for the remote.'

'I haven't seen this for ages.'

'I don't think I've ever seen it before. You both look so happy,' he said.

'We were.'

Jake yawned. 'I'm off to bed, Mum. See you in the morning,' he said as he kissed her on the cheek.

'Night, son.'

Grace curled up on the sofa with her legs tucked underneath her. She studied the photograph. It was the only surviving image of her and Nathan on their wedding day. Not one of the cheesy pictures the expensive photographer had made them pose for, but one taken by her Aunt Helen that they'd been oblivious to at the time. They were walking down the church steps with people milling about in the background. Nathan had his arm around her waist, his face buried in her hair as though he'd just said something in her ear. He was smiling, and Grace's head was thrown back in laughter.

As a child, Grace had loved to look at old photographs, particularly of her mum. She always imagined that the image was a piece of her mum's consciousness, frozen in time. And that if she went back to that place the image was taken, a part of her mum would still be there. She wondered the same about the photograph of her and Nathan. Did a part of them still dwell in that churchyard? The happy couple who thought that all they needed was each other. She used to look at it often. It reminded her that she wasn't crazy. That once upon a time, Nathan had loved her as much as she'd loved him. It was the life that could have been.

Grace rubbed the pad of her thumb across the image of the two figures on the glossy paper. She hadn't felt the need to look at it in a long time. If she was honest, it was too confronting. Sometimes it was like looking at a different person, one she no longer recognized when she looked in the mirror. She'd been a good person once.

Walking into the kitchen, Grace rummaged around her cutlery drawer until she found the old packet of matches. As she opened the back door to her garden, the warm air swept over her. Lighting one of the matches, she held it to the corner of the photograph until it caught fire. Dropping it to the floor, she watched as the orange flames burned effortlessly through the paper, until there was nothing left.

CHAPTER THIRTY-TWO

Twenty Years Earlier

'You all right, mate?' Ben laughed. 'You look a bit pale like.'

'Fuck off!' Nathan smiled, flicking the remains of his cigarette at him.

They were standing outside the church. Nathan stuffed his hands into his pockets to stop himself from fidgeting as he started to kick at a stone which was coming loose on the church steps.

Nathan had known Ben since they were thirteen. They'd been in a kids' home together when Nathan was sent there after a foster placement broke down. That's what the social worker said, anyway. Broke down – that was putting it fucking mildly.

They'd both hated the place, but before long they were practically running the joint, and had been best mates ever since. As far as Nathan was concerned, Ben was the only choice for best man.

They had got into, and out of, more scrapes together than Nathan could even remember. Although Ben was semi-legit, he worked in a garage during the day, he was a reliable fence too. Nathan had called on him occasionally while working for Tommy. The term built like a brick shithouse could have been written about Ben; he was a mountain of a man, but a gentle giant – not that you'd know to look at him. He'd never had the appetite for hurting people that Nathan did; he'd usually be the one trying to calm the situation down. But he'd always had Nathan's back when he'd needed him to.

Even as he was buttoning up his shirt that morning, Nathan could hardly believe he was getting married. Once he'd made up his mind to marry Grace, there seemed no point in hanging around. Everything about the two of them together made sense to him. Tommy had looked at him like he'd grown another head when he'd told him he'd asked Grace to marry him.

'You've only been together five minutes, lad. Are you sure?' his boss had asked him.

'Yes, I'm sure. I've never been more sure of anything in my life,' Nathan replied.

Tommy had insisted on paying for the do, and he'd shelled out a fortune. The best that money could buy. Tommy had pulled some strings to get them The Devonshire Hotel at short notice. Every face in Liverpool was going to be there. Tommy had always felt a sense of duty to Grace after her dad died and Nathan got the impression he was trying to make up for the fact her dad wouldn't be there. Not that Grace had any clue, of course. She still had no idea of her dad's connection to Tommy and Nathan was happy to make sure it stayed that way. She thought Nathan had paid for everything and Tommy was happy to let him take the credit.

After what seemed like forever the time came for everyone to head into the church. Nathan beamed with pride as he walked down the aisle and noted the number of guests in attendance. It was like the who's who of the Liverpool criminal underworld, and they were all there because of him. He had finally made it.

As he was standing at the altar, Nathan heard the music signalling Grace had arrived and was walking down the aisle. He was facing in the opposite direction, but Ben was looking right at the entrance.

'She looks stunning, mate, you're a lucky man,' he said.

Nathan turned then and saw her. She was the most beautiful thing he'd ever seen. Her long brown hair falling in waves over her shoulders; she was beaming at him and her smile lit up the whole church. He really was a lucky bastard.

Later that night as he lay in bed with his wife, he thought about how happy he was to be married to Grace. Despite everything she knew about him, about his past; and even though he didn't deserve it, she loved him. That knowledge was both comforting and terrifying to him. She had the power to destroy him. He pushed the thought to the back of his mind and concentrated on the feel of her skin against his; the taste of champagne that lingered on her lips; the smell of the coconut body lotion she always used – and he was lost to her.

CHAPTER THIRTY-THREE

Grace stared at Nathan's handsome face while he was sleeping. The sunlight highlighted his strong features as it penetrated the thin curtain of their hotel room. She wondered for the millionth time what she had done to deserve him; to be so unbelievably happy. Running her fingertip over the cool metal band of his wedding ring, she felt an overwhelming sense of joy and contentment.

Yesterday had been the happiest day of her life. She would remember every detail of it until the day she died. How she'd felt beautiful for the first time ever, walking down the aisle, feeling all eyes on her, but for once not being self-conscious or nervous. Her eyes were firmly fixed ahead, on Nathan. He looked so handsome in his suit, standing there waiting for her. The sun streaming through the stained-glass windows shone directly on him, illuminating him like some beautiful angel in the dim light of the church. She noticed that Ben said something to him, something which had made Nathan turn and look towards her. Then he smiled; the biggest and most beautiful smile she had ever seen. As she reached him he took her hand and whispered into her ear.

'Grace, you look beautiful.'

She'd never felt so happy in her life.

Grace would have preferred a small, quiet ceremony but Nathan was adamant that it should be a huge celebration. The church was packed to the rafters. Then afterwards they went to The Devonshire Hotel which was decked out like something from a Hollywood movie. The champagne flowed all night. People she'd never met or even heard of were stuffing envelopes into her hand, kissing her cheek, congratulating her and Nathan on their nuptials.

The best part had been when they'd finally gone up to their room that night. There Grace was, alone with her husband. He'd taken her in his arms and smothered her with a kiss. 'Let's go to bed, Mrs Conlon.' He grinned at her. Their wedding night was everything she could have hoped for.

Grace was still looking at Nathan when he started to stir.

'Stop staring at me, Grace,' he said, but she could see he was smiling.

She didn't stop, continuing to watch him. What had she done to deserve him? How could someone like him, love someone like her?

Taking hold of her hand, he opened his eyes. 'I told you to stop staring at me.' He smiled. 'It's very unnerving when I'm trying to sleep.'

'I can't help it.' She blushed. 'Anyway, you're my husband now, and that means I can stare at you all I want.'

He raised one eyebrow. 'Is that so, Mrs Conlon?' Before she could answer he rolled on top of her and silenced her with one of his incredible kisses. She thanked her lucky stars that she would get to spend the rest of her life as Mrs Nathan Conlon.

CHAPTER THIRTY-FOUR

Present Day

It was unusually hot, even for an afternoon in late August. The sweat trickled down Nathan's back. He'd been sitting in a stifling car for twenty minutes, waiting for Jimmy Dillon to make an appearance at the shithole he called a home. Jimmy had been trying to poach some of Nathan's customers, trying to undercut him. He claimed he had a better product, too. Jimmy had been around for a long time, but he was too much of a nutjob to ever make a serious bid to take over anyone's business. Besides, he'd had dealings with Nathan's firm before and had been given such a hiding, Nathan questioned how he'd ever even walked again. He was more suited to knocking off post offices and off-licences than he was selling drugs.

Nathan wondered what had prompted Jimmy's sudden change in circumstance, why he thought, after all those years, he could possibly get one over on Nathan Conlon. A warning from the man himself would ensure that Jimmy didn't dare take liberties again. But Nathan was becoming increasingly fed up of waiting.

Deciding he had better things to do with his time, Nathan

took his phone from his pocket and rang his newest recruit, Ste Jones.

'Find out where that prick is, Ste,' he barked at him, 'and fast.'

'Yes, boss,' Ste replied obediently.

Nathan phoned Jake as he was driving back to the club. His son's voice, bright and chirpy as ever, filled the car when he answered.

'All right, Dad.'

'Jake, come and meet me at the club for a few drinks.'

'Ah, I would, but I promised Mum I'd help out at the pub.'

'What? It's Friday night, you should be out enjoying yourself. Come and have a few drinks with your old man. Your mum won't mind,' he lied. He knew that she would. She loved spending time with her boy, especially when it involved him working in her precious pub. It made it all the more enjoyable to monopolize Jake's time as much as possible.

'Hang on a minute.'

Nathan could hear Jake's muffled conversation with Grace.

'I'll be there in an hour,' he said and hung up.

Seeing Jake would take Nathan's mind off that prick, Jimmy, at least for a while anyway.

The club was packed as it usually was on a Friday night. Some of the lads were regaling Jake with stories of their many misdemeanours and their near misses, showing off their various war wounds. Nathan watched his son laughing along with them and again it hit him how suited Jake would be to their line of work. He'd been so protected all his life, had never had a real fight as far as Nathan was aware. Never had any real brush with trouble. It wasn't right that he should go off into the big bad world without knowing how to protect himself. As Nathan's son, there would always be a danger someone would try and use Jake to get to him. He needed to prepare the kid. He was a big lad, and Nathan was sure he could have a good go, but it wasn't the same if you hadn't grown up around fighting. Even the smallest of men could knock you on your arse if they caught you just right.

'Enough of the war stories, lads,' Nathan said. 'Come with me, son.'

They took their drinks into Nathan's office and sat in the comfortable leather chairs.

'Would you know how to look after yourself if someone came after you, Jake?' Nathan asked him.

''Course I would,' he responded, puffing out his chest as if to prove it.

'It's just that there's a certain reputation that comes with being my son, and a risk too. Some people will always want what you have, and some will have the balls to try and take it. And I won't always be around to protect you.'

'Well, I've done all right for the past twelve years without you around, haven't I?' Jake snapped and it was the first glimpse of any sort of resentment towards Nathan that he'd seen – and it hit a nerve.

'Do you really think I left you and your mother to fend for yourself?' he bellowed at Jake. 'There was always someone looking out for you. Always!'

Nathan thought of Ben and John, and how they always kept a watchful eye on Grace and Jake, ready to spring into action if either of them were ever put in any real danger. Thankfully, they weren't. Jake shifted uncomfortably in his seat and Nathan knew he'd made his point.

'Now, you're going off to Leeds and I can't protect you the same way up there, that's all I'm trying to say. I just want to know that you can handle yourself, that's all.'

'Trust me, Dad. I can handle myself. I'm well aware of the reputation that comes with being your son and, believe me, it hasn't always been an easy one to live up to. I've had my fair share of having to defend myself simply because my name is Jake Conlon.'

'I didn't know that,' Nathan said, genuinely surprised.

'Well, why would you? You were in prison.' Just as Nathan thought he was about to be reminded again that he was an absent father, Jake added, 'And I didn't want to add to your worries. Besides, it was no big deal. I handled it.'

Nathan nodded. Time would tell if Jake could handle himself. 'Ever seen one of these?' he asked his son, pulling a Glock from his desk drawer.

'Shit. No.' Jake took the gun from him, his expression a mixture of trepidation and awe. 'Is this yours? Do you use it?'

'Not that one,' he told him. Nathan's gun stayed hidden, in the same place Tommy kept his – not that it had done him any good in the end. Nathan was not in the habit of carrying one about with him on a regular basis. He wasn't that stupid – at least not anymore. 'I'm moving this one on for someone.'

At that moment Ste came bursting through the door.

'We've found him, boss. He's in some flat on the new estate, with the Carter twins.'

'The Carter twins? What the fuck are they doing with him?' Nathan shouted as he grabbed his jacket to leave. That must be why the little bastard had become so cocky all of a sudden. Michael Carter's sons, Connor and Paul, were a pair of fucking idiots, but they were a pair of hard bastards and they traded on their family's reputation.

'You want to come?' he asked Jake, who stared at him open-mouthed. Nathan took that as a yes. 'Bring that with you then,' he told him, indicating the Glock. 'It won't do any harm to scare the shit out of the three of them.'

Jake tried to stuff the gun in the pocket of his jeans.

'For fuck's sake, son. You're gonna shoot your balls off if you're not careful,' Nathan snapped and snatched the offending item out of his son's hands. 'Keep it somewhere no one will see it,' he said as he tucked it into the back waistband of Jake's jeans, so it was covered by his jacket. 'There, now you look just like a pro.' Nathan smiled.

Jake smiled back nervously.

They pulled up outside the newly built block of flats, just Nathan, Ste and Jake. Nathan would have called a couple of the other lads for some backup, but he wanted to grab Jimmy before he figured out he'd been caught and did a runner. Ste could handle himself when he needed to but he wasn't Nathan's first choice for going into battle. And then there was Jake. Nathan had no idea how his son would react in any given situation. But now was as good a time as any to see if his boy had what it took.

Ste kicked in the door to the flat and ran in shouting at the top of his lungs. There's the element of surprise gone then, Nathan thought.

Nathan followed him, and Jake crept gingerly behind his father. They heard shouting and a woman screaming. Ste went off on one and started laying into Connor, who started shouting, protesting his and Paul's innocence.

Paul and Jimmy were nowhere to be seen. Nathan realized why, when he felt a searing pain to the back of his head. One of the little fuckers had hit him with something. Suddenly, Jimmy and Paul were on his back like a pair of wild animals.

Then everything happened so fast. He managed to elbow Paul in the face and he fell to the floor, blood spurting from his nose. Jimmy was still on his back, hitting him with something. Fortunately, most of the blows were being deflected by his arms. That's when Jake, who Nathan had almost forgotten was there in all the carnage, pulled out the Glock and stuck it right in Jimmy's face.

'Get the fuck off him now, before I blow your head off,' he said, although the tremor in his voice was easily audible.

Nathan could see that the boy's hands were trembling, but he had never been more proud of anyone in his entire life.

All Jimmy could see was the barrel of a gun in his face, and Nathan felt him slip from his shoulders, Jimmy's hands in the air in submission.

Nathan spun around and punched him in the face, feeling the satisfaction of Jimmy's nose break under his fist. He fell to the floor and Nathan started to kick him. He didn't stop until his leg began to ache.

'Don't you ever try and make a cunt of me again, Jimmy,' Nathan growled at him. 'Or I will let my boy put a bullet in your head. You fucking wanker.' He gave Paul a kick in the balls on his way out too, just for good measure.

Nathan shouted to Ste who followed them out. The collar of Ste's shirt was torn and he had a split lip and the beginnings of a black eye. It wasn't clear who'd come out the winner in his tussle with Connor. But Nathan was satisfied that Jimmy would not be fucking with him again.

'Jake, what the fuck?' Nathan said to him once they were outside. 'Where did that come from? You handled that like a pro, son,' he said, and he couldn't resist pulling him in for a hug and tousling his hair. He was smiling so much his face hurt. 'I'm so fucking proud of you.'

Jake, however, was green, and looked like he was about to throw up. 'Thanks, Dad,' he mumbled.

Nathan took the gun from him. 'I think this lad needs a few stiff drinks in him, and then I'd better get him home.'

'Well done, kid,' Ste told him with a pat on his back. 'Your first showdown! And you were a legend. Wait until we tell the lads.'

'No. Don't tell anyone, Ste,' Jake said anxiously.

'He won't be telling anyone, son. Don't worry,' Nathan assured him, giving Ste a look that said he meant it, too. The fewer people who knew about what had just happened, the better.

CHAPTER THIRTY-FIVE

'Be quiet, will you?' Nathan slurred. 'You'll wake your mother up.'

Too late, Grace thought as Jake and his father came tumbling through the front door like a pair of drunken oafs. It was seven in the morning and she'd been awake since six, wondering where Jake was.

'Shh, don't tell her what happened,' Jake said loudly, obviously believing he was whispering.

Grace walked down the stairs. 'Don't tell me what?' she demanded. A few months under Nathan's influence and Jake was already keeping secrets from her.

'About the gun,' he said to her, before breaking into a fit of giggles.

Grace thought she must be hearing things. 'The gun! What gun?' she said, trying to keep the anger from her voice. Her question was directed to Nathan, because she was sure he was behind whatever had gone on, and because Jake started to ramble incoherently about beer bottles and pigeons.

'Don't get your knickers in a twist, Grace,' Nathan said flippantly. 'There was just a bit of an incident tonight, that's all. And our boy here saved me!'

The look of pure pride on his face was unmistakeable. She

wanted to punch him right in the mouth, but she remained calm. At least she presented a calm facade anyway. She asked what the hell had happened, and why Jake was talking about a gun. Nathan proceeded to tell her that the two of them were ambushed by Jimmy Dillon and the Carter twins, and 'quick thinking' Jake scared them off by pointing the gun in Jimmy's face. Her heart almost stopped. She had so many questions. Why did Jake even have a gun in the first place? Why were they ambushed? Why had Nathan allowed their son to be in such a dangerous situation? All of which, Nathan failed to give her any credible explanation for.

As Grace understood it, from Nathan's drunken ramblings and Jake's incoherent babbling, Nathan wanted to give Jake the 'experience' of holding a gun. As he was doing this they were interrupted by Ste, who'd whisked them away on urgent business to see Jimmy. This is when they were set upon by Jimmy and the Carter twins and Jake had no choice but to defend himself, and Nathan of course. Afterwards they went back to the club and because Jake was in shock he drank himself into a stupor and then started demanding to shoot something. So, Ste drove them both into the middle of nowhere, so Jake could fulfil this 'ambition' and go through this 'rite of passage'. Nathan wanted Jake to shoot a pigeon, but of course he wouldn't do that, so he shot at an empty beer bottle instead.

'He missed, like,' Nathan said as though that made it all better.

'Why?' She just kept repeating the word, in her head and out loud. 'Why would you give him a gun? Why would you let him fire a gun anywhere? Didn't anyone hear it?'

'It was only the once, Grace,' he scoffed. 'And we were in the middle of nowhere. I told you.'

She stood there shaking her head, because she was at a loss as to what else to do. She knew what she would like to do, but fortunately for Nathan, she would never resort to violence in front of Jake. She would give that boy of hers what for once he sobered up, though. The stupid little bastard! What on earth was he thinking? He could have ruined his whole life just to show off to his idiot dad. She couldn't even bear to think of the many awful ways last night could have turned out. She was just glad he was going to university in two days' time and would be as far away from his lunatic father as possible. She told Nathan to leave.

'Good luck, son,' he shouted to Jake on his way out the door. Grace could hear him laughing as he walked to the waiting car.

As Grace escorted her sozzled son to bed, she wondered what the Carter twins were doing with Jimmy Dillon of all people. Michael wouldn't be happy about his boys hanging about with that lunatic. Dear God, what if Jake had shot one of them? Or they'd hurt him? What would she have done? She'd worked hard to keep Jake away from her other life. He knew Michael and Patrick as men who frequented the pub and did a bit of security work for her, anything more than that he was oblivious to. Things were getting a bit too close for comfort, and it was all bloody Nathan's fault.

Grace's head spun with the incomprehension of it all as she lay in bed staring at the butterflies on her bedroom wallpaper. The sooner she could get her son away from his father, the better. There was no way she was going to let Nathan ruin her son's life the way he'd ruined hers.

Jake was good. He was kind and caring and decent. Hell would freeze over before she would allow his bastard of a father to corrupt him. Grace would do anything in her power to ensure that their son turned out nothing like either of them had. He would have a proper, respectable job. One where he could go home every night with a clear conscience and not worry about who might knock at the door.

Grace needed a strategy. And as soon as her head was clearer she'd come up with one. She'd got rid of Nathan once. She would do it again.

CHAPTER THIRTY-SIX

Grace sat on the sofa staring at her son. Jake had chosen a suitably awful film for their final movie and takeaway night, and obviously, pizza was the selected cuisine. When he was little they would always watch a film and get a takeaway on a Sunday night. It used to be her favourite time of the week. It seemed fitting that they do that the night before her baby boy went off to live on his own, in another part of the country. As usual, Jake was allowed to choose what they ate and watched.

The film was full of blood and guts, just the type his father used to like making her sit through too, she thought. Of course, she feigned interest in it, but she spent most of her time looking at Jake. Her son, off out into the big wide world. Her heart could burst with love and pride whenever she looked at him, despite his little adventure a few nights earlier. He told her later it had been a mistake and that he was deeply ashamed of himself, and she believed him. She hoped he could put it behind him and move on. Connor and Paul Carter had been warned not to mention his involvement in anything. They were to forget he was ever there.

Jake was the best thing to ever happen to her. During her darkest times, she would have given up, had it not been for him.

He was her everything. Tears pricked her eyes as she thought about him being so far away. Even though she knew it was good for him to get away – especially from Nathan's influence.

'Stop staring at me, Mum. I'm only going to Leeds, and I'll be home every weekend, so you can do my washing.' He winked.

She knew that right then he really thought he'd be home every weekend. But she also knew that soon his life would be taken up with studying and all the new and interesting people he would meet, just as it should be, and he would visit her less and less. But that was okay. That's what she wanted for him. To be unrestricted. To have no ties; no responsibilities; just to work hard and enjoy himself. She stopped staring at him but continued to steal surreptitious glances at him for the remainder of the film. Her beautiful boy. From the day he was born he'd been her entire world. She'd known then that she would do anything for him; anything to protect him; to make sure that he got to live his life exactly the way he wanted to. Now that Nathan was back in their lives it had only made her more determined to ensure that her son was kept safe from harm. There'd be salmon swimming in the River Mersey before she would allow Nathan to do anything to jeopardize their son's future.

CHAPTER THIRTY-SEVEN

Reuben McBride sat in the chair across the desk from Grace in her office. He was a local thug who'd had his knuckles rapped by Patrick a few days earlier for causing a disturbance in the Rose and Crown. Unfortunately for Reuben, his hand was broken in the fracas and he was no longer able to participate as the getaway driver in an armed robbery. A venture that, if successful, would have been incredibly lucrative. He, and his co-conspirators, were incredibly pissed off about this fact, particularly as they'd been planning the job for months.

'Just what the fuck are you going to do about it then?' he barked at her.

Grace shrugged. 'Nothing. You should have thought about the consequences of kicking off in my pub, Reuben.'

'What?' he shouted. 'That ponce refused to serve me. All I did was pull him up on it.'

'Well, we don't tolerate that sort of homophobic language, or loutish behaviour in here. You got everything you deserved. And if Patrick had seen you barge your way up these stairs today and into my office then you'd have much more than a broken hand. Now get out.'

He stood up, his face scarlet with rage. 'You fucking bitch,' he snarled. 'I'll give you more than a broken hand, you jumped up cunt,' he said before launching himself across the desk at her. Before Grace could reach for the golf club beside her, she saw Reuben being pulled back by the scruff of his neck like a dog on a lead.

'Do you talk to your mother with that mouth, son?' Ben McKinley said as his large frame came into view.

He winked at Grace who mouthed a thanks to him.

Reuben yelped in pain as Ben took his broken hand and forced him back into the chair. 'Apologize to the lady,' he said.

'Fuck off,' Reuben said, earning him a swift heel to his groin.

'I said apologize,' Ben growled.

Sensing he was beaten, and probably in for a good hiding, Reuben looked at Grace. 'Sorry,' he mumbled.

'Don't you ever come anywhere near my pub again, you piece of shite,' she said as she stood up.

'Fortunately for you I'm not in the profession of mindless violence. If it had been any of the Carters who'd walked in here then you'd be eating through a straw for the rest of your days, lad,' Ben said as he pulled Reuben to his feet. 'Now you heard the lady, piss off.'

Just as Ben was about to push Reuben out of the door, Michael came bounding through it, breathing heavily and wild-eyed. 'Marcus called and told me there was trouble,' he panted.

Ben started to laugh. 'Oh dear. Your day has just got a whole lot worse,' he said to Reuben as he pushed him back down into the chair.

'It's handled. Just show this piece of crap out, will you?' Grace said.

'What's handled?' Michael asked.

'This young tearaway was about to lamp Grace when I got here,' Ben told him.

Michael glared at the intruder. 'About to hit a woman? Someone should teach you some manners, lad.' Then he turned to Ben. 'What the fuck are you doing here?' His gratitude for arriving in the nick of time and protecting Grace already forgotten.

'Just here to discuss something with your boss, that's all,' Ben replied.

'Such as?'

'None of your fucking business,' Ben snapped.

'Michael,' Grace said. 'It's fine. Just get rid of him, will you?' She indicated to Reuben who winced in his chair. 'Oh, don't flatter yourself, Reuben,' Grace said. 'I mean out of my pub.'

Michael glared at Ben. 'I'd rather see what this big oaf is here to see you about first.'

Ben bristled, and Grace felt the tension rising to an uncomfortable level. 'Whatever it is, I can handle it on my own,' Grace soothed, placing her hand on Michael's arm. 'Now please get him out of my sight.'

'Yeah, let the adults talk now.' Ben grinned.

'Fuck off,' Michael growled. 'I'll be downstairs if you need me, Grace. After I've seen to this prick.' He pulled a terrified looking Reuben up from his chair and out of Grace's office.

'Close that door, will you?' Grace asked once Michael was gone.

Ben did as she asked and walked over to her.

'Do you have to antagonize him?' she sighed.

'I'm sorry. It's hard not to.' He grinned at her.

'He wasn't supposed to be here at all today. I gave him enough work to keep him tied up for the afternoon. I could bloody kill Reuben. But anyway, it would make my life easier, if on the rare occasions you two do meet, you don't act like you're dying to punch each other's lights out.'

'Sorry Grace, but we're never going to get along, are we? As far as Michael is concerned, I'm Nathan's best mate and therefore your sworn enemy. And let's face it,' he said as he slipped his arms around her waist and pulled her to him, 'if he knew the

142

truth then he'd probably want to slit my throat, never mind have a few digs.'

She leaned into him, pressing herself into his muscular chest and inhaling the smell of oil on his clothes.

'Well, he'll never know,' she said.

She felt his muscles tense. 'That's exactly what I'm afraid of,' he said.

'What do you mean?'

'I mean we've been doing this dance for thirteen fucking years now, Grace. I'm tired of it. This has got to stop.'

'What do you mean, this has got to stop?' she snapped at him.

'It's all or nothing. No more sneaking around. I'm too old for this shit.'

'But, Nathan.'

'Fuck Nathan,' Ben snapped, releasing her from his embrace. 'We can't live the rest of our lives worried about hurting his feelings.'

'It's not about hurting his feelings. It's about him being a raging, jealous psychopath, and you being his best mate who had an affair with his wife. He will make you pay in ways you have never dreamed possible, Ben. I can't even think about what he'd do,' she said, tears pricking her eyes.

'I can handle myself,' he growled. 'Don't pretend this is about protecting me, Grace. I would have told him thirteen years ago, but you wouldn't let me. It's always something else. Well I'm fucking tired of waiting for our life to begin.'

'It's not just you though, is it? He'll kill me. And then what would happen to Jake? The thought of not being here for him ...' She didn't finish the sentence. She couldn't.

'I'd never let him hurt you,' Ben said as he met her gaze. 'But I can't do this anymore, Grace.'

Grace could hardly blame him. She'd been so unfair to him. Expecting him to wait around for her indefinitely. They'd broke it off so many times, but they always ended up drifting back together – like flotsam and jetsam. He'd even moved away for twelve months but he ended up at Grace's door again one night – and they'd fallen back into their on-off love affair like he'd never been away. That had been the year Grace had started working with Patrick. She wondered sometimes if she'd be where she was now if Ben had been around. No doubt he'd have tried to talk her out of it, telling her it was too dangerous. But would she have listened? Probably not.

She studied his face, sensing that this time he meant what he said. Could she live without him? Of course, she could. But did she want to?

'Okay,' she said and watched as the smile took over his face. 'But just give me a few months.'

'Always a catch,' he sighed.

Taking his face in her hands, she kissed him. 'Not this time. I promise. But I just need to take care of some things first.'

'I love you, Grace Sumner,' he said and kissed the top of her head. 'But I won't wait for you forever.'

'You won't have to,' she smiled. 'But you'd better get out of here before Michael comes back up to check on me.'

'Ah yes, your bodyguard,' he laughed.

'Don't start.' She gave him a playful shove.

'I'm not. I'm grateful that you have him around. He's like a loyal Rottweiler.'

'I'll meet you at the hotel instead then? Half an hour?'

'See you there, gorgeous.'

Grace watched as Ben walked out of her office. There was only one way the two of them could ever bring their relationship out into the open, and that was if Nathan was out of the picture – permanently. But could she do it or was she fooling herself? If she had the chance to wipe Nathan from the face of the earth, would she have the nerve to go through with it? She certainly hoped so. She'd done a lot of things in her life that she'd never dreamed she was capable of. A lot of things she wasn't proud of.

But Nathan was her son's father. How would she ever look Jake in the eye again?

As Grace picked up her coat and handbag, she thought about the night that changed hers and Ben's lives forever.

CHAPTER THIRTY-EIGHT

Thirteen Years Earlier

Resting her head on the pillow, Grace finally closed her eyes. She could sleep for a week. She and Jake had caught a stomach bug. He was just getting over the worst of his when hers kicked in. It had been an endless seventy-two hours of wiping up vomit. She settled him to sleep about half an hour earlier and then fell into bed herself, wearing only an old T-shirt because she hadn't had the time or energy to wash any of her vomit-stained pyjamas. She was exhausted; the place was a mess but it would have to wait.

She must have drifted off because she was woken by an intense pain in her scalp. She shrieked in pain as she realized Nathan was pulling her from the bed by her hair. He dragged her out into the living room.

'Look at the fucking state of this place,' he growled, grabbing her by the face. 'What the fuck do you do in here all day, Grace? This place is a fucking shithole. I even arranged for someone to manage the pub, so you could have more time to be a proper fucking wife.' He pushed her to the floor. She didn't answer him back. She was too exhausted. Too afraid. And she knew it would only make him angrier anyway.

'Get this place cleaned up now,' he snarled.

She started to pick up the toys and the dirty dishes.

'Look at the fucking state of you, Grace,' he snorted. 'Not only do I have to come home to you looking like shit, this place is filthy now as well. Don't you have any pride in yourself?'

The irony of his remark stung. Any pride she had in herself had been eroded by him, like the rock that was constantly beaten by the waves. Day in and day out. She didn't even look at him; she continued silently going about cleaning up as best as she could.

Her silence was obviously taken as some sort of slight against him, because the next thing she felt was a sharp kick to her stomach. She retched, relieved that there was nothing left inside her as she would have vomited it up onto the carpet. Getting up, she resumed tidying. All the while Nathan was sitting on the sofa, smoking a cigarette and flicking the ash onto the floor. She went into the kitchen, and he followed. Her apparent poor effort in mopping the floor was rewarded by some slaps to the head and a punch to the ribs. Again, she retched, but he didn't seem to notice, certainly he did not care.

The cycle continued for what felt to Grace like forever. She remained silent, hoping that he would get fed up and praying that Jake didn't wake up and leave the safety of his bedroom. She had told him so many times that if he ever heard Daddy home when he was in bed, that he was never to come out of his room unless she got him.

Grace's continued silence and apparent poor attempt at housework only seemed to anger Nathan more, until he got up and pulled her to him.

'How am I supposed to get it up for you, Grace? You disgust me!'

He managed to though, without any problem at all, after he tore her clothes from her body. He left shortly afterwards, to her

147

utter relief. She curled up in a ball on the floor and just lay there, whimpering like some wounded animal.

Grace had no idea how long she lay there. She wasn't sure how much longer she could live like this. If she didn't have Jake, she would just close her eyes and never wake up again. But she could never leave Jake without a mother, and in the hands of the monster that was his father.

Grace hadn't heard the door open or the footsteps coming towards her. She only heard the soft voice. 'Grace?'

Looking up, she saw the face of Nathan's best friend, Ben McKinley.

'What happened?' he asked.

All she could do was shake her head and scrabble to cover her almost naked form. What the hell was he doing here?

The next thing she knew, she was being wrapped in her fluffy bathrobe and carried to the sofa.

'What happened?' he asked again. 'Who did this?'

She looked at him. Was he serious? It must have been something in her face that gave her away.

'No. Not Nathan?' he shook his head. 'But ... I don't ...'

Ben lifted her face to look at him and she nodded. Then it all came out. Tumbling out of her mouth as though once she started talking, she couldn't stop. Ben sat and listened to it all. The look of disbelief on his face soon replaced by anger, and then something else. Something Grace hadn't seen in a long time – concern.

It was light when Ben left the following morning. Grace and he talked for hours, mostly about Nathan, but about Jake too. How she tried her best to protect him. How, fortunately, that child could sleep through an avalanche. Ben told her she should ring the police and get that bastard put where he belonged, but she couldn't do that. She was too scared. Instead, she made him promise he wouldn't tell Nathan what he knew. When he offered to beat the crap out of Nathan instead, she begged him not to.

He would only make her pay for daring to tell anyone what a monster he truly was.

Since that awful night, he'd called in on Grace regularly and she enjoyed spending time with him. He always knew when Nathan wouldn't be around. But it was two months later before Ben first kissed her. They were standing in Grace's kitchen and Ben had just finished his mug of coffee and was about to say goodnight. Grace leaned in for their usual parting embrace, but instead of wrapping her in one of his trademark bear hugs, his lips had found hers.

'Sorry,' he mumbled, red-faced. 'I shouldn't have—'

Before he could finish his sentence, she pulled him to her and kissed him right back. It was soft and hard. Slow and fast. All at the same time. Fervent and furtive; the threat of Nathan walking in on them at any given moment, only heightening the emotion of it all. She concentrated on the taste of his lips. The scent of his shampoo. The smell of the coffee they'd been drinking filling the kitchen. It felt so good to be kissed like that again; with passion; with feeling. By someone who had to kiss you, because they just couldn't not. She hadn't been kissed like that in a long time.

Nathan's advances were always unwanted by then; they were always either forced on her, or his clumsy attempt at easing his conscience every so often. It was the closest he ever came to an apology. He still told her he loved her all the time. He claimed that he needed her, and she responded with similar prose. But they were like two characters in a play that had reached the end of its run. They both knew their lines well, but there was no real conviction behind them anymore.

When Ben's hands moved lower and he started to unbutton her blouse, she didn't stop him. She knew it was wrong. She was a married woman, after all. But Nathan hadn't kept a single one of their marriage vows – so why should she?

CHAPTER THIRTY-NINE

Present Day

It was late when Nathan knocked at Grace's door. He waited patiently for her to answer and when she did, she looked surprised to see him. She was in her pyjamas, and he smiled when he realized he'd probably got her out of bed.

'Jake's not here, Nathan. He's at uni.'

He didn't move from the step. 'It's okay. It's you I want, Grace.'

She looked exasperated. 'Go home, Nathan. I'm tired and we have nothing to say to each other that can't wait until tomorrow.'

'Oh, I think you'll want to hear what I have to say,' he smiled. 'It's about Jake.'

Reluctantly she let him in and they went into the kitchen.

'What is it?' she asked, frowning at him, arms folded across her chest.

He smiled to himself thinking how soon her attitude would change. 'Well, I've been thinking,' he started, and he went on to tell her how well Jake had been fitting in at the club. How everyone respected him; how much he reminded Nathan of himself and how far Jake could go in the family business. He told her too, how much Jake seemed to enjoy working alongside him. And how, if he travelled up to Leeds and told Jake he needed him, he would leave university in a heartbeat and take his rightful place by his father's side. He told her how formidable they would be. How feared. They would be kings.

As he expected, she did not take it well. She stood staring at him, open-mouthed.

'Are you fucking serious, Nathan? Is this a wind-up? Why on earth would you want him to be anything like you?'

'He's already like me, Grace, and you know it.'

She laughed now. 'He is nothing like you, Nathan. Nothing!'

It was Nathan's turn to laugh. 'What? You think he gets his confidence and his good looks from you, do you? He is just like I was, when I was his age. He thinks he can conquer the world. And he can. With me to guide him, he can.'

'Do you honestly think I would let him give up his future for you? You sack of shit!' she screeched.

God, how she would regret that soon. 'That's a bit rich coming from you, isn't it? Given your recent career choices?'

'I do what I do so that my son won't have to,' she snapped.

'Well, I don't think you'll have much choice, Grace. He's a grown man now and he can make his own decisions.'

'And you think he'll listen to you over me, do you?' she laughed. 'He is dazzled by you, Nathan. Blinded by your money and your expensive suits and flash cars. But I have been here for him every day for the past eighteen years. He will listen to me eventually.'

Nathan lit himself a cigarette. He was strangely calm. Despite Grace's ranting and her apparent disdain for him, he knew that very shortly he was going to play his trump card. And then he would enjoy watching all the fight leave her body. He would enjoy watching her break. She would be his again, under his control, whether she liked it or not.

'By the time he realizes he should listen to you, Grace, it'll be too late. He'll be in way over his head. He'll be too involved, to just walk away. And I'll bet he probably wouldn't want to walk away. The power, the respect; it's addictive. You know that. And he would have both. Just because he's my son he would have that. But with his brains too, he would be a man to be reckoned with. Don't you want that for our boy, Grace?'

'If you bring him into this life, Nathan I swear I will—'

'You'll what, Grace?' he interrupted, pulling on his cigarette. 'Have one of your heavies beat me up? Kill me? I'd like to see them fucking try.'

'No. I'll tell the police what you did to Tommy,' she hissed.

He laughed again; he'd had a feeling she might bring that up. He knew she would think of anything, do anything to protect their son. Whenever he was forced to think about what he did to Tommy, he felt the bile rise in his throat. But his body only reacted that way out of habit now. Besides, Grace would never cross him. She might have the balls to take most people on, but not him. Because she knew exactly what he was capable of.

CHAPTER FORTY

Grace stared at Nathan as he laughed. Not a small chuckle, but a large guffaw. As though she had just told him the funniest joke in the world.

'Really, Grace?' He raised an eyebrow at her and took another pull of his cigarette. He had a huge grin on his face – mocking her. 'You really haven't changed, have you? You're still as thick as shit. You have no proof. You never actually saw me do anything. You saw me with what looked like blood on my clothes. There's no evidence, Grace. You're as guilty as I am. You destroyed my clothes – remember?'

'Did I?' she glared at him.

She watched his grin slowly turning into a frown. His eyes narrowed. 'You wouldn't fucking dare!'

'Try me, Nathan,' she said defiantly.

He took a step towards her, so his face was just inches from hers. She could feel the heat from him. His blue eyes looked almost black, smouldering like the dying embers of a fire. She could feel droplets of spittle hitting her face as he snapped, 'Don't fucking mess with me, Grace.'

She forced herself to smile at him. 'I have evidence, Nathan. I didn't burn it all. And if it should fall into the wrong hands …

well, who knows what would happen? You're not the only one with some of Merseyside's finest in your pocket, you know. I happen to be very good friends with a detective inspector and a couple of his sergeants.'

He raised his hand, and to her annoyance, she flinched. She assumed he was going for her throat, but instead he ran his index finger gently down her cheek. 'Where is it then?'

'As if I'd tell you,' she snapped.

'Well phone your police buddies then, Grace. Either we both go to prison, or neither of us do. It's your choice.'

Shit! What was her next move? Of course she'd destroyed the evidence. She'd done as she was told. Like she'd always done. And he knew it. God, he was the most devious, manipulative bastard she'd ever met in her life. But as good as he was, she was better.

She closed her eyes. She couldn't bear to look at his smug, smiling face any longer. He was going to pay for this. She'd make sure of it.

'Thought so,' he said. 'You might think you're a big player now, but you don't have the balls to cross me. You never will. Don't ever forget that.' He walked away from her and pulled out a chair before sitting on it and resting his feet on the kitchen table. He started to blow smoke rings across the kitchen. 'That was a good try though, Grace. You almost had me for a second there. Maybe you have learned something from me after all. But I'm very disappointed in you. Trying to use Tommy against me. I never thought you'd stoop so low. But your willingness to bring it up, and even incriminate yourself, to protect Jake, makes me wonder what else you'd do to protect our son.'

She frowned at him. What the hell was he on about now?

'You remember that gun Jake told you about the other night? The one he waved in Jimmy Dillon's face? Well that gun was used in an armed robbery the week before. That armed robbery where the driver was shot. Did you hear about it?'

154

Grace's heart started to beat at an alarming rate and her stomach churned.

'Well our Jake's prints are all over that gun because he fired it too. Remember? Now I also happen to know that Jake was sleeping off a hangover in my flat when that robbery happened. And what with me being his dad, and a convicted criminal, well I wouldn't be much of a credible alibi witness now, would I? As much as I could protest he was with me, who would listen, eh? The very fact that he's my son would be enough to convince anyone he could have done it. Now, I currently have that gun secured in a very safe place. But if for some reason, it should fall into the wrong hands,' he said, mimicking her earlier threat to him, 'then he would be looking at a very long stretch indeed. Don't you think?'

He smiled at her, the way he did when he knew he'd won. She hated that smile. She wanted to rip it from his face. She'd seen it so many times. She leaned against the kitchen counter for support. This couldn't be happening. She was the one in control now. Not him. Not anymore. But how could she fight this without hurting Jake?

'I warned you to be careful, Grace. I tried the nice approach and you were having none of it. Thought you were too good for me now that you've grown up a bit. Well it's about time that you learn, once and for all, who has all the power here. Me. You have none, Grace. You do what I say, when I say it, from now on. Do you understand?'

She could feel the blood draining from her face, as though it trickled from her head, all the way down her body and out through her feet. Time stood still. She needed to wake up from this dream, this nightmare, but she had a horrible feeling that it was all real. How could she be here again? She was free. She'd changed so much. Changed who she was. Done things that kept her awake at night. All to protect her and Jake so they would never be at the mercy of this bastard ever again. And yet here they were. Her heart felt like it had stopped beating, frozen in the eternal misery of this awful moment. She held her breath, because to breathe would be to go on living in this hell that had once again become her life.

A part of her couldn't believe what he was saying. She knew better than anyone that Nathan was a monster, an animal. She'd always known what he was capable of, or at least she thought she had. But to be willing to send his own son to prison, and to ruin his promising young life, just so that he could drag her back down into the gutter with him? Just to prove that he could still control her. She wanted to scream at him – *why can't you just let me go?*

It was almost as if her brain refused to accept what he was saying. She kept shaking her head like some crazy woman. She started to reason with herself. Trying to find some sense in his senseless words.

No, he would never carry out his threat. As callous and as cruel as he was, Jake was his child. She refused to believe he would do such a thing. She called his bluff.

'Even you wouldn't do that to your own son, Nathan,' she said confidently.

It seemed before she'd even finished speaking, he was on her. His hand around her throat, his body pressing hers into the kitchen counter. She could barely breathe. The feeling of his fingers squeezing her throat all too familiar. He glared at her, unflinching. His face hardened. A vein pulsed in his temple. His blue eyes ice cold.

'You know better than to underestimate me, Grace,' he growled.

In that moment, she knew this man would destroy her without a second's hesitation, even if it meant destroying their son too. She was frozen. Nineteen again, alone and at the mercy of a monster.

Nathan smiled as he climbed into his car outside Grace's house. Checking his reflection in the rear-view mirror, he noticed the deep red scratch on his neck. He'd enjoyed putting Grace back in her place just as much as he'd thought he would. She was much feistier than she used to be – he quite liked that. He'd been worried for a while that she'd become too independent while he'd been inside. She wasn't afraid of him like she used to be. His usual tactics didn't have the same effect on her they once did. The incident with Jake and the gun had been like a gift from the gods. It was just the thing to ensure that Grace did exactly as she was told from now on.

Looking down at his shirt, Nathan saw tiny splatters of blood on one of the cuffs. Shit! He loved that shirt, and blood was such a pain in the arse to get out. He'd have to get cleaned up before he went home, or he'd never hear the fucking end of it from Kayleigh.

Pulling away from the kerb he felt an overwhelming sense of contentment, like a warm blanket settling over him. Grace was back where she belonged. The world felt right again. She didn't need to know that he'd wiped that gun clean, his prints were on it too, after all. And he'd never grass on his own son. He wasn't a fucking monster! But she didn't need to know that either. She just had to believe he was capable of doing monstrous things.

And if she had forgotten that, he had certainly just reminded her.

CHAPTER FORTY-ONE

As she half-listened to Patrick's breakdown of the previous week's business dealings, Grace thought about Nathan and the events of the previous night. Absent-mindedly running her fingers across her neck, she suppressed a shudder as she remembered his hands on her throat – on her body. There had to be a way to get rid of him without putting Jake, or anyone else, in danger.

She was vaguely aware of Connor and Paul Carter as they fidgeted in their seats. Chomping at the bit to get in on a slice of the action, no doubt. She was pleased they were keeping their mouths shut though as they listened to their grandfather. She'd agreed to take the twins on at the request of their father, Michael, after they'd become embroiled with Jimmy Dillon. Jimmy was a loose cannon who didn't abide by any rules. And he was a raving lunatic – anyone was fair game in his opinion. Old women, kids, gangsters – he didn't care who he ripped off. One day he was going to upset the wrong person and Michael wanted his boys far away from Jimmy when he did, particularly as they'd recently had a run-in with Nathan, one of the most dangerous and unpredictable men in Liverpool.

'Now that we've sorted the usual business out, I need to talk to you about a much more delicate, and urgent, matter,' Grace said to the three men.

'Oh?' Patrick frowned. He was usually aware of the agenda items for their weekly meetings.

The twins looked at her wide-eyed, eager for something to do and a chance to prove themselves.

'I want Kevin Mitchell to run the Manchester deal for a few months. He's going to be our liaison with Sol for the time being.'

'What?' Patrick said, his mouth hanging open.

'You heard me, Pat.'

'But why? We're already doing more business than I'd like with that slimy bastard.'

'Yeah, he's a fucking knobhead,' the twins chorused. 'Doesn't know his arse from his elbow.'

'Well you two had better start getting along with him because you're going to be working with him. Think you can handle that?'

''Course we can,' Paul said.

'Hang on a minute,' Patrick interjected. 'The Manchester deal is a nice earner for us. We've never had beef with Sol. Why do we need Mitchell all of a sudden?'

'We don't need Mitchell, but we could use his muscle. It's just a short-term arrangement. Things will go back to normal in a few months. Mitchell and his lads will do as they're told. Trust me, Pat. He won't give you any bother at all.'

'But why, Grace?' Patrick shook his head, and the twins looked on in disbelief.

Grace sighed. 'Nathan is digging into my business dealings and it's only a matter of time before he finds out about our arrangement with Sol. You know he would shoot his own granny to get in on that action. He has no idea Sol was even in the market for a new supplier. Fortunately for us, he doesn't keep his ear as close to the ground as he once did. I need some distance from it all right now, that's all. But it's not a permanent arrangement, don't worry. I've already squared it with Sol too.'

159

'But why the hell are you bothered if Nathan finds out? We could squash him like a bug.'

'I know we could. But let's just say he has me over a barrel right now. I need to be careful. And I don't want to let him into my life anymore than he already is. If he digs deeper and finds out the truth, he'll try and muscle in on our deal. I'd rather allow Mitchell in on it for a short while on my terms, than let Nathan within a sniff of it.'

'But we could handle him, Grace,' the twins said.

'Don't be stupid,' she snapped. 'Nathan is dangerous and unpredictable. I know what I'm doing. Trust me. Anyway, you two get out of here. I told Mitchell you'd meet him at his place and fill him in on what he needs to know.'

Paul and Connor bounded out of her office, chattering to themselves. When it was just her and Patrick left in the room, Grace told him about Nathan's threats to her, and her belief that he was entirely capable of carrying them out.

'Fucking bastard,' Patrick spat.

'You see why I have to tread carefully then? But am I making a big mistake teaming up with Mitchell? Can the twins be trusted to behave themselves?'

'I think you know what you're doing, Grace,' he said. 'And the twins won't let you down.'

Grace nodded. She had to do something about Nathan, and this was just the beginning. Tensions were already high between Nathan and Kevin Mitchell's firms, the pair of them had a long history and hated each other with a passion. All she had to do was keep stoking that fire. She couldn't bear one more second of Nathan's smug, self-entitled arrogance. And there was always the possibility he might do something stupid with that gun. If anything happened to Jake, she'd never forgive herself.

It would all work out fine though. She had a plan.

Grace swirled the brandy around her glass as she leaned back in her chair and watched as Patrick counted the mountain of ten

160

and twenty pound notes into piles. She contemplated how far she'd come from the foolish young girl who'd first met Nathan Conlon. Some of the most feared and respected men in Liverpool were at her disposal now. Day or night, she just had to say the word and they would come running. It wasn't because they were scared of her either, not like Nathan's minions. It was because they were loyal to her. They all owed her something. She smiled to herself. Sometime soon, Nathan would be out of hers and Jake's lives for good, and everything would be perfect.

CHAPTER FORTY-TWO

Grace and Patrick were sitting in silence, enjoying the peace and quiet of the pub after hours when they heard the pounding on the double doors. As soon as Patrick undid the large steel bolt, his grandsons Connor and Paul Carter burst into the otherwise empty pub.

'What the hell has happened?' Patrick asked them, his brow furrowed in concern.

Their pale, wide-eyed expressions suggested it wasn't something good.

'We shot Kenny Lennox,' Paul said while Connor stood behind him shaking his head.

'What? Why?' Grace asked, assuming the boys had been defending themselves. After all, there had to be some plausible explanation for them shooting one of Nathan's closest associates.

'We were aiming for Nathan,' Paul replied.

For a second, Grace thought she must have misheard. Surely, they wouldn't dare. Her stomach lurched. They had just started World War Three. Nathan had obviously just escaped the twins' bungled attempt on his life and he would raise hell to find out, and destroy, whoever was involved. But what if they had shot Nathan as they'd planned? What would have happened then?

While it would have been a far better outcome than the one they were facing, it still would have caused an all-out war. Nathan's minions wouldn't take his assassination lightly. They'd all be vying to prove themselves worthy of his crown.

'What the hell have you two done?' she demanded.

The two of them started to explain. Stammering and stuttering. The adrenaline coursing through their bodies making them almost incomprehensible.

'Calm down, lads,' their grandfather soothed. 'Paul, tell us what happened, son.'

'We waited outside The Blue Rooms for Nathan. We know he stays there late on a Sunday. We saw him coming out. We were on a scrambler and we rode over to him. Connor pulled the gun and he fired, but ...'

'I missed him.' Connor shook his head. 'That stupid old bastard, Kenny Lennox, jumped in front of him. He's definitely dead. Took a bullet right to the face.' He shuddered. 'Nathan dived behind a car and we couldn't get to him. We didn't know if there was anyone else in the club so we had to get out of there.'

Grace's heart was beating so fast in her chest she thought it might explode. She rose from her chair. 'You pair of stupid fucking idiots,' she shouted. 'Who the hell gave you permission to go after Nathan?'

'No one,' Paul said sheepishly. 'We did it for you, Grace. We thought it would help.'

'You thought it would help?' she sneered. 'I don't pay you to think. I had a perfectly good plan to get rid of Nathan, and you two have fucked it right up.' She walked away from them before she completely lost the plot. 'Fucking help,' she muttered.

'What happened then? Did anyone see you?' Patrick asked, trying to defuse some of the tension.

'We got away down the alley. Dumped the gun and the scrambler and came straight here,' Paul replied.

'You pair of fucking amateurs,' Grace snapped as she walked

back over to them. 'If I'd wanted Nathan shot then I'd have asked your father to do it.'

'We're sorry, Grace,' they both said in unison.

'At least no one saw them,' Patrick said, still trying to defuse the tension in the room.

'What?' she shouted. 'Look at the two of them. Identical twins. Pair of them built like brick shithouses and you think he won't have recognized them? Come on, Pat. Are you having a laugh?' She turned to the twins. 'So, you took it upon yourselves to shoot Nathan. Why didn't you at least finish the job then? At least then there'd be something to show for this mess.'

'I know, but once Kenny went down, Nathan bolted and we panicked. We just wanted to get out of there,' Connor said.

'I should hang you two out to fucking dry. I should ...' She didn't finish her sentence. The thought that Nathan had just survived a murder attempt was too much to contemplate. The fallout from this was going to cause mayhem. He might not think she had anything to do with it, but he would know it was the Carter twins. Thankfully, Nathan had no idea that the twins were on her payroll, but they were, and she couldn't help but feel responsible for the whole Carter family. When Michael found out he'd have a bloody canary fit.

'We're sorry,' they both said again.

Patrick remained quiet.

'Get out of my sight and start thinking about how you're going to make yourselves disappear for the foreseeable future until I can sort this mess out,' Grace barked at them.

As the twins left, Patrick sank into his chair, his head in his hands. Grace put a hand on his shoulder. In her own panic, she'd overlooked the implications of this for him. His grandsons had just started a war with a raging sociopath. They were all in it together now.

'What's our next move?' he asked as he looked up at her.

Always looking to her to tell him what to do. The weight of

being the one who always had to make the decisions sat heavily on her shoulders.

She shook her head. 'Right now, Pat, I don't know. But I'll take care of this somehow. I promise. Until then, we all need to be extra vigilant.'

'Shall I tell Michael?'

Grace swallowed. 'No.' She shook her head. 'Let me take care of that.' It was a conversation she wasn't particularly looking forward to. Michael Carter was a bad-tempered sod. Fortunately, he was in Spain on some business for her, that would give her time to think before she saw him next. Grace always kept him on a very short leash. Perhaps now she'd have to consider letting him loose.

CHAPTER FORTY-THREE

Grace heard his voice before she saw him. He came bounding up the stairs of the pub to her office.

'Grace, are you up here?' he bellowed.

She groaned inwardly. She'd been waiting for this conversation and really wasn't in the mood for it now.

'Michael.' She smiled at him as he strode into her office.

'What the hell, Grace?' he shouted. 'I'm gone for five minutes and I find out my boys have tried to take out your ex-husband.'

'Look—' she started, but he interrupted her.

'But not only that, they failed miserably and now my dad tells me you've got them hidden in the middle of nowhere. What the fuck is going on?'

'If you stop ranting for a minute, I'll tell you exactly what's going on,' she snapped.

'Explain away,' he said sarcastically as he took a seat on the chair opposite her.

'For a start, lose the attitude. You were the one who begged me to give your boys a job after they got caught up with that prick, Jimmy Dillon, and had a run-in with Nathan. And your fuckwit sons took it upon themselves to try and take Nathan out. Just like that. No discussion with me, or even your dad. They thought it would be as easy as walking up to him and pulling a trigger. Well you know as well as I do that fucker has more lives than an alley cat. They killed poor old Kenny Lennox instead. They have fucked up big time, Michael, and now I'm the one trying to clean up the giant pile of steaming shite they've left in their wake.'

Michael shook his head. 'I didn't realize that, Grace. I assumed they were acting on your orders.' He put his head in his hands and they both sat in silence until Michael spoke again. 'They're a pair of fucking idiots. But they're my kids, Grace. What can I say?'

Michael would do anything for his boys, just like she would for Jake. He'd wanted them to choose a different path to the one he had. He'd sent them to the best schools and paid a fortune for private tutors, but it had made no difference. The twins had wanted to be just like him. They'd inherited his temper and his build, but unfortunately not his brains. She knew he must be worried sick about them.

Michael rubbed a hand over the stubble on his chin. 'I don't understand why they did it. What the hell were they thinking?'

Grace sighed. 'Who knows? They thought they were helping me out, apparently. Nathan has been up to his usual tricks, trying to make my life a misery, and they wanted to make things a bit easier for me,' she snorted. 'Instead they've created a fucking shit-storm.'

'I'm sorry,' Michael said again, shaking his head.

'Stop bloody apologizing,' she snapped. 'I'll handle it. Nathan doesn't know the twins work for me – yet! So, that buys me some time at least. The boys are safe. They're at my place in Scotland.'

'Scotland? What place in Scotland?'

'I have a place there. I rent it out as a holiday let. Your dad helped me find it when he was up there last year. They'll be safe there until we can figure something out. As long as they don't go blabbing about where they are.'

Michael nodded. 'I'll make sure they don't.'

'Good.'

'Any other things I don't know about you, Grace?' Michael asked.

'Plenty,' she said.

Standing up, he walked over to her. 'And here was me thinking I knew everything about you,' he said against her ear. 'What other secrets are you hiding?'

'If I told you, I'd have to kill you,' she said and then she pushed him. 'Get out of here, you menace. You've got work to do.'

'Anything you say, boss,' he said before bounding out of her office.

CHAPTER FORTY-FOUR

It had been a little over a week since someone had murdered Kenny Lennox. Although Nathan knew he had been the intended target. Two men on a scrambler bike had fired shots at him and Kenny as they were leaving the club. Ever the loyal soldier, Kenny had pushed his boss out of the way and taken a bullet to the face for his trouble. It had ripped right through his jaw and out through the back of his head. Not that Nathan had hung around to pay much attention to his fallen comrade. He'd been out of there quicker than a rat up a drainpipe.

Nathan hadn't been able to get a good look at the shooters because they were wearing motorbike helmets. But from what he did see, they were both of a similar build and the way they handled that scrambler suggested they were a couple of young lads. The fucking Carter twins. He was sure of it. The cheeky cunts! Who the fuck did they think they were to try and take him out? He was Nathan fucking Conlon, and they were nothing but a pair of thugs. He'd had every man at his disposal looking for the pair of them, but they seemed to have vanished into thin air.

Nathan sat back in the expensive leather chair in his office and watched as Ben McKinley walked into the room. He hadn't seen much of Ben lately as he'd been on one of his frequent visits to Ireland sorting out his gran's estate. It was distracting him far too much for Nathan's liking.

Nathan poured them both a generous measure of Scotch before offering Ben one of the sweet-smelling Cuban cigars he'd just had imported.

Ben shook his head. 'No thanks, mate. So, what's going on? Why the urgency to see me?'

Setting his glass down on his desk, Nathan looked at his best mate of almost thirty years. 'Someone tried to kill me last week,' he said.

Ben put his own glass on the table, his mouth open in shock. It was a few seconds before he spoke. 'What? Who?'

'I can't say for sure, but I think it was the Carter twins. Kenny's dead. He took the bullet for me, the dozy bastard. Too stupid and too loyal for his own good. I've had feelers out for information, but no one seems to know anything. Can't find the little fuckers now though, so that tells me all I need to know.'

'Poor Ken,' Ben said. 'He should have retired years ago and been sunning himself in the Costa del Sol by now. But why would the Carter twins try and take you out? It makes no sense. You have no beef with the Carters, do you?'

Nathan shrugged. 'As far as I can figure out, Grace has Patrick and Michael on her payroll, if you can believe that,' he snorted. 'But not the twins. I heard they've just started working with Kevin Mitchell, but he wouldn't dare order a hit on me. He hasn't got the balls. Grace and Michael might have had a bit of a thing years ago, although she denies it. But even if they did, there's no major issue there between us. Michael and Patrick wouldn't start a war over a woman. They're not that fucking stupid. The twins are a different story though. Me and Ste had a bit of a kick off with them the other week. They were in the wrong place at the wrong time, but the pair of them took a bit of a pasting. Obviously, they have very fragile egos.'

Ben downed his whisky in one gulp and shook his head. 'Fucking hell, mate.'

'Anyway, that's why I phoned you. It's strange that no one seems to know anything. It could even be an inside job. They knew exactly where I'd be. I don't know who I can trust. So, I'm trusting no one on this. Except you, and John.'

Ben looked at him like he'd grown another head. 'But, what can I do?'

'If I can't find the twins, then I'll settle for the next best thing. I just need you to have my back, mate.'

Ben nodded. 'Of course. I always have, haven't I?'

They were interrupted by the vibration of Nathan's mobile phone on the desk. John Brennan's name flashed on the screen.

'Yeah?' Nathan answered.

'I've found him, boss.'

'Good. I'll be there as soon as,' he said as he stood up. Grabbing his coat from the back of the chair, he nodded to Ben. 'Time to get to work, big fella.'

CHAPTER FORTY-FIVE

Taking her phone from her handbag on the passenger seat, Grace saw it was Sean Carter calling.

'Hey, Sean,' she said.

'Grace. You need to come down to the Royal. It's my dad. He's in intensive care.'

A chill ran down her spine. 'I'm on my way,' she said and ended the call. She didn't want to waste valuable time asking what had happened, she could find that out when she got to the hospital. But she already knew it was something to do with Nathan and the failed attempt on his life. Her heart raced as she started the ignition. Poor Pat. What had that bastard done to him?

Grace arrived at the hospital and saw Patrick's sons, Sean, who stood ashen-faced outside the intensive care unit, and Michael, pacing up and down cursing under his breath.

'What happened?' Grace asked as she hugged Sean.

His eyes filled with tears. 'They found him, half dead, down the dock road. All we know is he's in a really bad way. If the ambulance hadn't got to him when they did, he'd be a goner.'

'Who called the ambulance?' Grace asked.

Sean shook his head. 'We don't know. They said it was anonymous. Someone just phoned and reported him lying in the gutter. They reckon he was dumped there. Maybe it was just someone passing by?'

Grace nodded in agreement.

Michael bounced over to her then. 'They left him to fucking die in the road,' he shouted. 'Like a fucking animal.'

'Keep your voice down, the police are over there,' Sean warned him.

Michael lowered his voice. 'I'm going to put a bullet in that fucker's head, Grace,' he said.

Before she could respond to him, a doctor came out of the double doors facing them.

'Your father is stable for now,' he said. 'But he's still in a critical condition. He's conscious, so you can see him now, but he needs to rest. He's very lucky to be alive.'

Michael and Sean shook his hand in turn. 'Thanks, Doctor,' they said.

'Are you family?' the doctor asked Grace.

'She's our sister,' Sean lied.

'You can see him for a few minutes, but then he really needs his rest. And I'm sure the police will want to talk to him as soon as he's up to it. It's only two per bedside in ICU, I'm afraid. So you'll have to decide who's going in first,' he said before walking away.

'You two go in first, of course,' Grace said.

They nodded and Grace watched as the two brothers walked into the intensive care unit.

Grace thought about her next move while she waited. Was this all her fault? Should she have just gone along with Nathan's demands and kept her trap shut? At least everyone she loved would be safe. God, she could kill the twins for their stupidity. She'd had the perfect plan to get Nathan out of their lives for good and they'd fucked it all up. And Nathan, that evil bastard. When she was through with him he would wish he'd never laid eyes on her.

Ten long minutes later, Sean and Michael came back into the waiting room. The pain etched on their faces was clear to see.

'You can go in now,' Sean said quietly. 'Just keep calm when you see him, okay? Don't freak him out.'

'I won't,' she replied, wondering at the state Patrick must be in for such a warning to be merited.

It took all of Grace's strength not to burst into tears when she saw Pat lying on the hospital bed with tubes sticking out of him. His hands and head were bandaged but she could see the dried blood and bruising which covered the skin that was exposed.

'God, Pat, you had us worried for a minute then. Anything for a few days off, eh?' she said jovially.

He winced as he tried to smile and her heart almost broke. Sitting down in the chair beside his bed, she gently placed her hand over his bandaged one. 'You're the toughest man I know, Pat Carter. But I'm going to make him pay for this. Do you hear me?'

Pat closed his eyes and she knew he was fighting sleep. Standing up, she kissed him gently on the forehead. 'Get some rest now, I'll see you tomorrow.'

Grace and Michael drove back to the Rose and Crown in silence while Sean followed in his car. It wasn't until they were safely inside the pub and Grace had poured them all a generous brandy that they dared to mention the state they'd just seen Patrick in.

'Those bastards cut two of his fingers off,' Michael shouted. 'Smashed his kneecaps. Broke almost every bone in his body.'

'We know,' Sean said. 'We were there too.'

Sean's phone rang. It was his wife, Sophia. He spoke to her in hushed tones while Grace and Michael took a seat at one of the tables.

'I've got to get home, the kids are worried,' Sean said. Then he turned to Grace. 'I don't care how you do it, but make sure that prick never comes anywhere near me or any of my family ever again.' Then he downed his brandy in one before walking out of the pub.

Grace locked the doors behind him.

'I'm going to go round there now and fucking end him,' Michael growled.

'No you're not,' she snapped.

'What?' he shouted. 'This is my fucking dad we're talking about here. My dad who could end up a fucking cabbage because of that cunt.' He slammed his glass down onto the table.

'I know he's your dad, Michael. He's like a dad to me too. Don't you think I'm hurting as well? But we have to use our heads. Going off half-cocked is just going to get someone else hurt. Just leave it for now until I can figure out what to do. If we retaliate now, more people are just going to caught in the crossfire.'

'I don't fucking care,' he growled, almost foaming at the mouth. 'I'm going to kill him.'

She glared at him then. 'I said leave it,' she snapped.

Michael stared at her. He rarely saw her angry. Annoyed, yes. But rarely angry. 'I owe you everything, Grace. I would do anything for you,' he said, his tone softer now, sufficiently chastised. 'But this is my dad we're talking about.'

He stood up and walked away from her, and she followed him. 'Have I ever let you down, Michael?' She stroked his cheek with her fingertips. 'I promise I'll sort this. But we can't handle this your way. You have to let me do my thing. There's still the twins to think of too.'

He took hold of her hand. 'I wish you'd let me finish this now. I hate sitting around doing nothing.'

'I know that. But you trust me, don't you?'

He nodded and pulled her close to him, close enough that she could smell his aftershave. It was Tom Ford – her favourite.

'I wish I could kiss you,' he said.

She knew if he did, he'd taste of peppermint and coffee. He

always did. 'You have a wife at home waiting for you. Remember?'

He released her from his grip. 'Let me know when you've decided what we're doing, Grace.'

Then he was gone too, and Grace sat in the pub alone. It was only after she'd bolted the door behind Michael that she finally broke down, her sobs echoing in the empty pub. Her beloved Pat tortured and left for dead. Nathan seemed intent on ruining her life. He just couldn't seem to let her go. And now Patrick had paid the price.

Grace knew one thing for sure, if she was going to be rid of Nathan for good, she had to do it herself. He was a hard man to get to at the best of times, but after being shot he'd be extra cautious. And now he was on the warpath. She had to figure out a way to get close to him. He would never suspect a thing. He hadn't before. Not even when she'd contacted the police and told them all they'd needed to know to earn her husband twelve years in prison. She supposed she was responsible for Michael's and Sean's sentences too. The evidence the police found in Nathan's lock-up had led to a whole load of arrests and prosecutions. The irony of that didn't escape her. Michael and Sean thought they owed her – but it was really her who owed them.

CHAPTER FORTY-SIX

Twelve Years Earlier

Grace's cheek was stuck to the cold linoleum floor. She was lying in something wet and sticky. The metallic taste of blood filled her mouth, and its acrid, tinny smell flooded her nostrils. She was shivering and then she realized it was because she was almost naked. Her clothes were lying in shreds somewhere in the near vicinity. Nathan had really lost it. Despite the crazed blonde woman turning up on Christmas Eve, they'd managed to have a pleasant enough few days after Christmas. But after the New Year's Eve celebrations at the pub, Nathan had suddenly taken offence at the fact that Grace wasn't paying him enough attention.

She'd barely batted an eyelid when the blonde, who Grace had later learned was a stripper named Candy, had come bursting into the pub the week before, screeching like some crazed banshee, demanding to know why Nathan had forced her to abort their baby. According to Nathan's warped way of thinking, the fact that Grace hadn't responded with anger and indignation, as Nathan had, meant that he'd lost face. How did it look if his wife didn't care that he got a stripper pregnant? She really couldn't win.

So obviously, he'd decided to make her pay. She thought he

was going to kill her. Perhaps she was dead. Maybe this was purgatory – or hell? He was in a rage like one she'd never seen before. He was shouting about how she didn't care about him; that all she cared about was herself.

The last thing she remembered was him slamming her head against the kitchen counter and then nothing.

Everything was black.

It was nice there, though. No pain. Just nothing. Maybe she should go back there? Escape the pain that was starting to invade every part of her body. If she just closed her eyes …

Soft, little pads of warmth started to work their way up her arm, gently squeezing her, coaxing her back to reality. Then she heard the softest whisper.

'Mummy. Mummy. Wake up, Mummy.'

Jake! Her eyes snapped open and she looked down to see the little dark mop of hair. Jake's body curled into hers. Grace's heart broke into a million, tiny pieces. What had she done? All that time she'd been telling herself that she had always protected her son – that she had shielded him from his father. And yet she looked at him now and realized none of that was true. Her poor, sweet boy.

Grace lifted herself up. Taking Jake's little face in her hands, she forced a smile.

'Mummy is okay, Jake. I'm never going anywhere without you. I promise.'

Somehow she found the strength to get herself cleaned up. Then she sat on the sofa with Jake and they watched cartoons. She could have almost cried when she heard his little laugh again. She was worried it might have disappeared. She knew that her only goal in life had to be to get away from Nathan. The man she fell in love with, the one she married – he was long gone. She'd been hoping that he'd come back one day. Praying that one day he'd finally wake up and see what he was doing – but she realized that day was never coming. And in the meantime, she was endangering the most precious thing in the world. Her son.

Grace vowed there and then that Nathan would be out of her life as soon as possible. Unbeknownst to him, she had all the details of the next big job he was planning. He thought so little of her intelligence, and had become so arrogant in his belief that he was untouchable, that he discussed specifics while she was sitting in the same room. All in some pathetic code, of course, as if she was too stupid to realize what he was really on about.

The day before the big event, she phoned Crimestoppers and told them everything they needed to know to catch him red-handed. He was charged with 'Possession of a Firearm With Intent to Resist Arrest; Conspiracy to Supply Class A Drugs and Money Laundering'.

Even during the trial he'd never suspected a thing. She sat in the public gallery every single day, looking every inch the dutiful wife. She was no stranger to a courtroom, having sat through two previous trials. Once shortly after she met him, when he'd been charged with GBH. And again a few years later when he was charged with ABH and got eight months. But when they'd handed him an extended sentence, twelve years in prison with an extended licence of six years, Grace had almost fainted. It was longer than she'd dared to dream of. He would be eligible for parole after nine years, but even nine years away from him felt like an eternity.

After Nathan was taken down to the cells, Grace stumbled out of the stuffy courtroom. She couldn't breathe. Beads of perspiration trickled down her back making her thankful she was wearing a jacket over her thin blouse. The room started to spin. Her knees buckled. Fortunately, Nathan's barrister was with her, and caught her before she hit the floor.

Manoeuvring her to the nearest seat in the waiting room, he asked. 'Are you okay, Grace?'

She nodded. 'It's just a shock, that's all.'

'I'm sure it is. I'm so sorry. I didn't think he'd get so long, but the Old Bill laid it on thick, and that probation report didn't help either. Once they assessed him as a danger to the public, well, there was nothing more I could do for him. They've basically made an example of him because he was the ringleader.'

She just sat in the moulded plastic chair, nodding at him, thinking she must look like one of those stupid dogs she hated to see in the back of cars.

'Are you sure you're okay, dear?' he asked again.

She straightened herself up. 'Yes, I'm sure, Jack. I'll be fine. You get on, I'm sure you must be busy.'

He made his excuses then and left for his next court case. She walked to the car park in something of a daze and before she knew it, she was at the car. She couldn't remember getting there; it was almost as if she was operating on autopilot.

It wasn't until she unlocked the car and climbed inside that the tears, which had been threatening since she was in the courtroom, finally came. Deep, gulping sobs – sobs of pure relief. She was free! For at least nine years he wouldn't be able to hurt her, wouldn't be able to touch her. She would be able to live in peace in her own home. To take charge of her own life and do the things she wanted to do. She could take control of the pub again, could go back to running the place herself. Have her own bank account with her own money. The potential future unfolded before her like an endless stream of possibilities. The start of Nathan's prison sentence signalled the end of hers.

She couldn't have been happier.

CHAPTER FORTY-SEVEN

Present Day

Michael came out of his father's hospital room with a grim look on his face. It had been two days since Patrick had been admitted to hospital and he'd finally been moved from the ICU to the trauma ward. He was still in a state, but was no longer critical.

'He said he doesn't want to see you, Grace,' Michael said as he shook his head.

'What? Why?' she asked. That didn't make any sense to her.

'He wouldn't tell me. He said that Nathan finally told him the truth and you'd know what that meant. What the hell's he on about?'

She swallowed. 'I don't know.'

'Don't bullshit me, Grace,' Michael said. 'I can tell by your face. You look like you've seen a ghost.'

'Maybe I have,' she replied. There was only one thing it could be. She had few secrets from Pat. And Nathan only knew about one of them. Because if he'd found out about the others, she'd already be a dead woman. He would kill her, and he wouldn't care if there were a dozen witnesses.

'So what the fuck's going on? My old man treats you like his daughter. He thinks you're the second coming. So, what can you have possibly done to make him refuse to see you?'

'I don't even know where to start.'

'Let's go for a coffee downstairs. And you can start at the beginning.'

'Later. Right now, I have to be somewhere.'

Michael looked at her with concern. 'Where are you going?'

'I'll be back later,' she said, ignoring his question.

'If you're going to see him, I think I should come with you.'

She shook her head. 'No. I'm going alone.'

'Grace, don't be stupid,' he pleaded.

'I said I'll see you later,' she said as she walked off down the corridor.

Grace's stomach bubbled with anger as she climbed into her car. Nathan had gone too far this time. He was poison. He had the exact opposite of the Midas Touch – everything he touched turned to shit. She wasn't going to let him hurt her or anyone she cared about anymore. She'd wondered whether she really had it in her to end Nathan Conlon – and now she knew.

Grace pulled up outside Nathan's club. Her heart was hammering in her chest. Her hands trembled. She took a moment to compose herself. She couldn't show him any weakness.

Walking through the double glass doors of The Blue Rooms, she headed towards Nathan's office.

'Do you have an appointment?' a young brunette in a black miniskirt and purple crop top asked her as she approached the door to Nathan's office.

'No,' she snapped, pushing past her and opening the door.

Nathan looked up as she entered the room. 'Grace, darling,' he grinned.

Closing the door behind her, Grace walked over to his desk. 'You're a fucking animal,' she spat.

'Woah. Is that any way to speak to the man you love?' he laughed.

'How could you do it, Nathan?'

'What are you on about, Grace?' he said dismissively.

'Pat Carter. I assume you're the one responsible for his current situation?'

Nathan shrugged. 'Can't believe the old bastard's still breathing to be honest.'

'What?'

'He had it coming, Grace. Trust me. You're just pissed off because I told him your big secret. And now Pat won't be your bestest friend anymore,' he mocked her.

'Why did you tell him about Tommy?' she shouted. 'Why?'

'I thought you were happy for all that to come out now? You were the one who brought it up the other week.' He smiled and leaned back in his chair with his hands behind his head.

Grace wanted to punch him in the mouth – anything to put a stop to his constant, smug grinning.

'You're not the only one who can make threats, Grace. I can too. But I follow up on mine. He's a hard bastard that Pat Carter, though. Cut two of his fingers off and he didn't even flinch. I smashed his kneecaps with a hammer and he still wouldn't tell me what I wanted to know. He didn't make a sound. But when I told him about what we did to Tommy, well I saw his little heart break. I think that hurt him more than anything I did.' He shook his head in mock disbelief.

'You bastard,' she spat.

'Be careful, Grace,' he warned. 'There's only so much leeway I'll give you. I know you're upset so I'll let this little episode slide. But stay away from the Carter family from now on.'

'Why?'

'Because I told you to,' he snapped. 'It's for your own good.'

'The Carter's will have nothing to do with me anymore anyway after your little stunt. So, thanks to you, my business has gone to shit,' she lied.

Nathan shrugged, unable to hide his happiness about that fact. 'What can I say, Grace. This is a tough game.'

'Is that why you hurt Pat? Because of me?'

He nodded. 'In part, yeah.' She knew he'd let her believe she was responsible if it meant making her feel bad.

'I knew it,' she said. 'Well, that's why I've come here anyway.' She sat in the chair opposite him. 'You win, Nathan. I'll do whatever you want. I won't fight you anymore. I don't want anyone else hurt.'

Pushing his chair back from his desk, he stood up and walked over to her, his eyes dark with lust. He stood in front of her. Taking hold of her chin, he tilted her head to look up at him.

'Prove it,' he growled.

Grace closed her eyes and tried to think about anything but where she was and what she was about to do. Despite her skin crawling as though it had been swarmed by a million scurrying ants, she forced herself to smile, and thought about how one day soon, she would bring Nathan Conlon to his knees – and he would beg her for mercy.

CHAPTER FORTY-EIGHT

Fourteen Years Earlier

'You wanted to see me, Tommy?' Nathan asked as he walked into the office in The Blue Rooms. It was early morning and there was nobody else around. Tommy looked up from his books. His face was drawn. His eyes red. His usually clean-shaven face had a distinct shadow.

'Nathan, yes, come in, son. Fancy a drink?'

Nathan nodded as he sat in the chair opposite, sinking into the old leather. Taking off his coat, he put it over the arm of the chair as Tommy poured him a whisky – he hoped it might dull the effects of the copious amount of Charlie he'd been snorting all night. Although Tommy was not usually one for drinking so early in the morning. In fact, his phone call to Nathan had been odd in many ways. It made Nathan suspicious.

'You been here all night, Tommy?'

Tommy nodded as he ran his hand over his chin. His day-old stubble making an unfamiliar rasping sound under his calloused hands. 'Never mind me. How are things, Nathan?'

'All good, mate.'

'And Grace? Jake?'

'Yeah, they're fine.'

'The pub doing well?'

'I suppose so. Look, Tommy, I know you didn't ask me here this early in the morning to make fucking small talk, what's this really about?'

Tommy shifted uncomfortably in his seat. 'All right, if you want me to get to the point, I will. I've been hearing some things, Nathan.'

'Such as?'

'Such as you doing your own thing, having me off, cutting my gear with all kinds of shit to make it go further, and then keeping the extra profit for yourself.'

'And just who the fuck has told you that, Tommy?' Nathan snapped.

'That doesn't matter right now, what matters is whether it's true. I will kill the fucker who told me myself if it isn't, but is it true?'

Nathan thought about his response. He could have gone on feigning his outrage and anger, but if he was honest, he couldn't be arsed anymore. And anyway, what would be the point? Someone had sold him out, and even if he denied it, it was only a matter of time before it all came out. Tommy would be watching him now, like a fat man watching a hot dog. He wouldn't be able to move in future. And God knew who else had been told about his indiscretions. He'd always earned a little extra on the side doing this and that, but he'd started making some serious money during the past twelve months. The stuff they'd been importing was good quality. A bit too good for the likes of people around there, in Nathan's opinion.

Tommy was an old-fashioned businessman and he prided himself on selling a good quality product. But as Nathan was the man in charge of distributing and cutting that product, he'd decided that no one would notice if he made it go that little bit further. So, for every hundred grand Tommy made, Nathan made another twenty-five or so on the side. It had been a great little earner for him. Tommy was getting soft in his old age. Nathan probably would have got away with it forever if he hadn't brought that stupid little slut, Shannon, in on it with him. He needed somewhere to cut what he had siphoned off, somewhere that no one else knew about and Shannon's place had seemed the obvious choice. She was an old friend of his who had no connection to Tommy or anyone else he knew. But, she must have blabbed to someone. The stupid bitch. He'd deal with her later.

'What do you think, Tommy?' he said, staring the older man down.

'I think that if it is true, you're the greediest, stupidest bastard I've ever met. I've treated you like a son, and I would hope this is not how you repay me. So, answer me, is it true? Look me in the eye and tell me that it's not.'

Nathan looked him in the eye, but he didn't say a word, and in that moment, Tommy realized that the rumours were not rumours at all.

Nathan knew that Tommy had invited him to his office on his own for several reasons. Mostly, because he expected him to say that he was still a loyal soldier, and that he'd never double-cross the great Tommy McNulty. Because Tommy respected him, and also because of Tommy's arrogance, and his belief that he was untouchable. That was a big mistake. It was Nathan who was untouchable. He was fucking invincible.

Before Tommy could reach for the gun, which Nathan knew he kept under his desk, Nathan had pulled the knife from the pocket of his coat on the chair. He plunged it straight into Tommy's throat. He watched the horror and disbelief in Tommy's eyes as he started to slip away, choking on his own blood. Nathan continued stabbing him repeatedly, with each thrust the rage in him abated, until finally he barely had the strength to lift his arm.

Nathan looked at the scene he'd created, almost as if he was standing outside looking in, like someone else had committed the horrific act. He was covered in blood. It was as sobering as an ice bath. The realization of what he'd done began to sink in. He'd killed Tommy McNulty. His mentor. His friend. The Boss. There was no one to help him cover it up. No one to get rid of his clothes or the body for him like they usually would. He couldn't trust anyone with this, not even Ben. He realized there was only one person he could trust with his life, the only person who could save him.

Grace.

He cleaned himself up as best as he could, careful not to leave any bloody prints behind. Returning the knife to his pocket and putting his coat on, he zipped it up in an attempt to hide his bloodstained clothes. Leaving by the back entrance, he ran to his car, making sure no one saw him. He drove home as quickly as he could. He had to make certain he came out of the situation on top. He needed to plan his next move. Of course, there would be some people who would suspect it was him and if they were stupid enough to say that out loud, he would shut them up permanently without a second's thought. But most people would think it was a rival firm. Tommy had plenty of enemies, and everyone knew how close he and Nathan were, how Tommy treated him like a son.

Nathan had built a fearsome reputation of his own. Anyone who knew the score would keep their mouths shut even if they did suspect him. Nathan was sure of that. Even the police wouldn't fall over themselves trying to solve Tommy's murder. This was how it always had to end for people like Tommy. If you lived by violence and intimidation, then you died that way too. It was just the way their world worked.

Nathan would shout louder than anyone that they needed to avenge Tommy's murder. He would break bones and bust heads open in the name of seeking revenge. No one except Grace would ever know the truth, and as Tommy's right-hand man, Nathan would be the natural choice to take his place. This could all work out well for him, if he could just convince Grace to help him.

CHAPTER FORTY-NINE

Grace was clearing up the breakfast things. She smiled when she heard Jake laughing at the cartoons he was watching in the living room. He was such a good boy, so sweet and thoughtful. She heard the front door open, signalling Nathan's return home.

'Grace, I need you,' he said, sticking his head into the kitchen. 'Now!'

She put down the plates she was holding and followed him obediently into the bathroom. He locked the door behind her and she wondered what fresh hell he had in store for her. Surely, he wouldn't do anything while Jake was awake and sitting happily in the next room? He'd never been that reckless before. She noticed a look on his face that she'd never seen before; if she didn't know better, she'd say it was fear.

As he took off his coat, she almost passed out from the shock. His pale blue T-shirt was covered in blood, making it appear almost entirely purple in colour. It was only then that she noticed his jeans had blood on them too. And his arms, and his neck – it was everywhere.

'Are you okay? Are you hurt?'

He ignored her questions. 'I need you to help me get rid of these, Grace, quickly!' He pulled off his clothes. 'Take them to

Uncle Billy's allotment; he's got a firepit there. Put them in that and burn them. Make sure no one sees you. I'll watch Jake while you go.'

'What have you done, Nathan? Whose blood is this?' she asked, acutely aware of the tremor in her voice.

'Just do as I fucking say, Grace. Now!'

'I'll take Jake with me then,' she said, desperate not to leave her baby with him, this monster who had clearly just done something terrible.

He grabbed her by the arm. 'You can't take him with you, you fucking idiot,' he snarled. 'What if he sees something? Leave him with me.'

So, she did as he asked, because she was too terrified not to. Terrified of what he would do to her, and to Jake, if she refused. But he would never hurt Jake. Not his own son? She reassured herself that Jake would be safe while she made the quick trip to the allotment. She wondered at the ease in which Nathan had asked her to become an accomplice in whatever heinous thing he'd done. But more so, at the ease in which she had complied.

Grace stuffed Nathan's clothes and trainers into the nearest thing she could find – a plastic 'Happy Shopper' bag which she and Jake had used the day before on a trip to the park. She noted the irony of the paradox of the bag's most recent contents as she emptied out Jake's football and cars and filled it with his father's blood-soaked clothes.

She told Jake that Daddy was looking after him for an hour while Mummy popped to the shops. He started to cry to go with her, but she placated him with the promise of returning with some sweets. She thought about picking him up and running. Going to the police with Nathan's clothes and telling them that she thought he'd killed someone. But how could she be sure they'd be kept safe? Nathan and Tommy were well-connected men. They had several police officers on their payroll, and who knew what they were capable of covering up between them? Then

Nathan – or someone else – would kill her – and what would happen to Jake? No – she needed to protect Jake, and herself. And the only way to do that was to do what Nathan wanted, at least until she could figure out a way to escape him for good.

Grace left the flat and drove to the allotment, almost as if on autopilot. Uncle Billy was her Aunt Helen's ex-husband. Grace had kept in touch with him sporadically over the years, but more recently, with no other friends or family to turn to, she'd contacted him again after Nathan had bumped into him in town one day.

Grace knew it was too early for Billy to be there yet. She and Jake visited the allotment occasionally. Jake loved it, playing in the dirt and planting potatoes. She saw a couple of faces that she recognized but she passed by relatively unnoticed. She set her bag down by the firepit which Billy used for warmth on the cold nights he liked to spend there. She had often wondered what he burned in there and thought then whether Nathan had ever used it for such a monstrous purpose before.

She emptied the bag's contents into the pit, along with the bag, and set it alight using Billy's matches and some old newspaper. She watched as it burned, making sure all of it was gone before she left. Seeing the picture of the round smiling face on the carrier bag melting in the flames, made her wonder whose face would never smile again; whose blood was on those clothes, and whose life she was helping to erase. When she had finished, she drove back home, remembering to stop at a sweet shop on the way.

The smell of burning would stay in her nostrils for days.

192

CHAPTER FIFTY

Nathan scrubbed himself over and over in the shower, making sure that he removed every last trace of blood. It was everywhere, under every fingernail, in every crease of his skin. When he'd finished, he dressed and went into the living room to sit with Jake, who beamed at him as he entered the room.

'What are you watching, son?' Nathan asked him, tousling his hair.

'*Fireman Sam*, Daddy,' he replied happily, climbing onto Nathan's knee as he sat down.

Nathan wondered where he got the kid from. He was so innocent and pure. He looked like Nathan but was nothing like him. His mother's influence no doubt. They were still watching *Fireman Sam* when Grace arrived home.

'Is it done?'

She nodded. She pulled some sweets from her pocket and gave them to Jake.

'Go and play with your toys in your room for a while, sweetheart,' she told him and being the good little boy he was, he skipped off to his bedroom.

Grace sat down on the sofa next to Nathan and he knew she was waiting for an explanation. He could try and blag her, spin her some yarn or other, but part of him wanted to, needed to, tell someone what he'd done. And he owed her the truth this once.

'I killed Tommy,' he said, and saying it out loud suddenly made it all seem more real to him. Completely unexpectedly, he broke down in tears, sobbing. He hadn't cried like that since he was a kid. Why had it affected him like that? Tommy was certainly not the first person he'd killed, and he wouldn't be the last.

Perhaps he reminded Nathan of the only other real father figure he had in his life? When he was stabbing Tommy over and over, maybe he was imagining someone else.

'What? You killed him? Tommy? Why, Nathan? Why on earth would you do that?' She stared at him, wide-eyed and open-mouthed. Her cheeks, usually flushed, were now as pale as the white lilies he would buy her when he was feeling particularly guilty.

'Because it was either him or me, Grace,' he sobbed.

'But you were covered in so much blood!' She looked at him in horror. 'What did you do to him? Why are you always so angry at the world?' She shook her head, unable to comprehend him. How could she? She didn't have a vicious bone in her body. So, for the first time in Nathan's life, he tried to explain.

'Because I love it, Grace. I love hurting people, the power of it, the way it makes me feel.'

He told her about the day he discovered the power of using real violence, the kind that changed the very essence of your being. He was thirteen years old. He'd been in the foster home for four years, and it was unusual for him to have stayed somewhere for so long. Usually people had got fed up of him by then. He had been an insecure, needy, mixed-up kid for a while; he couldn't imagine now that he was a picnic to be around. He would have loved to get out of there though. His foster dad, Malcolm, was an animal. Him and his wife, Shirley, had three kids of their own, all younger than Nathan. Malcolm would beat them on an almost daily basis, and Shirley would pretend it wasn't happening. He didn't beat Nathan often though. No, he reserved his other vile tendencies for him.

At first Nathan liked Malcolm, he was nice to him – bought him sweets, told him he was a good boy. He told Nathan that he loved him. No one had ever told him that before. But then it started. For almost four long years he was tormented, abused in the most heinous and sickening ways.

It was a sunny afternoon in August when it happened. Malcolm was in the kitchen eating his breakfast. Nathan remembered it vividly – Malcolm was eating bacon, sausage and beans. Beans and tomato sauce were dripping off his double-chin and onto his yellowed vest. No one was home except the two of them. Nathan was sitting at the table waiting for Malcolm to finish, as he'd been instructed to. Nathan hated that filthy bastard more than he had ever hated anyone, or anything, in his life.

Malcolm dropped his fork on the floor.

'Pick that up,' he ordered.

Nathan made his way around to the other side of the table and retrieved the fork. As he raised his head to stand up, Nathan saw that Malcolm's trousers were unzipped, exposing his white, mottled flesh. Nathan knew what he expected him to do then: something he'd made him do countless times before. But this time something in the young Nathan snapped. He'd already become an angry little bastard, years of abuse had seen to that, but he'd never had anything more than the odd schoolyard fight before.

Nathan took that fork and he stabbed Malcolm right in the cock with it. Over, and over, and over again until he was writhing in pain. Howling like the animal that he was. Blood was spurting everywhere. Then the rest of his foster family came home. Nathan often wondered if he would have killed Malcolm if they hadn't. Murdered him with a fork!

Nathan was sent back to the care home the very same day. No

one ever told them why though. No one ever came to ask what happened. Malcolm and Shirley were too scared to say what actually happened – terrified Nathan would tell everyone what a pair of sick twisted monsters they really were. Malcolm was packed off to hospital – had a gardening accident apparently! And Shirley played the doting wife and mother, while Nathan was the troubled foster kid who just couldn't fit it in anywhere.

Nathan didn't care what they said about him though. He was happy to be out of that place, but nothing compared to the euphoria he felt when he stabbed that fucker. The noise and the feel of the fork piercing his flesh for the first time. Seeing the blood oozing from him, pooling at his feet, like the tomato sauce he was so fond of eating. Nathan had never felt so powerful. He was invincible. He was experiencing life in full glorious Technicolour, for the very first time. Ever since that day he'd been chasing that feeling, that rush. God knows he'd tried to find it in other ways. Drink, drugs, sex – but nothing came close.

Nathan finished reliving the trauma of his childhood for Grace and realized that he had his knees tucked up to his chest like a frightened child. After all this time, that bastard could still make him feel like that. Grace put her arms around him and kissed the top of his head, and it was his undoing. He broke down in her arms and begged her to never leave him.

Grace had never seen Nathan in such a state before. She could barely comprehend the events of the last few hours. He was so vulnerable and yet so terrifying, at the same time. It broke her heart when she thought of what he'd endured as a child at the hands of the animal who was supposed to be protecting him. Although she wasn't sure what was more tragic – what that monster did to him, or the monster he'd helped him to become.

She was so shaken by his confession that he'd killed Tommy of all people. His friend. How could he do that? And what was she thinking helping him to cover it up? She'd known for a long time that his lifestyle involved inflicting pain and misery on others. But she always reasoned that if she didn't know about it, she wouldn't have to acknowledge it. Now the truth was there with them, and it was inescapable.

She wrapped her arms around him as he sobbed. This great hulk of a man, this hard man, weeping like a frightened child. His shoulders moved rhythmically up and down with each sob. She kissed him on the top of his head because she couldn't think of anything else to comfort him. To show the frightened little boy in him that he was loved. Despite all that he was and all that he had done, she loved him still. Loved him and hated him in equal measure. But she had never been more afraid of him than she was at that moment.

It was as though someone had shone a torch into the dark recesses of her brain. Finally, she realized that it wasn't her who made him angry. It wasn't that she'd said the wrong thing, dressed too provocatively or asked too many questions. It was him; all him. His true nature was the violent monster and not the charming, caring man she'd fallen in love with. The monster was the side of him which he was constantly trying to suppress, but the one who would always win out in the end.

In that moment, she felt such pity for him. To have to live your life like that, never knowing true happiness, knowing that you could only be whole when you were hurting someone else.

He looked up at her then as if he was reading her mind. She saw the fear in his eyes.

'Please don't leave me,' he pleaded.

'I'm not going anywhere, Nathan,' she told him.

'Promise me you'll never leave me, Grace. Promise me.'

So, she promised him. Because, despite how much she wanted to, she couldn't see a way she could ever escape him.

CHAPTER FIFTY-ONE

Present Day

The scalding hot water ran over Grace's body. She'd jumped into the shower as soon as she'd got home after her visit to Nathan at his club. It had been tougher than she'd thought it would be, to smile at him and pretend that to even be in his company didn't want to make her vomit. But to allow him to touch her, to touch him and pretend that it didn't make her want to tear her own skin from her body, it had taken every ounce of strength she had. But it would be worth it. The quickest way to Nathan's heart was through his trousers.

As she dried herself off with a towel, Grace was busy formulating her plan. Nathan would pay for everything he'd ever done to her, to Jake, and to the people she cared about. She'd worked hard to build a life without him – a better life than any she could have ever had with him, and he was intent on ruining everything for her. Why couldn't he just leave her alone? He had Kayleigh, more money than he knew what to do with, his club, even a good relationship with his son, despite everything. Why wasn't that enough for him?

Why did he need to have her too? It was as though he couldn't bear to see her happy. To even go as far as telling Pat about Tommy's murder, there was no reason for that, other than to cause pain. It was just cruel. Well, if he liked sharing secrets so much, then she had a belter to share with him. One that would bring his perfect little world crashing down around him.

Before she set those wheels in motion, she was going to meet Michael. It was important that he and Patrick were out of the way for the foreseeable future. She had to focus on Nathan and couldn't be worrying about them every five minutes. And she wanted to explain to him why his dad was so angry with her. It was about time he knew the truth.

She wondered if Patrick would ever be able to forgive her for lying to him for all those years. Particularly as sometime soon, she was going to betray his confidence too, and reveal a secret he'd made her promise to keep. But she'd always known that was a promise she'd break one day. The information was too important, and too useful to her, not to share it with Nathan. After all, it was him who it would hurt the most.

CHAPTER FIFTY-TWO

Six Years Earlier

''Night, son,' Grace whispered as she closed Jake's bedroom door. He didn't answer. Always sound asleep before his head hit the pillow.

Patrick walked into the living room carrying two plates of spaghetti bolognaise. 'Here you are, boss. Get that down you,' he said as he handed her the food.

'Did today go to plan?' Grace asked.

'Yep. Not a hitch.'

'Good,' she nodded. 'So, we're all set then? The lads know what to do?'

'Of course. And they'll make sure to stay away from Nathan and John Brennan's turf. Our lads will be focusing on the city centre pubs and clubs. I've squared it with Barry.'

Barry 'the Biceps' Peterson was the head doorman for Storm Securities. They controlled most of the doors in Liverpool city centre. Getting them onside was crucial if you wanted to sell drugs without any hassle in their venues. Grace made sure that she gave Barry and his lads a decent cut of the money they made. She always made sure her partners were well compensated – it usually ensured they remained loyal and didn't bother looking elsewhere for business. If anyone tried undercutting her, she was happy to negotiate new terms. All via Patrick and Michael, obviously. They were the public face that people dealt with so that Grace was able to remain in the shadows. Ever the respectable businesswoman.

Patrick often joked that her rise to the top of the criminal ranks was one of the best kept secrets in Liverpool. Grace liked it that way. She was happy for him and Michael to take the credit for her success, and in turn take most of the aggro too.

'It must be nice working with Michael again?' Grace said.

Patrick shrugged. 'Bittersweet really. It's great to work with my lad, but I'd hoped he might go legit after he got out of the nick. But he's never been cut out for a nine to five. He takes after me.'

'Yeah. He wasn't happy just working in the bar, was he? And he's great at what he does, Pat. You taught him well.'

Patrick couldn't hide the look of pride on his face. 'I did, didn't I? What about Jake? What if he wanted to go into the family business?'

Grace shook her head. 'No chance. That boy is going to university and getting a proper job,' she laughed.

If Patrick was offended, he didn't show it. 'Michael wants the same for his boys too,' he sighed. 'I'm just not sure they've got it in them. Did you know they've been expelled again?'

Grace shook her head. 'That's three different schools now, isn't it?'

'Yep. Michael's having a word with the head to see if he can *persuade* him to take them back.'

'The things we do for our sons eh, Pat?' She laughed as she took a sip of her wine.

'Well we love them. Have to, don't we? Do anything for them, all of us. Michael, you, me, your dad, even Tommy.'

It took a few seconds for Grace to register what he'd said. 'Tommy?' she asked when she did. 'He had a son?'

Patrick's face flushed faster than an automatic toilet. He stared into his plate of food as though it held the key to life's mysteries.

'Pat?' she snapped. 'Did Tommy have a son?'

'No … I don't know what I was saying,' he stammered.

'Come on, Pat. I'm not daft. I can tell by your reaction. Just tell me.'

'I can't, Grace.' He shook his head.

'Pat. You can tell me anything. You know that.'

'I promised him I'd never tell anyone.'

'I won't breathe a word to anyone, I promise,' Grace said, placing her hand on his.

'It won't be that easy for you, Grace,' he whispered.

'What? Why?'

'Promise me you'll never tell him, Grace.'

Grace's heart started to hammer in her chest. What the hell was he on about. Tell who?

'I promise,' she lied, because she needed to know who Patrick was talking about more than she'd needed to know anything in her life. 'Who is Tommy's son?'

Patrick looked up at her with a look of horror on his face. 'Nathan,' he whispered.

Grace felt like someone had punched her in the stomach. 'What? How? Why doesn't anyone know? Why didn't Tommy tell him?'

Patrick shook his head. 'He was ashamed. Embarrassed that he'd abandoned his son. Tommy swore me and your dad to secrecy. He was married to his first wife, Marie, then. And she couldn't have kids. She would have murdered him if she'd found out. Plus, by all accounts, Nathan's mother was a fucking lunatic. She thought she'd landed the jackpot when she bedded Tommy though, but he would never have left Marie – not even for a son. So, Tommy paid her off and that was the end of it. But Tommy regretted his decision every day of his life.'

Grace ate her spaghetti and shared a bottle of wine but she

barely registered anything else Patrick said. She hardly tasted the food or the drink. Her head spun with so many questions. It was crazy – but it all fit together. Tommy had treated Nathan like a son, almost from the moment they met. He was always considered untouchable as far as Tommy was concerned. Nathan, in his arrogance, assumed it was because he was so great at his job.

After they'd finished their meal, Grace made excuses about feeling tired and asked Patrick to leave, telling him she had an early start. She had to confirm that what Patrick had told her was true, and she could only think of one other person who might know the truth after all those years.

CHAPTER FIFTY-THREE

Walking up the path to the redbrick house, Grace noted the stone fountain in the middle of the lawn, and the various garish ornaments which festooned the front garden. If the exterior was any indication, this house was as ostentatious as its owner.

A large golden door knocker adorned the shiny red front door, longing to be used. She rang the doorbell instead and listened to the tune of 'Greensleeves' filling the air.

The door was opened quickly, as though the occupier were expecting someone. She had hardly changed at all.

'Sharon.' Grace smiled at Tommy McNulty's widow.

Sharon stared at her for a moment, trawling the recesses of her brain to recall how she knew the younger woman. When she realized, she half-smiled, showing a row of perfect white teeth.

'Grace Conlon? As I live and breathe. What brings you here?'

'It's Sumner now.' She smiled. 'I just wanted to talk to you about something, Sharon. Mind if I come in?'

Sharon frowned in response, weighing up whether to allow this long-lost acquaintance to step into her plush cream-carpeted hallway. Seconds later she opened the door wider and allowed Grace inside.

Sharon was the perfect hostess. She'd always been all about

presentation. She went to the kitchen to make tea, while Grace sat in the stuffy, overly furnished sitting room. Returning a few moments later, Sharon made polite conversation about the weather. She asked about Jake and told Grace all about her holiday home in Spain. Grace smiled and answered politely until she could bear the pretence no longer.

'As I said, there's something I wanted to ask you about, Sharon.'

Sharon placed her china teacup onto its matching saucer. 'Go on.'

Grace was planning on broaching the subject gently, to try and determine if the older lady knew the truth or not. But maybe it was the ten minutes of inane chatter or the fact that this room was suffocating her, she got straight to the point. 'Was Tommy Nathan's father?'

Sharon's hands trembled and she placed the teacup and saucer onto the marble coffee table. God forbid she should spill a drop on her shagpile.

'I don't know what you mean, love,' she stuttered.

'I think you do, Sharon. Was he?'

'Where did you hear such a thing?' Sharon composed herself quickly and shook her head, attempting to dismiss Grace's question as nonsense, but her immediate reaction had revealed otherwise.

'From someone who knew Tommy well.'

'Ridiculous,' she huffed.

'Don't you think people deserve to know the truth, Sharon?'

'No.' She shook her head. 'Tommy wouldn't want it to come out now.'

'Then what about Jake? Don't you think he deserves to know who his grandfather was? What a great man he was?' Grace almost balked at that last comment. Jake's grandfather was indeed a great man, but his name was Pete Sumner, not Tommy McNulty. Grace saw Sharon soften.

'But Tommy didn't want anyone to know. He was ashamed,

205

you see. Ashamed that Nathan had to grow up the way he did. Tommy was young, and he was married to Marie then. And Nathan's mother … well – she was a raving nutter. When Marie died, he wanted to contact the lad, but Nathan would have been a teenager by then, and Tommy thought it would have messed him up too much to have his long-lost dad suddenly turning up out of nowhere. Tommy tried to make up for it when Nathan was older. That's why he gave him a job, and took him under his wing, like.' She shook her head. 'And why he let him get away with bloody murder.'

Grace took a sip of her tea to compose herself. If only she knew!

'If I had only known that Tommy was Jake's grandad,' Grace said as she shook her head solemnly. 'It would have been wonderful for Jake to have known him. And you too, Sharon. You would have been terrific grandparents.' Grace stared at the older woman intently, hoping that her little act had been convincing enough.

'Wait here,' Sharon said suddenly, before disappearing out of the room. Grace could hear her moving things around upstairs and wondered what she was doing. Oh, please, let there be proof, she thought. Let me have something over that bastard for once.

A few minutes later, Sharon came back into the room carrying an old biscuit tin. Handing it to Grace, she wiped a tear from her eye. 'I found these after Tommy died. He kept them all those years,' she sniffed.

Grace opened the tin and took out the photographs. They were faded, with well-thumbed edges. She wondered how many times Tommy had looked at them. Smiling at his son – or crying at the childhood he was never a part of. She stared at the chubby face of Nathan as a baby. It could almost be Jake looking back at her. There were letters too. She took one out of the yellowed envelope, and opened the crisp, carefully folded paper. She read them all. Some were from Nathan's mother, demanding money

206

for her silence. Others from a foster home. From the dates and the contents, she realized they were from *the* foster home. The one where Nathan had learned to become the monster that he was.

Tommy had found out where Nathan was and had wanted to make contact. Nathan's foster father – that animal – had dissuaded Tommy from contacting his son, telling him how happy and settled Nathan was there. What if Tommy had known the truth? How different would Nathan's life have been? How different would Grace's life have been?

'Could I borrow these, Sharon?'

She shook her head. 'I don't think so. I told you, this can't come out. Nathan must never know. It would kill him.'

'I wouldn't tell Nathan about Tommy. I promise. But I'd like to show Jake his dad's baby pictures,' she lied. 'They look so alike.'

Sharon continued shaking her head. 'I'm sorry, love. I can't have anyone else seeing these. In fact, I should have burned them after Tommy died.'

Grace smiled. 'I understand. Thanks for your time, Sharon.'

Leaving Sharon's house a minute later, Grace thought about the biscuit tin and the evidence within it. She needed to get her hands on it before Sharon did something stupid.

So, Nathan had murdered his own father. How about that. He'd spent so much of his life longing for love and acceptance, wondering who his father was. To think he had that from Tommy – his actual father, and he had thrown it away. Who knew how that would affect him if he knew. Not in any good way, she could guarantee. It would eat away at him. It would make him question everything. Who he was. What he'd done. She smiled to herself as she realized she now had information that could bring her ex-husband to his knees.

CHAPTER FIFTY-FOUR

Craig Snell sauntered over to the bar of the Rose and Crown looking very pleased with himself. All of five feet two inches and built like a whippet, he looked much younger than his nineteen years. The large backpack he carried was almost as big as him. Grace watched him from her vantage point. She'd recently finished eating lunch with one of her girlfriends.

'I'm here to see Grace,' Craig said to Marcus as he approached the bar.

'What for?' Marcus asked. 'Shouldn't you be in school, son?'

'I'm here for a job interview, aren't I?' he snapped.

Getting up from her seat, Grace approached the bar.

'Is this right?' Marcus asked, indicating his head towards Craig with a look of bemusement on his face.

Grace nodded. 'Come through, Craig,' she smiled.

Craig followed Grace up to her office. Once they were inside he took the battered metal biscuit tin from his backpack. 'As promised,' he smiled, showing off the gap in his teeth.

'You didn't take anything else though?' Grace queried.

He shook his head. 'Nope. Waited till the old bird was out and was in an and out quicker than a virgin on prom night. She had some good stuff though, Grace. Could have slipped a few quid's worth of bling out of there with me, no problem,' he sighed.

'And there's no sign of a break-in? No one will know you were there?'

'No. I told you, I'm the best.' He grinned.

As much as he looked like a scrawny schoolboy, yet to hit puberty, Craig Snell was one of the best thieves this side of the Mersey. He could get in and out of almost anywhere without leaving a trace. His considerable skills had earned him the nick-name 'Baby Houdini'.

'Well this is worth more to you than some jewellery,' she said as she threw the bag of money onto the table.

Craig picked it up and looked inside. 'Two grand?' he asked.

'As agreed.'

'So what's in there that's worth so much to you?' Craig queried as he placed the carrier bag into his now-empty backpack.

'Don't tell me you didn't look inside, Craig.' She raised her eyebrows. 'I know you better than that.'

''Course I did.' He shrugged. 'Just a load of letters and photos.'

'Well let's just say they have sentimental value. Come on, I'll show you out.'

He followed her back down to the bar. 'Bye then,' he called as he walked out of the pub.

'Did you really interview him?' Marcus asked. 'He looks like he should still be on the boob, never mind the ale.'

Grace shrugged. 'A favour for an old friend.'

'I thought I was in charge of hiring and firing?' he pouted.

'You are,' Grace soothed as she touched his arm. 'I was never going to give him a job behind the bar. It was just a favour, I told you.'

Marcus smiled, and she knew he'd already forgotten about it. She thought about the tin upstairs. Sharon had refused to give her any evidence of Nathan's parentage. Terrified that it could fall into the wrong hands. For now, the information would be securely stored in her safe. As much as she would never betray Patrick's confidence if she could help it, she knew a day would come when she would have no choice.

CHAPTER FIFTY-FIVE

Present Day

Grace linked her arm through Michael's as they made their way to the hospital café. Patrick was still refusing to see her. Would he ever forgive her? She couldn't bear the thought of never speaking to him again. At the very least, she wanted to explain what had happened all those years ago.

Grace took a seat while Michael ordered their coffees. A few moments later he walked over to their table with two Styrofoam cups.

'This looks like shit, but it's hot and wet.' He smiled. 'I'd make a joke about that, but I sense you're not in the mood?'

She shook her head.

'Fucking hell, Grace. What the hell could you have possibly done that was so bad?'

Grace told him everything. All about the part she'd played in helping Nathan after Tommy's murder. About her visit to Nathan earlier that day, and the details of her plan to get him out of their lives for good.

Michael sat quietly as he listened to her talk. When she'd

finished, he sat there shaking his head. 'Well, fuck me, Grace I wasn't expecting that.'

'Do you think your dad will ever forgive me?' she asked.

Michael nodded. 'Of course he will. You didn't have much choice, did you?'

'I know, but after all these years I never told him. All that time he didn't know who killed Tommy and I did. I should never have kept it from him.'

Michael placed his hand on hers. 'We all do what we need to survive, Grace. My old man included. He'll see that eventually. I promise.'

Staring into her coffee, she mumbled. 'I hope so.'

'But about this plan of yours. I'm not so sure about that.'

Grace's head snapped up. Immediately back in charge. 'It's the only way to keep us all safe.'

Michael shook his head. 'Well I beg to differ. You must understand I can't just sit back and do nothing after what he's done?'

'It's the only way, Michael. I know it goes against every instinct you have but you have to trust me. Even if you could get to Nathan, which is unlikely now given that he's upped his security, one of his minions would step up and take his place and they'd come after us instead. Not through any sense of loyalty to him, but because they'd be looking to prove themselves worthy of his crown. My way, nobody gets hurt except Nathan. No one will come looking for us. We can all walk away unscathed.'

'You're crazy, Grace. But if you could pull it off …'

'I will.'

'So this is it then? I have to just disappear?'

Grace nodded. 'Only until it's over.'

Running his hands through his hair, he sighed. 'But what if it goes wrong. What if he figures out what you're doing? What if he hurts you?'

'Trust me, there's nothing he can do to me that he hasn't already done. I'm a tough old bird. Don't worry about me.'

'You're the toughest woman I know,' he said softly. 'But what if you need me? I'll be too far away to help. I feel like you're putting me out to pasture.'

Grace laughed. 'You? Out to pasture? Never. I just want you all to be safe while I sort this out. Take your dad and Hannah to Scotland to stay with the boys and take care of your family.'

'You are my family.'

'And you're mine. Which is why I need you all out of here.'

'And what about Sean? Steph? Sophia? The kids?'

'I'll take care of it. They'll be safe. I promise.'

'Fine,' he sighed. 'Are we getting too old for all this shit?'

Grace nodded. 'I think we might be.'

'Maybe we should run off into the sunset and leave it all behind?'

'Nice idea. But it would never work.' She smiled.

'Worth a try.' He shrugged.

CHAPTER FIFTY-SIX

Untangling herself from the soft cotton sheets, Grace slipped out of bed.

'Do you have to go right now?' Ben grinned at her. 'I haven't seen you for two weeks and I was just getting ready for round three.'

'You're insatiable,' she laughed as she started to dress. 'Yes, I have to go.'

Standing up, he walked across the room and she took the opportunity to admire his naked body. Slipping his hands around her waist to her behind, he pulled her towards him. She ran her fingers through the tight curls on his muscular chest as he kissed her long and hard. Her resolve to leave weakening with each passing second.

'Right now?' he asked again.

'Yes, right now,' she groaned.

'Hmm okay. I'll let you go. Same time tomorrow?' he asked, raising one eyebrow.

She stroked his cheek, enjoying the feel of his day-old stubble under her fingertips. She wished it didn't have to end again. He could tell that she had something on her mind. He knew her far too well.

'What's wrong?' he asked, his voice full of concern.

'We need to stop seeing each other for a while.' She looked at the floor, because she couldn't bear to look him in the eye.

'What?' She could hear the exasperation in his voice and she couldn't blame him. 'Why do you do this to me, Grace? Every time I get close to you, you push me away. I can't keep doing this with you. You told me to give you a few months and I did, yet here we are again.'

He walked away from her now and sat on the bed with his head in his hands.

'I'm sorry,' she told him honestly. 'We just can't be together right now. It's too dangerous.'

He looked at her. 'Nathan?' He spat the word out as though it was a poison that left a bad taste in his mouth.

'We can't risk him finding out yet. You know he would kill us both if he found out. You know that. And it's just too risky with him hanging around all the time.'

Taking hold of her hand, he pulled her towards him. 'But he's been out for over six months and he hasn't found out. Besides, I thought we agreed we were going to stop sneaking around anyway?'

'I've got so much on my mind right now. With Patrick in hospital. I've got things I need to sort out. I can't be worrying about you and me being caught as well as all the other shit going on.'

'You always have shit going on, Grace,' he said. 'That's just an excuse.'

'Look. It's just different now,' she snapped.

'Different how?' he asked, and she could hear the frustration building in his voice.

'Because he's going to be around a lot more. And he'll know if I've been with someone else now, that's why.'

It took a few seconds until the proverbial penny dropped. 'What? I really don't believe you,' he shouted. 'How can you let

215

him anywhere near you? How can you let that fucker touch you? You've been trying to get away from him for years, and now you're going back to him? I don't fucking believe it. Are you forgetting who he is?'

'Of course not. But this is something I have to do. It's the only way,' she whispered, and then she told him everything. All about Nathan's threats, the Carter twins' stupidity and her plan to be rid of Nathan once and for all.

'And you expect me to be okay with this?' he said.

If she was honest she couldn't give a flying rat's arse if he was okay with it or not. It was her body and her choice. This was the smartest way to keep everyone safe. Why couldn't they all see that?

'Be okay with it, or don't, Ben. Either way, it's happening. Jake always has and always will be the most important thing in the world to me. I'm doing this to protect him. He is my main concern – not your ego. Anyway, if you really want us to be able to build a life together, then we need there to be no come back on this. Not from anyone. Not the police, John Brennan. No one.'

She felt like crying. Why did she keep having to do this to this man who loved her? He wanted nothing from her except for her to love him back and would do anything to make her happy. Closing her eyes, she tried to stop the tears coming, but one escaped anyway, and she felt it running down her cheek. He reached up and brushed it away with his thumb and that simple gesture was her undoing. Sinking to her knees, she started to sob. He was the only man she'd ever cry in front of. The only person she could be her true self with. He said nothing, stroking her hair until she was spent.

'Why didn't you tell me any of this before? I'll fucking kill him,' he growled.

'Don't be ridiculous,' she said. 'It's too dangerous. You know what he did to Pat. I won't have you on my conscience too.'

216

'It kills me not to see you, Grace,' he said pulling her up onto the bed with him. 'I love you.'

She loved him too. She'd never told him that, but she did. What would be the point in telling him? They could never have any sort of normal relationship while the spectre of Nathan loomed large in the background. It was better to keep him at arm's length; it was kinder to them both. She kissed him instead and they fell back onto the bed.

'There is something you could do for me,' she said as he kissed her neck. She loved the way he kissed her. The pleasant scratch of his stubble on her throat.

'Anything,' he mumbled.

'Do you think you could find out where he's keeping the gun? He still trusts you.'

'Consider it done.'

Grace watched his dark head disappear under the covers as he trailed kisses down her body. Thirteen years they'd been doing this dance together. It would be kinder to let him go and allow him to find a woman who could give him everything he deserved. But she couldn't. As unfair as it was to him, she couldn't let him go. A wave of guilt washed over her, leaving a sour taste in her mouth. She wondered sometimes what their life could have been like together if only she'd have been brave enough to tell Ben the truth …

CHAPTER FIFTY-SEVEN

Twelve Years Earlier

The plastic chair creaked as Grace shifted uncomfortably in her seat. She looked around the small waiting room. Its pale green walls were festooned with posters and pamphlets, each one as incongruous as the next. It was empty except for a young couple who fidgeted nervously, making idle small talk with each other, as though it might detract from the awful thing they were about to do. Grace was there to do the same thing. Although she had no one to have such banal conversation with. It felt right that she was alone though. She had made this decision alone. She would carry her guilt and shame alone.

She often thought about the other baby she lost, and wondered what he or she, who'd have been almost two years old by then, would have been like. Lost! It was such an odd term to use in the circumstances, wasn't it? It sounded careless. Like she'd left it on a bus or forgotten to take it out of the supermarket trolley. It was too casual a word to use for such a precious little life. Nathan had kicked it out of her stomach before she could even tell him she was pregnant.

She supposed that whenever she thought about this baby, she

wouldn't be able to claim to have lost it at all. She was choosing to end the poor child's life, to destroy it before it even had a chance. She couldn't bear the thought of having another child of Nathan's. What if it turned out like him? What if the monster was in his DNA? She had been lucky with Jake, he'd escaped it, but another child might not be so fortunate.

She was being selfish too. She didn't want anything else to tie her to that bastard; she was already chained to him more than she could bear.

But if she was honest with herself, the probability was that this baby wasn't even his. It was more than likely Ben's baby. And the fallout from that was unimaginable.

So, there she was, alone. She'd spoken with a doctor and two nurses a few minutes ago. They wanted to assess her mental capacity to make such a decision. That was a laugh, she thought. Anyone with half a brain should have been able to tell she was merely a shell of a human being. But they didn't. In a few moments, they would call her back in, give her some tablets to take and then send her on her merry way. It would all be over – just like that. She knew without a doubt that the guilt of the decision would hang over her, haunting her. She would never escape it; and she didn't want to. As far as she was concerned, she should be reminded every day of the life she was so carelessly tossing aside.

CHAPTER FIFTY-EIGHT

Present Day

Sean looked up from his laptop as Grace walked through the doors of Grazia's. A plate of uneaten pasta sat on the table beside him. It was Monday afternoon and the restaurant was quiet. He always did the books then.

'Unless you're here to tell me your ex-husband is currently having his heart carved out with a spoon, or is already pushing up the daisies, I'm busy,' he snapped.

'Not yet, unfortunately,' she said as she took a seat on the chair opposite him.

'Then why are you here, Grace?'

'Have you seen your dad today?' she asked, ignoring his question.

He sighed. 'Yeah. He still looks terrible. He'll probably be in a wheelchair for a long time. He'll fucking hate that.'

Grace nodded. 'I know.'

'He's insisting on signing himself out in a few days though.'

'I know,' she repeated.

He looked at her. 'You could have put a stop to all this a long time ago. You know that, don't you?'

Sighing, Grace looked at him intently. 'Don't start. I feel bad enough already. I don't need this from you.'

'You don't need this?' he snapped. 'My dad will never be the same again after what happened. All because of your psychopathic ex-husband.'

Grace bristled, sitting up straighter in her chair. 'Oh, fuck off, Sean,' she said. 'Don't you dare lecture me on morality. It wasn't so long ago you, and your dad were running around Liverpool giving out similar beatings yourselves – or paying someone else to do it. Don't forget who put you here in your fancy restaurant and your suit and tie. If your idiot nephews hadn't screwed up and taken it upon themselves to make decisions way above their paygrade, then none of us would be in this mess. I'm going to deal with Nathan in my own way. I always was. He's not some no-mark dealer you can just take out with no repercussions. He's a fucking lunatic with an army behind him. Not to mention, he's my son's father.'

Sean glared at her, but he didn't challenge her any further. He knew she was right. 'Michael tells me you've got a plan to fix everything?'

'Yes. Did he tell you what it is?'

'I got the gist. For what it's worth, I think your mental. It's brilliant, but mental all the same.'

Grace shrugged. 'So, you know him and your dad and the boys will be out of the way for a while.'

He nodded. 'I've told Sophia to take the kids to her mum's. And Steph's going to go with them. She doesn't want to leave Antonelli's when we're only just getting established, but I told her to think of it as a working holiday. If she can bring some authentic Italian dishes back with her, it will only help the restaurant.'

'And she believed you?'

'No, she's not stupid. But she's a good girl. She'll do as I ask.'

'And what about you?'

'I'm going nowhere.'

Grace knew it was no use trying to convince him otherwise. He wasn't as pliable as his brother and father – he never had been. He was a stubborn sod when he wanted to be. It was one of the things she admired about him.

'Fine. But stay out of the way.'

He nodded. 'I won't go looking for him, Grace. But if he should find me ...'

'Fair enough. But I plan on keeping him very busy,' she said as she stood up to leave.

He took hold of her arm. 'Be careful,' he said softly.

'I will.'

CHAPTER FIFTY-NINE

'Hiya Mum,' Jake said, a huge grin on his face.

'Jake, what are you doing home?' Grace asked as she leaned over the bar to give him a hug.

'I've been invited to a birthday party,' he said.

'Oh whose?'

'Siobhan Davies,' he smiled.

Grace rolled her eyes. Siobhan was a bright, funny girl with flaming red hair and an infectious laugh. She and Jake had been friends all through school but had drifted apart once they went to different colleges.

'Better get your best clobber out then, hadn't you?' Grace said to him.

'Yeah, about that. Any chance of a few quid to buy something new, Mum?' he asked her, tilting his head slightly, knowing she would never refuse him.

'Of course, son. Marcus is upstairs in the office. Go and tell him how much you need.'

Before Jake could move from the bar, Nathan stepped up behind him. Grace hadn't even seen him come in. But then he'd become like a part of the bloody furniture lately. Always skulking around the place. Lingering like a rotten smell.

223

'Hello, son,' he said as he put his arm around Jake's shoulder. 'What are you doing home?'

'Hiya, Dad. I'm going to a party. Remember that bird I was telling you about.'

'Jake,' Grace snapped. 'Do not call women birds.'

'Sorry, Mum,' he said sheepishly.

'For fuck's sake,' Nathan muttered, and Grace glared at him. It was bad enough that Jake looked up to his dad so much, without Nathan's terrible attitude to women rubbing off on him as well.

'So, you might get lucky then?' Nathan smirked.

Jake shrugged. 'It's just a party.'

'How's uni then, son?' Nathan said as Grace continued to glare at him.

'Great, the lads I'm living with are a good laugh.'

'Well I hope you're staying out of trouble,' Nathan said. Then looking directly at Grace, he gave Jake's shoulder a squeeze and went on. 'It would be a shame if things got screwed up for you, wouldn't it?'

'Of course I am, Dad,' Jake said, oblivious to the menacing undertone in his father's words.

'You'd better go and see Marcus before he locks the safe,' Grace said to Jake.

'Oh yeah. I'll get straight off when I've seen him, Mum. See youse later,' he said before heading off to Grace's office upstairs.

Once he was out of earshot, Grace leaned over the bar towards Nathan. 'If you ever threaten my son again, I will fucking end you, Nathan Conlon,' she snarled.

'Don't forget who you're talking to, Grace,' he snapped back. 'Don't forget I still have that gun. Be careful, love,' he grinned. 'Don't forget our little agreement.'

'If you ever do anything to harm him. If you ever use him to intimidate me again, then all bets are off.'

224

To her fury and annoyance, he laughed. 'I'll see you later, babe,' he winked. Then, still laughing, he walked out of the pub.

Grace realized she was wringing the bar towel in her hands. She hated that man with a burning passion. The sooner he was out of hers and Jake's lives for good, the better. It was time to put the next stage of her plan into action.

CHAPTER SIXTY

Grace climbed out of her Mercedes and straightened her clothes. She was wearing a tight-fitting pencil skirt, the type that made Nathan's eyes glaze over. Her long hair fell in waves over her shoulders. She walked into The Blue Rooms, her high heels clicking on the tiled floor. It was midday and there was no one else around. Nathan was expecting her. She'd phoned him earlier to tell him she wanted to see him.

She walked into his office making him look up from what he was doing.

'Grace,' he leered at her. 'I'm so glad you phoned me. I knew you couldn't resist me really.'

'Here. I have something I need to show you,' she told him as she handed him a small bundle of photographs. He snatched them from her hand and stared intently at the one on the top of the pile.

'Is this Jake?' he frowned. He knew it wasn't. It looked a lot like Jake, but anyone who knew him as well as Nathan and Grace did, could tell it wasn't him.

'No. Not Jake. Take a look at the back.'

Nathan turned the photograph over in his hand and read the carefully written handwriting. *Nathan. 18 months.* His skin paled, as though all the blood had drained from his face in an instant. His features distorted in anger and confusion.

'What the fuck is this? Where did you get these?' he shouted as he thumbed through the remaining pictures.

'There are letters too,' she told him, holding up the yellowed envelopes.

His head snapped up. 'What? Where did you get this stuff, Grace?' The tremor in his voice clearly audible.

'From a mutual acquaintance of ours,' she said trying her hardest not to smile as he became increasingly bewildered. The beads of perspiration started to trickle down his forehead. His hands trembled as he reached for the letters. She handed them to him, ensuring that she held the envelope the right side up, so he had a clear view of the addressee: *Tommy McNulty.*

'Tommy?' he stammered. 'But why?'

'He was your dad, Nathan.' She enjoyed delivering that piece of information.

Nathan sank further into his chair as though someone had just hit him full force in the stomach with a cricket bat. Running his hands though his hair, he started to take deep, gulping breaths.

'But this doesn't make any sense,' he looked at her wild-eyed. His hair, usually so well groomed, was damp with sweat, sticking up at odd angles from his head. 'Why didn't he tell me?'

'From what Sharon told me, I think he was ashamed of not being there for you when you were a kid. I think he was scared you'd reject him if you found out the truth. But he kept the photographs all those years, Nathan. He must have loved you. That's why he gave you a job. You should read the letters,' she told him, knowing they would bring him untold pain.

He shook his head. 'Sharon told you? No. It can't be true, Grace.'

She touched the top of his head, gently, soothing him. 'I thought you deserved to know.'

He looked up at her, his eyes wet with tears, and nodded. 'But I killed him, Grace.'

'I know,' she whispered.

'He was my dad and I killed him?'

'You should read the letters,' she said again as she picked up her handbag and left his office. Smiling, she strode out of the double doors and into the bright sunlight. That would keep him occupied for a while and give her some much-needed breathing room.

She would enjoy watching him unravel, watching his perfect world come crashing down around him.

CHAPTER SIXTY-ONE

Nathan's hands shook as he pulled the bag of Charlie from his jacket pocket. Dipping his finger into the bag, he scooped up a mound of white powder and snorted it. He didn't take it often anymore and it hit him straight away. He immediately started to feel more focused. Picking up a new bottle of whisky from a box beside his desk, he broke the seal and took a long swig, enjoying the feeling of the liquid burning his throat on the way down.

Scanning the desk in his office, he saw the bundle of letters and photographs sitting there, taunting him. He had no idea how long he'd been sitting like that. He'd read the letters after Grace left and realized it was true. Tommy was his dad. His fucking dad. He could have saved him from that horrible foster home, but he'd just left him there to rot, like he was nothing. But he'd wanted to come for him, he had – and that filthy bastard had stopped him.

Nathan had killed his own dad, right in the very office he was sitting in. He remembered how stupid he thought Tommy was to confront him without any backup, but he was never intending to take him on.

Why didn't he just fucking tell me? Why? I killed my own fucking dad!

That day was still as vivid for him then as the day it happened. He could still smell the blood; still hear the noise of Tommy's final breaths as they left his body. He was sure if he looked hard enough he could have found some of Tommy's blood somewhere in that office.

Without any warning, he vomited the most recent contents of his stomach onto the desk. The foul-smelling liquid trickled off the side of the desk and onto his trousers. But he didn't move.

He couldn't.

He'd killed his own father.

'What the hell happened to you last night?' Kayleigh shrieked as Nathan opened his eyes. He was at home in bed, but he had no idea how he'd got there. His mouth felt like he'd been licking the bottom of a skip. His head spun as his eyes tried to adjust to the bright light of the bedroom. Kayleigh jabbered on in the background, but he tuned her out.

What the fuck had happened?

As his mind regained its focus, he remembered. Grace had told him that Tommy was his dad and she had the proof too. How long had she known? Days? Months? Years? Had she kept it to herself and then used it to hurt him? Was it all just part of some sick, twisted game she was playing?

No. Grace wasn't that cruel. Was she? He swallowed the bile that lurched from his stomach and into his throat.

'Shut the fuck up, you stupid bitch,' he barked at Kayleigh as he stumbled out of bed.

She stared at him, mouth hanging open, like he had three heads.

If he'd had the strength, he'd have slapped her face for daring to look at him like that. Instead he staggered into the living room and sat on the sofa. He couldn't breathe. He felt like someone had their hands inside his chest and were squeezing his insides, until there was no breath left in his body.

There was an open bottle of vodka on the coffee table. He picked it up with a trembling hand and took a swig. His chest started to feel looser, and he could breathe again. Closing his eyes, he leaned back against the sofa. He needed to stop thinking. He needed to do something. He needed to get out of there before he stopped Kayleigh's whining and snivelling for good.

CHAPTER SIXTY-TWO

Holding the phone to her ear, Grace checked again that she'd locked the front door. She didn't want anyone accidentally walking in on her. She had been put on hold by the receptionist a few seconds ago.

'Hello, Rebecca speaking,' a chirpy voice filled her ear.

'Hi Rebecca. My name is Grace Sumner. I understand you're Nathan Conlon's probation officer?'

Grace heard a small sigh before Rebecca said. 'I'm sorry Grace, but I can't discuss individual cases.'

'I know that. I'm sorry. I'm not looking for information. Nathan told me you were his probation officer, and I'm just worried about him, that's all.'

'Well I can't give information, but I can listen. Perhaps you could tell me why you're worried?'

'Well, I really don't want to get him into trouble. And I don't want him to know I've phoned you. He would think I'm interfering, you see.'

'If you're worried about him, Grace, then I think you should tell me why. I can assure you any information you provide will be treated confidentially.'

'Okay,' Grace said, as though Rebecca had convinced her to

tell all. 'Well … Nathan's been struggling lately. I'm not sure why. Maybe it's being out after such a long time inside? He seemed fine at first. But now … well, he's drinking every day, and I know he's back on drugs.'

'Oh, and how do you know that?'

'I see him almost every day in my pub drinking. And as for the drugs, I've known Nathan for a very long time, and I know when he's using. I'd say cocaine and possibly other stuff too – but I'm only guessing at that. I still care about him, we get on really well you see, and our son, well he idolizes him. I just want him to get some help before he starts to go off the rails again, so I thought I'd let you know.'

'Thanks for the information, Grace. As I said, I can't discuss an individual case with you. But I appreciate your call. If you have any concerns in the future, then please call me and I'd be happy to listen.'

Grace thanked Rebecca for her time and ended the call. She put the kettle on to boil as she started to make her second call of the morning. After three rings the automated service kicked in. Once she had answered the necessary questions, Grace listened to the recorded message telling her she was being connected to the appropriate control room. It was a few minutes before she heard a man's voice on the other end of the line.

'Merseyside Police.'

'Hi,' she said nervously. 'I wasn't sure whether to even call about this, but I think someone has been sneaking into the flat above my pub and stealing some whisky.'

'Okay, may I take your name, Miss?'

'Grace Sumner.'

'And the address where you say the break-in took place.'

'The Rose and Crown. Smithfield Street. But I don't think there's been a break-in. There's no sign of forced entry. I think they may have a key.'

'Well, who would have a key?'

233

'Just me and my son. The bar staff don't have a key for the upstairs.'

'So could it be your son?'

'No. I don't think so. He's at university now in Leeds.'

'Ms Sumner. Are you reporting a break-in or not?'

'No. There's been no break-in. It's just I can tell someone's been here, that's all. And they've definitely taken some whisky.'

'Look, you can come into the station and make a statement if you want to report a crime.'

'No,' she said. 'I'm being silly. It's probably nothing. I was just panicking, that's all. I'm sorry I wasted your time.'

'Do you have CCTV, Miss Sumner?'

'Yes, but it's not working at the minute. It hasn't worked for a few months.'

'Well, I would recommend you get it fixed.'

'Yes, I will. Thank you for your time.'

She put the phone down. No doubt the operator thought she was a complete idiot. But she didn't care. There would be a record of that phone call, and that was all she wanted.

CHAPTER SIXTY-THREE

It was almost closing time when Nathan fell into the pub. Grace hadn't seen him for almost three weeks – not since she'd given him the news about Tommy. He could barely stand, let alone walk and he looked rough. He was still wearing his trademark designer suit, but it was creased and grubby and his hair and beard were unkempt.

He stumbled over to the bar and just about managed to sit on one of the stools. He looked up at her, his eyes bloodshot and heavy. He didn't say anything. He just stared at her, or through her, like he was waiting for her to say or do something. She couldn't help but feel a twinge of guilt, because she was responsible for his present misery. Not directly responsible, she knew that. The blame lay with Tommy, and with Nathan of course. But she had used the situation to her own advantage.

She thought to see Nathan in pain would somehow bring her some relief, or some redemption. But it did neither. She could feel nothing but pity for him as he sat there. She only saw the lost little boy he had always tried to silence. She couldn't deny it had been good not having him around those past few weeks. Not having to put up with his unwanted advances. Not having to pretend that her skin didn't crawl every time he touched her. And it had given her some space to think, and to plan her next move. She had to remind herself that this was all for Jake. Nathan might have been a drooling shell of a man right now, but it wouldn't last. It never did. Something, or someone, would snap him out of it soon enough, and he'd be back to himself.

'Are you okay?' she asked him.

He shook his head and she saw tears in his eyes. 'I can't,' he mumbled. 'I don't understand ...' Then he put his head on the bar and started to sob. His shoulders moving up and down to the same beat of the cheesy eighties song that was playing quietly in the background. People were starting to stare.

She placed her hand on his hair. It was damp with sweat. 'Come on. Come upstairs.'

He looked up at her as though he was a starving man and she'd just offered him a three-course meal. He nodded and slid off the stool. She asked the bar staff to close up and helped Nathan up the stairs to the flat. He clung to her like she was a lifeboat in a storm. He smelled of stale whisky and she wondered when was the last time he'd been even mildly sober.

She helped him into bed and he curled up in the foetal position, mumbling to himself. As she started to walk out of the room, he wailed. 'Grace! Stay. Please.' And then he started to sob again.

Sighing, she made her way back over to the bed. She could barely stand the smell of him; he was in desperate need of a shower. But at least she wouldn't have to spend the night fighting off his wandering hands.

She lay beside him and he curled his body into hers, the way Jake used to when he was small. The exact same way he had that night he'd found her, after Nathan – this sobbing man-child, had almost killed her. No. She could never forget what Nathan was capable of. Not for one minute could she afford to overlook how dangerous he was. He was suffering right now, and because of that he was vulnerable, like a wounded animal. But he was a survivor. He had been through worse. He would get through this. And armed with the knowledge that he'd killed his own father, he would no doubt be even more dangerous than before.

Grace got up before Nathan and made a pot of strong coffee, before phoning his friend John Brennan to come and collect him. She took a cup into the bedroom, and if only for the sake of her sense of smell, persuaded Nathan to take a shower.

John arrived within twenty minutes of her phone call.

'Hey, Grace.' He smiled as he took a seat at the kitchen table. 'How are you?'

'Okay thanks, John. And you?'

'All the better for seeing you.' He winked, ever the charmer.

He flinched as Nathan emerged from the bathroom. Such open flirting with Grace, someone Nathan essentially considered his property, could on occasion incur his epic rage. But if Nathan heard him, he didn't acknowledge it. He walked towards them, pale and drawn, but smelling a little fresher at least.

'Hey, mate,' he mumbled to John.

John nodded at him in return before taking a sip of the coffee Grace had just handed him. She and John made some small talk while Nathan continued to stare into space, occasionally nodding to acknowledge something one of them had said. As things became increasingly awkward, John made his excuses and ushered Nathan out of the front door.

Picking up her mug of coffee, Grace leaned against the kitchen counter. Nathan looked terrible, even worse than she'd imagined he would. He'd taken so many drugs when he was younger, she'd thought they barely affected him anymore. But anyone who saw him couldn't miss the fact that he was off his head. Back when they were married, he could have snorted Charlie for breakfast, washed it down with half a bottle of whisky and still looked presentable. In fact, she could only recall one occasion where she'd seen him looking worse than he did currently. At the time, she'd thought he was going to die.

If only he had.

CHAPTER SIXTY-FOUR

Fourteen Years Earlier

As he paced up and down the small office that once belonged to his former boss, Tommy McNulty, Nathan downed his drink in one large gulp. His hand trembled slightly as he set the tumbler down on the desk, the ice clinking in the bottom of the glass. Licking the remainder of the whisky from his lips, he sat in the big leather chair. Tommy's old chair. He was waiting for Kenny Lennox and some of the lads to get back to the club.

They'd gone to see Mickey the Fence; he was the last link in the chain. They had broken bones and rearranged faces in the search for Tommy's killer. If Mickey didn't know anything, or if he was clever enough to keep his trap shut if he did, then the trail went cold and Nathan was in the clear.

He could hear them in the hallway. He touched the gun that was taped under the desk, as if to make sure it was still there should he need it. Kenny came in first followed by John Brennan and Fat Gavin; all three of them seemed in good spirits.

'Nothing, boss,' Kenny said, taking the packet of cigarettes from the desk and lighting himself one. 'Not a dickie bird, no one seems to know a fucking thing.'

Nathan feigned his outrage. 'How can no one know anything? He was Tommy fucking McNulty, for fuck's sake!'

Kenny took a step back, unsure whether his boss's wrath was directed at him for not looking hard enough. Nathan didn't say anything to make him feel better. It wasn't his style.

'Did you get anything at all from Mickey?' Nathan asked finally.

'Not a sausage, about Tommy, boss. But …'

'But what, Kenny?'

'That knob, Kevin Mitchell, has been mouthing off again. Telling anyone who'll listen that you're a cunt, and he's going to sort you out. His words, not mine.'

Kevin Mitchell was, at one time, Tommy and Nathan's main rival. But they had successfully taken over most of his business and now he was a nobody.

'Does he have a fucking death wish or something?' Nathan snapped.

Kenny shrugged. 'Want us to shut him up for good?'

'Well, that would require you fucking finding him first, wouldn't it, Kenny?'

Kenny's face reddened. Nathan had asked him to find that little prick, Kevin, weeks ago and he was still waiting. Nathan was aware he was in danger of getting drawn into yet another argument, and he needed everyone to move from the whole saga now. He tried to appear indifferent.

'Don't worry about it, Kenny. He's a fucking nobody. I'll take care of him myself – when I've got a spare half hour.'

Nathan had every intention of dealing with that little prick as soon as he could find him. But, now that he was free and clear, he felt like celebrating. Everything had worked out better than he could have imagined. There were a few whispers that he was involved, but not from anyone worth listening to. People assumed it was those who had it in for him, like Kevin, or those who didn't want him running things, just trying to cause shit. And of course, as far as anyone else was concerned Nathan had been at home

240

in bed with Grace when it happened anyway. No one was more shocked and outraged than he was that someone could butcher their beloved Tommy like that.

Tommy's loyal soldiers were now Nathan's loyal soldiers and he couldn't help but smile at the irony of that. Nathan was the man who controlled it all. Nothing happened in Liverpool without Nathan's say-so.

Walking out into the club, he ordered a round of drinks for the lads. They made a toast to Tommy, and it was understood that they had put the search for his murderer to bed.

A few hours later and Nathan was suitably off his face. He and the lads had attracted the usual type of women who liked to hang around with their kind. One of them honed in on Nathan, well aware of who he was – the power was a massive attraction for some of them. Her tits were far too big for the dress she was wearing and she wasn't shy of rubbing them against him every chance she got. She was wearing the flimsiest dress he'd ever seen in his life; he wondered why she'd even bothered putting it on. He smiled at her while he pictured how good she would look bent over his desk in the very near future, with that dress around her ears. Taking a small bag of white powder out of her handbag, she sniffed a tiny amount from her finger.

'Want some?' she asked him.

Assuming it was Charlie, he snorted the entire contents of the bag.

She looked at him and laughed. 'You're crazy, I've never seen anyone do that much ket at once before.'

'Ket?' He laughed. 'I thought it was Charlie?' He shrugged his shoulders; he'd done more drugs in one night before than most people did in a lifetime, a bit of ketamine was nothing.

Nathan was looking at the glass of whisky which the barmaid has just brought him. It was only inches from him on the glass-topped table, but he couldn't reach it. He tried to raise his arm, but it wouldn't move. People around him were starting to talk very slowly, or he was hearing slowly. His brain had turned to pea soup. Suddenly he couldn't move any part of his body. He tried to stand up. In his mind, he was doing it, but he wasn't actually moving. People were still talking and laughing and drinking around him, unaware that he was paralyzed. He started to panic then, his breathing becoming erratic. What the fuck was happening? Why couldn't he move?

'John, John.' he slurred at the nearest body to him. 'I can't move, mate. I can't fucking move.'

'What are you on about, Nathan?' John said amiably, plonking himself on the seat next to his boss.

It took a few minutes, hindered by Nathan's slurred speech, to convince John that he was telling the truth.

'What the fuck did you give him?' John snapped at the blonde, grabbing her by the arm.

'Just some ketamine,' she shrugged. 'Don't worry, he'll be fine. Some people just have a bad reaction, that's all. And he took a shitload of it. He'll be okay once it wears off.'

John pushed her roughly out of the way 'Come on, mate. Let's get you home.'

John and Kenny drove Nathan home and carried him upstairs to the flat. He was in and out of consciousness by that point. Nathan could hear snippets of their conversation with Grace.

'He'll be fine ... Ketamine ... Just keep an eye on him ...'

Then they were gone, and Nathan thought that he might be a goner too.

CHAPTER SIXTY-FIVE

'Grace, Grace, are you in there?' A voice Grace didn't recognize said quietly at her bedroom door, followed by a light knock, rousing her from sleep.

'Grace!' A bit louder this time.

Who the hell was it? She glanced at the clock and saw it was just past midnight. Taking the baseball bat Nathan kept under the bed she tentatively opened the door. She saw a round, pale face she didn't recognize looking at her. His eyes were wide, like a frightened rabbit.

'Grace?' he asked. 'It's John. I'm sorry to get you out of bed, but it's Nathan. He's not well. He's in the living room.'

She followed John out of the bedroom, and saw another man she didn't recognize, as well as Nathan, who was lying on the sofa, looking like he'd passed out.

'Are you kidding me?' she said to John. 'He's just drunk, or off his head on something, as usual.'

'He's had some ketamine,' John said. 'But he's had a bad reaction. He's paralyzed, he can't move a muscle. It'll wear off eventually, but you'll need to keep an eye on him.'

John looked at her with a worried expression on his face. She wondered briefly how worried about him he and his colleague would be if they knew what their beloved Nathan had done to Tommy.

John jabbered on. 'I've seen him take shitloads of drugs in my time, Grace, but I've never seen him like this. Ket just mustn't agree with him.'

'Which idiot gave it to him then?' she asked.

John and the second man exchanged a surreptitious glance at each other, leaving Grace to suspect she'd rather not know the answer to that question.

'Well, thank you for getting him home safe,' she told them and quickly showed them out.

Grace lifted Nathan's legs onto the sofa and lay him on his side in case he vomited. His skin was hot to the touch and beads of perspiration trickled down his forehead. She put a cold cloth on his forehead in an attempt to cool him down while she pondered their current situation. So, the great Nathan Conlon was paralyzed. And apparently unconscious. A terrible thought forced itself, unbidden, into her consciousness. She could put a pillow over his face right then and he would never wake up. It would all be over. But of course, she would never do that. Or maybe she could call the police? Tell them that he'd murdered Tommy McNulty. No, of course she couldn't. She'd helped him cover it up. She was an accessory to murder. Nathan had made sure to explain that to her. And then what would happen to Jake? She couldn't go to prison, and certainly not for her rotten husband.

So instead, she sat on the armchair and watched him, like she would do a small child who had a fever. He looked so helpless and pitiful, lying there, drooling. She remembered how he used to make her heart race just to look at him. How she'd feel dizzy with excitement whenever he touched her. She felt nothing but disgust for him right now. Totally off his face on God knew what. Ketamine, they said. What the hell was that? The great, Nathan Conlon – reduced to a dribbling wreck.

Why would anyone choose to live like that? To want so desperately to escape reality.

She wished that she was enough for him, that Jake was enough for him. She hated him. She hated the things he did to her. She hated the way he made her question everything – even her own sanity. But she loved him too. She wished she didn't; that she was not so connected to him as she was; that her happiness and her sadness were not his to control. She supposed that he loved her in his own messed up way, and she knew that he loved Jake. But she also knew that their normal life could never be enough for him – and it broke her heart.

It was almost daylight when Nathan started to stir. Grace watched him from the armchair. He still struggled to move his limbs, but he opened his eyes and looked at her.

'Nathan, you scared the hell out of me. What were you thinking?'

He mumbled something about not knowing what he was taking. She knelt beside him on the floor, taking the damp cloth from his forehead and pushing his hair from his face.

He tried to reach his arm out to touch her but couldn't quite manage it.

'I love you, Grace. I'm sorry,' he said, and in that moment, she believed he actually meant it.

'It's okay. You're going to be okay.'

'No, I'm sorry for everything, Grace, I really am. I'm going to do better I promise.'

She nodded at him. She'd heard it all before.

CHAPTER SIXTY-SIX

Present Day

'Have you seen Dad lately?' Jake asked Grace as he took a packet of crisps from behind the bar.

'Not for a week or so, son. Why?'

'I've not heard from him much, that's all. I phoned him a few times, but he didn't get back to me.'

'You know your dad, he's probably just got a lot on,' she said as she busied herself clearing some glasses.

'You don't think he's pissed off with me or something, do you?'

She gave Jake her full attention now. 'No, of course not. Why would he be?'

'I don't know,' he shrugged. 'He usually phones me all the time.'

'I'm sure he's just busy.' She feigned a smile. She despised how much Jake idolized that man. It made her stomach churn to see how anxious he was for his father's approval. He should have been enjoying himself in university and instead he was worrying about not hearing from Nathan. That hold on his son was what made Grace fear Jake joining Nathan in their line of work one day.

Jake sat at the bar with a glass of Coke and his packet of crisps, and Grace couldn't help but remember all of the Saturday afternoons he'd spent there doing the same thing when he was younger. He'd come back from football and help himself while she finished her afternoon shift. She always took Saturday and Sunday nights off to spend time with him. But now, instead of the smiling chubby-cheeked little boy staring at her from across the bar, she saw the face of an anxious young man.

'Do you think I should go and see him?' he asked.

'No,' she replied a little too quickly. 'I'm sure he'll be in touch when he finds the time.'

'Do you think he's fed up of me hanging around with him.'

'Look, Jake,' she said as she leaned on the bar next to him, 'I know your dad better than anyone, and I can guarantee he's not fed up of you.'

'So why do you think he hasn't phoned me then?'

Grace had to stop herself from groaning. She wanted nothing more than to tell Jake that he should be grateful that his rotten bastard of a father was out of his life – she was. But Jake could never know just how much she hated Nathan. Not if her plan was going to work.

'Look, Jake. This is just how your dad operates,' she said.

'What do you mean?'

'He's like a toddler with a limited attention span and a new best friend every week. One minute, you're the best thing since sliced bread, and the next, well, you're not. Don't take it personally. It's just who he is. There's only so much charm to go around.' She smiled.

Jake looked down at his crisps like she'd just told him Everton had been relegated from the premier league. 'Don't worry,' she soothed. 'It won't last. He'll remember who you are soon enough and then he'll be back.'

He smiled at her then. 'Thanks, Mum,' he said, before downing his drink and hopping off the barstool. 'I'll see you later.'

'Where are you going?'

'I'm going to see Dad,' he grinned. 'Remind him who I am.'

She forced a smile. Bloody hell, this kid was too nice for his own bloody good.

'Bye, son.'

CHAPTER SIXTY-SEVEN

'For fuck's sake, Nathan. What the hell is wrong with you?' John shouted at him.

Nathan's head snapped up. There were very few people who could speak to him like that and live to tell the tale – fortunately for John, he was one of them. Nathan had heard his voice, but he'd no idea what the other man had said.

'I just told you that some little gobshite has been trying to move in on our patch, and you sit there staring at your fucking desk like a moron.'

Nathan glared at him. 'Who the fuck do you think you're talking to?' he growled.

John put his hands on the desk and leaned towards his boss. 'I thought I was talking to Nathan fucking Conlon, but I don't have a fucking clue who you are, mate. You've been off your fucking face for weeks now. I don't know what's gone on. I don't fucking care. But snap out of it. Fucking wake up – before there's nothing left for you to wake up to.'

Before Nathan could respond John stomped out, slamming the door behind him as he did. The sound reverberated around the small office, rattling Nathan's brain in his head. He shook his head to stop the ringing in his ears as there was another knock at the door.

'Fuck off,' he shouted, but the door slowly opened, and Jake popped his head in gingerly.

'You all right, Dad? You look bloody awful.' He half-smiled, but the concern on his face was clear to see, making Nathan wonder at the state he must be in. He looked down at his clothes – un-ironed and stained. He couldn't remember the last time he'd been home or changed his clothes.

He attempted a smile. 'Yeah, just had a rough few days, that's all.'

'Jesus, you don't say,' Jake laughed as he sat down in the chair opposite him. 'I thought you might fancy a pint? There's a good band on at the pub, my mate's the drummer.' He looked at his father, full of youthful exuberance.

He didn't have a care in the fucking world, Nathan thought. He'd been just like him once, hadn't he?

'Yeah, sounds good, son. Give me half an hour and I'll be with you.'

Nathan had always kept spare clothes at the club, and everything else he'd ever need if he planned on not going home for a few days, in the bathroom attached to his office. Stepping into the scalding hot shower, he let the water wash away the weeks' worth of grime. If only it was as easy to wash away the guilt and self-loathing. His head had already started to feel less cloudy, like he could see and hear again. As though he'd been watching an old television and someone had finally fixed the focus. He trimmed his beard with the electric razor and brushed his teeth before putting on a fresh suit and tie. Looking himself over in the mirror, he smiled.

It was good to be back.

Striding into the club, Nathan saw Jake and John sitting at one of the tables. They looked up as he approached. He leaned on the table, his face close to John's. 'You ever speak to me like that again and I'll rip your nuts off.' He grinned. John knew he was only half joking. 'Find out who's trying to have us off. I want a name by tomorrow. Then we'll make the cunt wish he'd never been fucking born.' Nathan stood up and straightened his tie. 'Tonight, I'm off out with my boy.'

John nodded. 'Yes, boss.'

Jake bounded into the pub like an excitable puppy and Grace couldn't help but smile. She groaned inwardly as she saw his father close behind him, although her grin remained fixed on her face.

'Hello, you two,' Grace said as they approached the bar.

'All right, Mum,' Jake asked.

'Grace.' Nathan nodded.

Nathan looked fresher than when she'd last saw him. It seemed he'd had a shower and changed his clothes at least, but his face looked drawn, and his tailored suit didn't quite fit like it once did.

'Two pints please, Mum.'

'Pints? No whisky, Nathan?'

Nathan shook his head. 'Not tonight. Stella will do fine.'

While Jake chatted to his friends, Nathan sat alone at the bar, staring into his pint of lager as though it held the key to life's mysteries. Grace took him a fresh drink. She had never known the phrase, a shadow of his former self, to fit someone so aptly as it did him right now. But he had brought all of his misery on himself; she couldn't let herself forget that.

'How have you been, Nathan? I've not seen you much.'

'I know, sorry,' he said, mistaking her observation as a complaint. 'It's just been hard to get my head around stuff.'

She nodded sympathetically. 'I can imagine.'

He looked up from his glass. His eyes shining; he was clearly drunk. 'I've missed you, Grace.'

She smiled in response. What was she supposed to say to that?

Well I haven't missed you at all, Nathan. In fact, not having you around here has been heaven. I only wish you'd remained a dribbling wreck a little while longer. Of course, she didn't say that though. *Just keep him sweet, Grace – for now.*

'But we can catch up later, eh?' he grinned.

She forced her face to remain frozen in a smile. She knew exactly what he meant by catching up. He suddenly sat up straighter, his shoulders no longer hunched over his drink. The smile reaching his eyes. She could see glimmers of the Nathan she knew all too well, breaking through the cracks of his self-pity and doubt. Well, it had been nice to have him off her back for a few weeks at least. It had given her the time and space she needed. But now he was back. She'd give it a week before he was behaving like his usual arrogant, lecherous self again.

Everything was almost in place. It was just a matter of time before she could put the final part of her plan into action.

But she had a use for Nathan first.

CHAPTER SIXTY-EIGHT

'Hello, Grace.' Kevin Mitchell smiled as she walked into the tiny room in the back of a bookmakers that he called an office.

'Kevin.' She nodded at him, not in the mood to exchange pleasantries. He was a smarmy bastard. Greasy hair and podgy fingers. Always rubbing his hands together as though he was expecting something. 'What can I do for you?' she asked as she took a seat, placing her new Hermes handbag down beside her.

Kevin had phoned her earlier and asked to meet with her. He'd suggested coming to the Rose and Crown to see her, but she didn't like to conduct business with his sort in the pub. He was one of those people who would see it as an invitation to 'drop by' whenever he fancied.

'Business is going well,' he said, not answering her question.

'Yep.' She nodded, not even bothering to try and hide her irritation.

'Your attack dog not with you today, then?' he asked.

'Clearly not.'

'Haven't seen him or his old man about much.' He grinned.

'Well you wouldn't. They're out of town,' she snapped. 'You still haven't answered my question.'

'Oh yeah.' He smirked. 'It's not me, you understand. It's my lads.'

Grace smirked. Kevin was blaming his lads for wanting more money because he knew she still had evidence of his mistress and their aborted child. He was always careful not to push her too far.

'They've been getting a lot of hassle from Nathan and his firm,' he went on.

'So? It's what they're paid for.'

'I know that,' Kevin replied, sucking air in through his teeth. 'But they're getting a bit edgy about it all. They'd like something for their trouble.'

'You mean more than what I'm already paying them?' Grace asked incredulously.

'Let's call it danger money.' Kevin smirked as he sat back in his chair.

Grace took a deep breath. Pricks like Kevin could really push her buttons. But losing her cool with him wasn't going to help matters. Besides, that wasn't how she operated.

'Kevin.' She smiled. 'If your lads are whingeing about not being paid enough money, then I suggest you either bring them in line, or find yourself some new employees. I pay you fucking well for what you do. Just because Michael and Patrick aren't around, don't think for one second that you can dictate terms to me. I don't need their backup. I'm perfectly capable of handling myself,' she snapped as she stood up.

Kevin stared at her, mouth open, but he didn't respond.

'Don't contact me again unless you actually have something worthwhile to discuss.' Picking up her handbag, Grace walked out of his stuffy little office. She rubbed her temples as she walked to her car. As if she needed anymore problems to deal with.

Little did Kevin know that some of his *loyal* employees were actually working for Grace. She knew most of his lads were more than happy with her arrangement with their boss. It was Kevin who was getting greedy for more. Obviously, he thought he'd chance his arm while Michael and Patrick were out of the way. Cheeky bastard. Why did men assume that women needed a man to back them up? Grace's way of dealing with people might be different, a little more subtle that smashing someone's skull open with a hammer, but in her experience, it was much more effective.

Grace was also aware that Kevin was keen to branch out into other areas – firearms to be precise. It was something she'd never had an interest in herself. They were too risky. There was no telling where a gun might end up once you'd passed it onto someone.

But obviously, Kevin had been given a taste of working with the big players for a few months and stupidly thought that gave him the credentials and the experience to set up an operation on his own. Grace would put a stop to that – well, Nathan would. Not that he'd have any idea he was doing it for her. She smiled to herself. This was all going to work out perfectly.

CHAPTER SIXTY-NINE

'Where's your mother today?' Nathan asked Jake, trying to appear indifferent.

'Dunno, probably at the pub, why?'

'She's not. I went there before I came here.'

'She's probably out with a mate, then.' Jake raised an eyebrow at him. 'Why are you so interested in where mum is?'

'I was looking for you, dickhead. And I'm not that interested. I was just wondering, that's all. Anyway, out with a mate? Your mother doesn't have any mates, does she?'

Jake laughed at him. ''Course she does. What, do you think she just sits in this house all the time when she's not in work?'

Nathan frowned. That's exactly what he thought she did. Now that she no longer had the Carters at her disposal, her burgeoning criminal empire seemed to have been taken over by Kevin Mitchell, of all people. So, what was she doing with her time? Maybe she was with that Sandra bird? Nathan had forgotten all about her in the midst of all the recent drama.

Jake laughed again and shook his head as he put on his jacket. 'Come on then, where are we going?'

Nathan was still pondering Grace's whereabouts as they drove to the scrapyard. Where was she and who the fuck was she with?

It bugged him more than he had expected it to. He'd phone her, but Jake was with him and he would definitely get suspicious then. He was becoming increasingly annoyed. He'd gone to find her at the pub earlier that afternoon because he was hoping for a quick fuck. She usually did the books on a Saturday afternoon in the office upstairs. No one would have even known he was up there.

When she wasn't there, he went to the house to find her, only to find Jake there instead.

Nathan had to pretend he was looking for him. Although it turned out in his favour anyway, as Jake could help him out with some business he had on that afternoon. And he could do with having someone with him he could trust. Especially as John appeared to have gone AWOL that afternoon too.

Nudge Richards was waiting for Nathan in his office. Nudge had a very unfortunate 'accident' with a machete when he was young. He was left with a scarred face and lasting nerve damage in his right eye – giving him the appearance of a permanent wink. It started as a joke whenever anyone saw him – 'nudge, nudge, wink, wink'. And was soon shortened to nudge – hence the name. In addition to his facial disfiguration, he was over six feet tall, and was a huge, hairy fucker. He always reminded Nathan of a gorilla. Quite frankly, he scared the shit out of most people he met. Not Nathan though. He had the measure of him.

Recently, Nudge had developed a significant Charlie and gambling problem. He was also partial to a beautiful woman. He'd built up quite a debt in Nathan's club, and had also developed something of a crush on one of their dancers, Mandy. It turned out he was surprisingly loose lipped when she was sucking him off. It seemed Nathan's old friend, Kevin Mitchell, was looking to make a bigger name for himself. He was looking to get his hands on some decent guns, and he had come to Nudge to supply them.

Guns were Nathan's thing. Or at least they were once one of

his things. They made him a lot of money. Their acquisition and disposal, used to be a particular area of expertise of his. And he didn't like the idea of some other fucker, least of all Mitchell, having that honour. It should have been Nathan people came to, and in future they would.

Nudge offered to make them both a brew. Nathan noticed the cups were chipped around the edges, and they looked like they hadn't been washed since 1974, so he politely declined.

'So, you want me to make sure the guns I get him are duds, but look like the real deal?' he asked Nathan incredulously.

'That's exactly what I want, Nudge.'

'But what about my reputation? And what if that fucker comes after me for screwing him over?'

'Mitchell is too much of an arrogant prick to tell anyone that you were the one who supplied them. He wants people to think he can import them himself, without a middle man. And by the time whoever he passes them onto realizes they are blag, then the damage will have been done. I've heard who he's trying to get these guns for. And believe me, once they realize he's given them dodgy merchandise, he won't be going after anyone.'

Nudge looked uncomfortable, but both of them knew that Nathan had him by the balls. Nudge might fear Mitchell, but he was more afraid of the psychopath who was currently standing in front of him. Nevertheless, Nathan reminded him of the benefits of his plan.

'Look, Nudge. I know you're feeling a bit twitchy, but it's a win-win for both of us. You're going to make a shitload of money selling him restored pieces of shit that are as reliable as a whore with a coke habit, and I'm going to be back to being the go-to man for supplying firearms. And if Mitchell gets a good kicking as well, then that's the cherry on top, isn't it?'

Nudge lit a cigarette and took a large gulp of his tea.

'All right then. But no one can know it was me who supplied him with them. Okay?'

'Of course not.' Nathan gave him his most convincing smile.

'Is Mandy on tonight?' Nudge asked, his eyes full of lust now.

'Yeah, she's on. She'll be waiting for you, mate.'

Nathan got up to leave then and Jake followed his lead. 'He doesn't seem Mandy's type,' Jake said as they got into the car.

'He's not.' Nathan sighed. 'She fucking hates him. She'll have a fit when I tell her she's got to entertain him all night. He's not even a good tipper.'

'What if she says no?' he asked, reminding his father how young and naive he was.

'She'll do as she's fucking told, son.'

They drove back to the club, and Nathan gave Mandy her instructions for the evening. She had a bit of a strop, as he expected she would, but she knew the score.

'I'd much rather be entertaining you all night, boss,' she whispered in his ear. Her hand ran down his chest and dangerously close to his groin. He was still frustrated at not finding Grace earlier and still having no idea where she'd been. He rubbed his temples which were starting to throb.

'Not tonight,' he barked at her and signalled to Jake that they were leaving.

'Let's go somewhere no one will bother me,' Nathan said as he drove them both to the Rose and Crown.

As soon as Nathan opened the doors he saw her behind the bar, smiling and laughing, like she hadn't a care in the fucking world, while he'd been losing his mind, wondering where she'd been all day. Jake wandered off to catch up with some of his mates, and Nathan went straight to the bar. She had him a whisky ready before he even sat down.

'Where the fuck have you been all day, Grace?' he barked.

The colour drained from her face. 'What do you mean?'

'Didn't you hear me or something? Where the fuck have you been? It's a simple question.'

'I was out with a friend,' she said.

'What friend? And where did you go? I came here looking for you, and then I went to your house, but you weren't there.'

'I went into town for a coffee and a look around the shops. I met up with Joanne, she used to work here. We keep in touch and meet up every now and then. That's all. I wasn't aware I had to check with you if I went anywhere, Nathan.'

He could see she was regaining her composure. She stared at him; her eyes narrowing; jaw set defiantly. She was a lot feistier than she used to be. Sometimes he liked that, enjoyed it when she fought back. He glared at her, studying her face for clues. He decided she was telling the truth.

'In future, just let me know if you're not going to be around,' he snapped.

'Yes, Sir,' she replied sarcastically and gave a mock salute. He would slap her for that right there if they weren't in the middle of a crowded pub with so many witnesses; including their son who, Nathan noticed, was watching the whole exchange.

Jake and his mates left once the band had finished, off to find somewhere more exciting. Nathan remained though, and sat at the bar, enjoying the free whisky and the view. He watched Grace all night, the way she moved effortlessly behind the bar, like she was born to be there. It was obvious it was her place. He admired the curve of her arse in the tight pencil skirt she wore. She'd developed a habit of pulling her long hair over to one side, leaving the right side of her neck exposed. It made him hard just thinking about kissing her there, having his face buried in her neck, and what he was usually doing at the time.

He thought of all the beautiful women he knew. Kayleigh was sitting at home waiting for him. She was undeniably gorgeous, but she'd never held the same pull for him that Grace did. None of them had. He'd tried to convince himself that he was over her, that he could make it work with Kayleigh, but Grace was like a drug to him. And the more she seemed not to want him, the more he needed to have her.

When she hadn't been around earlier, he'd been surprised by how much it affected him. Maybe he should stop being such a prick and tell her that he was bluffing about Jake? Tell her that he would never do that to his own son. Ask her to give them another chance. Tell her that he would never hurt her again, if she would just take him back. He almost laughed out loud. What the fuck was wrong with him? It must have been the old place messing with his head. Even he knew that was a promise he couldn't keep.

When closing time came, he was desperate to touch her, to run his hands over her bare skin, to taste her.

'I'll help Grace close up,' he told the three bar staff who were left. 'You can get off home.'

They all looked at her, seeking her approval. She was the boss after all, not him. Not anymore.

'Yes, go on,' she smiled at them.

Nathan practically pushed them out of the door.

CHAPTER SEVENTY

Nathan closed the heavy front doors as he let out the last of Grace's staff, fastening the huge steel bolt behind them. The noise echoed around the empty pub. She imagined that was what a prison cell door sounded like when it was closed and she winced at the irony.

She wondered what sort of games he would be in the mood for playing, although she noticed that his earlier frustration at not being able to find her seemed to have dissipated and he appeared in a much more affable mood than usual. She was relieved that he didn't pursue the topic of where she'd been today any further, seemingly accepting her story that she'd gone to meet an old friend. If he knew she'd spent the afternoon in a hotel room with the man he believed to be his best mate, then she doubted she would see the light of another day. Despite her efforts to distance herself from Ben, he'd convinced her to let him help her with her plan. If she was honest, it was good to have someone on her side.

She started to busy herself clearing the last of the tables when she felt him behind her. His arms around her waist, he spun her around to face him.

'Do you remember the first time I ever kissed you? It was in this pub, Grace. Almost on this very spot, in fact.'

'Of course I remember.'

'After you'd been eyeing me up all night like a piece of meat,' he laughed.

'No I was not,' she started to say in her defence, until she realized he was teasing her.

'Okay. When I think about it, maybe it was the other way around.' He winked and she was struck unexpectedly, by how handsome and charming he could still be when he chose to. Although he didn't fool her. Not even for a second.

'You looked at me like I was something special, Grace. Like I was something. Those big Bambi eyes, gazing adoringly at me.' He was still smiling.

'Love yourself much?' she retorted, and he laughed again.

He took her face in his hands then. Not roughly, like he usually did, but as though she was fragile. Precious. 'Would you go back and change it if you could, Grace?' he asked, his tone serious now.

She had to think about her answer. Not only because she had to think about everything she said to him, but because he'd caught her off guard, and she really didn't know. How did she explain that she would change everything and nothing? Because despite it all, she was a big believer in fate and everything that had ever happened to her, had made her the woman she was. She had always believed that in the end, everyone ended up exactly where they were supposed to be.

'No,' she told him honestly. 'Would you?'

If he was surprised by her answer he didn't show it. 'I'd change a lot of things. But mostly, I'd make sure that you never stopped looking at me like that.'

Jesus Christ, what had got into him? He rarely expressed any regret or remorse. He perceived them as weaknesses – and Nathan was never weak.

'Can we pretend then, just for tonight, that we are those people we were when we first met?' he asked her. 'We'll stay upstairs. In our flat. In our bed, and pretend that we're young again?'

If only it were that simple, Nathan, she thought. Before she could answer him, he was kissing her. Softly at first, and then urgently. As though they were long-lost lovers, who'd finally been reunited after years apart. She could taste the whisky he'd been drinking, smell his expensive aftershave, and feel the scratch of his beard on her skin. He pulled her skirt up to her waist and pushed her back onto the table.

'I love this skirt on you, Grace,' he groaned.

If only to make the whole situation more bearable, she tried to pretend. She tried to remember how it had felt to love him with everything she had, when he was the Nathan she had met a lifetime ago. He smelled good. He always did. His lips were still as soft as she remembered. He'd once made her the happiest woman alive and she couldn't bear to be without him.

He made it easy to remember those people they were when he was in one of his good moods. Those two young lovers, who thought all they needed was each other. How blind and naive they were. But she would never forget. She couldn't. Her skin crawled where it once burned. Her eyes closed in anguish now rather than pleasure. She let him do what he needed to. She needed him to think that she still loved him; still wanted him.

Grace had come to terms with the fact that she would never escape Nathan Conlon. That he would always be a part of her life, a part of her. Ever since she met him he'd had an unnatural hold over her. Her happiness, her misery, had been his to determine. There was a certain sense of relief that came with accepting your fate, with realizing your role in life. So, she didn't fight it anymore. She didn't fight him anymore. She let him do what he needed to do. She told him what he wanted to hear. Because it was easier to be with him than against him. Then he would never see it coming.

CHAPTER SEVENTY-ONE

It was dark when Grace pulled into Nudge Richard's scrapyard. She shuddered as she stepped out of her car. These places gave her the creeps even in daylight hours.

The Portakabin door opened and Nudge's distinctive silhouette appeared in the doorway, the light from inside shining behind him.

'Hello, Grace, love,' he called. 'Come on up, I've just put the kettle on.'

Climbing the rickety wooden steps, Grace almost slipped on one of the loose planks of wood. She silently cursed the expensive heels she was wearing, wishing she'd opted for more appropriate footwear.

'Cup of tea, girl?' Nudge asked as she walked into his office.

'Yeah, I'd love one,' she lied. His cups were always filthy but Nudge considered himself a good host and she knew it would offend him if she said no. She was fond of Nudge, and besides he'd just done her a huge favour.

'So, Nathan came to see you then, Nudge?' she asked as he frantically searched for some teabags in his numerous cupboards.

He turned his attention to her. 'Yep. Brought your lad with him too. Seems like a good kid.'

Grace bristled. So, that's where Jake had been all the previous afternoon. She'd thought he was out with Siobhan. She could kill Nathan. How dare he involve Jake in his business with Nudge. It seemed he was determined to put their son directly in harm's way. God, he made her blood boil.

'Looks just like his dad, doesn't he?' Nudge went on.

'Yes,' Grace groaned. 'Thankfully it's only Nathan's looks he's inherited.'

'Hmm.' Nudge nodded. 'He's still a cocky little fucker, isn't he?'

'Yep. So, tell me, what happened?'

Nudge sat down, forgetting about the cup of tea. 'It was just like you said. I told that Mandy bird about Mitchell wanting me to source him some shooters and she went straight to her boss and blabbed. He's asked me to give Mitchell duds.'

'Good. I thought he would.'

'And obviously when Mitchell's buyers find out that he's supplied them with dodgy merchandise, he'll wish he'd never even thought about getting involved in the firearms business.'

Grace contemplated what Nudge had told her. Kevin Mitchell was becoming a massive pain in her arse. Every time she met with him, he seemed to be pushing for more money or a bigger cut of her business. Since the Carters had gone into hiding, he'd become even more obnoxious. Obviously, he thought that Grace was a pushover without her hired muscle around. How wrong he was.

When she'd heard he was making noises about creating a name for himself in the firearms business, she'd thought of the perfect plan.

Starting a feud between Kevin and Nathan would distract them both for a while, and hopefully take one of them out of the game on a permanent basis. Nudge was the perfect co-conspirator. He had ready access to guns and he was an old friend of Grace's. He'd come to her for some help a few years earlier when he was being blackmailed by an associate of his. He'd heard Grace had

266

a way of digging up damaging information on people, and thanks to Sandra's trawling of the NHS computer system, Grace was able to find out some much more interesting and salacious information on Nudge's blackmailer.

The plan was for Nudge to approach Kevin, but she'd almost cried with laughter when Kevin had phoned her a few days earlier and asked her if she knew anyone in the firearms game. He made it so bloody easy, it almost took the sport out of it.

Grace stood up to leave. 'Thanks for the update, Nudge.'

'No problem, Grace. You didn't get your brew. Sorry.'

'That's fine. I need to get home. Jake's making me a curry. Keep me updated, won't you?'

'Of course I will. Bye, Grace,' he said as he bent to kiss her on the cheek.

'Bye, Nudge,' she said as she closed the door of his Portakabin.

Grace smiled to herself as she drove home. Soon enough, either Kevin or Nathan would be out of her hair for good. She hoped it would be Nathan, it would certainly save her a job, but she wasn't sure Kevin was quite up to the task of taking out one of the biggest players in Liverpool. He was too slow, and always seemed to be a few steps behind everyone else. It made him easy to manipulate and was one of the reasons Grace had chosen him to front some of her operations for a while. In all likelihood, it would be Nathan who would come out on top in any dispute between the two. But once that was over she could get on with the final stage of her plan.

CHAPTER SEVENTY-TWO

Grace noticed Kayleigh had been at the bar on her own for the past half an hour. Nathan was sitting at a table with some business associates of his and was clearly deep in conversation. Kayleigh was knocking the vodkas back like they were about to announce a prohibition, and she signalled to Grace for a refill. Grace took her a fresh drink over and could see she was more than a little drunk.

'How did you do it, Grace?' she slurred.

'Do what?'

'Get that fucker to marry you,' she spat. 'He barely even notices me anymore.' She was almost crying. 'Except when he fancies a quick shag anyway, and he hasn't even done that for ages.'

Grace couldn't help but feel for her. She was desperate for the attention of a man who didn't seem to pay her much at all; a man who didn't deserve her. She wanted to tell Kayleigh that she should be grateful for small mercies and that she should run for the hills while she still could. But of course, she didn't. It would only cause trouble for both of them. And she doubted Kayleigh would listen to her anyway. She had that look Grace knew all too well; she was completely besotted with him, blind to his many flaws and content with the snatched moments when he made her feel like the only woman in the world.

'How am I supposed to live like this? I thought the baby would make him change, force him to spend more time with me. To love me again, but it didn't.'

'The baby?' Grace exclaimed, about to take her drink away.

'Don't worry, he made me get rid of it.' Kayleigh was sobbing then. 'He was furious with me, said I'd trapped him and I had to choose – it was either him or the baby. I just wanted to make him love me again. So, I got rid of it,' she wailed.

Suddenly, Nathan's recent coldness towards his girlfriend and his complete lack of attention to her all made sense now. He didn't like to be pushed into corners, to be manipulated or put in situations which were not of his own making. So, poor Kayleigh was being punished for trying to do just that. God, he was such a heartless bastard. How many lives did he need to destroy before he'd think about the consequences of his disgusting behaviour? How many women had he forced into having an abortion? How many women had he terrified into keeping his dirty little secrets?

Grace blinked back the tears as she remembered the two babies she'd lost. She thought about them often. They would be fourteen and twelve years old by now. Would they have been boys or girls? Would they have looked like her? Three children milling about the place instead of just one. She'd always wanted a big family, but Nathan had taken that from her, just as he'd taken everything. Then there was poor Eddie, who'd had to grow up never knowing his father. Nathan had forced his mother, Sandra, to lie to her son for all those years. How could Nathan know he had another son out there and not feel anything for him?

It was Kayleigh's loud sobbing that brought Grace back to the matter at hand. 'Why don't you come through the back with me, love, and we can have a drink there?' she said to her soothingly, aware that the younger woman was starting to draw attention to herself and Nathan would not like that one bit.

'Okay,' Kayleigh sniffled, and she obediently followed Grace into the back room.

Grace made her a coffee instead of vodka and gave her some tissues.

'Was Jake planned?' Kayleigh asked as she wiped her eyes with the tissue.

'No, not exactly. But he was very much wanted.'

'By Nathan too?'

Grace knew it would hurt her, but she couldn't lie and say that Nathan wasn't over the moon when he found out about Jake. That would be so unfair to both of them.

'Yes, by Nathan too.'

'Why didn't he want our baby too then, Grace? I did do it on purpose, you know,' she whispered. 'I saw how much he loves Jake, and how much he idolizes you, and I wanted that too.'

Grace almost laughed then. 'Trust me, Kayleigh. Nathan does not idolize me. In fact, that couldn't be further from the truth.' She wondered where the girl got such a notion.

Kayleigh looked at her, eyes and her mouth wide in shock. 'Are you kidding?' she sniffed. 'You're the only one he's ever really loved, Grace. You are the yardstick by which we are all measured.'

Grace smiled in response. What the hell was she supposed to say to that?

'Why didn't he want our baby?' she howled again, and Grace could see she had a flair for the dramatic, while realizing that she hadn't answered Kayleigh's original question.

'Maybe it was just too soon, Kayleigh.' she said softly. She really wanted to scream at her though, or even slap some sense into her. What the hell was she thinking?

'What's the fucking matter with her now?' Nathan bellowed as he walked through the door to the back room.

Kayleigh looked at him wide-eyed with fear, making Grace want to wrap her in her arms and protect her from the monster, but she didn't of course.

'She's just had a couple of drinks too many, that's all, and was feeling a bit ill, weren't you, love?' Grace said to Kayleigh as she helped her up from the stool.

Kayleigh nodded frantically as though she'd been worried Grace was about to tell him the truth. Grace put her hand on Nathan's arm. 'She really needs to get home and get to bed,' she told him. 'Lots of TLC is what you need, eh, Kayleigh?'

'All right, let's go,' he said gruffly and led her out of the door.

As she was leaving, Kayleigh mouthed a thank you to Grace, who felt like a fraud. It was gratitude she didn't deserve. She should have rescued that poor girl from him; but who was she kidding? She hadn't even been able to rescue herself.

But now all that was about to change …

CHAPTER SEVENTY-THREE

Leon James was a man with a mission. According to him, he was about to pull off the biggest heist since the great train robbery. He sat talking to Nathan in the darkest corner of the Rose and Crown. It was a quiet night and the pub was nearly empty. Anyone thinking of sitting near them would give them a wide berth anyway, once they saw Leon and his two sons. The only time the three of them were seen together was when there was trouble brewing. They cut imposing figures. Always dressed entirely in black. Their long dreadlocks hung loose around their shoulders and they rarely smiled. Leon junior and Jerome rarely spoke, although Leon certainly talked enough for the three of them.

Nathan had brought Ben and John with him. They were the two men he trusted more than anyone else to have his back should anything kick off. Not that he expected it to. Leon knew that Nathan didn't fuck about either, and together with Ben and John, they were more than a match for Leon and his sons.

Leon was an expert in his field, and he was not a man to be messed with. Unfortunately for Kevin Mitchell, but opportunely for Nathan, Leon was very upset with him. Mitchell had supplied him with some guns for his upcoming job. Nathan pretended to be surprised by this revelation. His little talk with Nudge Richards had obviously paid off. As Leon told it, Mitchell swore the guns were the real deal.

'One hundred per cent clean and reliable, that's what the fucker told me.' The big man's jowls wobbled as he shook his head in anger and disbelief. 'Good job I fucking tested them, Nathan. The triggers jammed on two of them, and one misfired. Nearly shot my fucking knob off.' He winced.

Professionals like Leon did not use restored replicas or converted antiques. They couldn't afford to.

'Well, I can guarantee that what I get you will be the dogs bollocks, Leon. Scouts' honour.' Nathan smiled, taking a sip of his drink. 'But obviously, it'll cost you. Quality doesn't come cheap.'

'Of course.' Leon smiled. 'I'm sure we can come to an arrangement that suits us both.'

'And what about Mitchell?' Nathan asked.

'He will rue the day he ever fucked me over,' Leon said calmly.

Nathan winked. 'Well, make sure you tell him I said hello.'

They were finishing off their drinks and smoking some of the excellent weed Leon junior had brought with him when Nathan noticed Kayleigh out of the corner of his eye. She was talking to Grace and gesticulating wildly. He couldn't hear what she was saying but he would bet it was nothing pleasant. All he needed was her and Grace becoming mates; that would be a truly unholy alliance. She followed Grace through to the back and he decided he'd better get her out of there.

'Gentlemen,' he said, standing up. 'I think the girlfriend has had a bit too much to drink. I'd better be going. Leon, I'll be in touch once I have what you need.' He shook the big man's hand and then said his goodbyes to Ben and John.

He could hear Kayleigh snivelling as he walked through to the back of the pub. Maybe he should give her something to fucking whinge about, he thought. One thing about Grace, she was never a whiner. Sure, she'd have a cry now and again, but it was usually for good reason. She certainly knew how to take a punch, his Grace. Better than most men he knew.

Grace was comforting her; she gave Nathan some bollocks about Kayleigh feeling sick, but he would bet she'd been whining about how tough her life is. Yes, with her designer clothes and her constant trips to the hairdressers or the nail salon. Fucking awful time she had, did Kayleigh. He got her out of there as quickly as possible and took her home.

'Just what the fuck do you think you were doing tonight, Kayleigh?' he snarled at her once they were inside the flat. 'Look at the fucking state of you. Snot running down your face. You can barely even stand up!'

She sobbed her reply. 'You left me sitting there on my own.'

'What?' he shouted now. 'I was working; keeping you in fucking clothes and hair extensions. You stupid bitch. So what? You had to sit on your own for ten minutes. You're a big girl, aren't you?'

She was still sobbing, tears and mascara running down her face. He could barely even look at her. He pushed her into the bedroom.

'You have one fucking job, Kayleigh. To make me look good. If you can't do that, what fucking use are you to me? Sort yourself out,' he barked at her before slamming the bedroom door and heading back out.

He was raging as he closed the front door. He was sure she'd told Grace all about her little scam to trap him. As if her getting pregnant would make him marry her or something. He could guarantee she'd made him out to be the bad guy as well, forcing her to get rid of it. He bet she neglected to tell Grace that she purposely stopped taking the pill to get pregnant, without even consulting him. What was it with these women and their inability to use fucking birth control?

He went straight back to the Rose and Crown. It was almost

closing time and the last few regulars were finishing off their drinks. He sat at the bar, and Grace poured him a large whisky.

'Is Kayleigh okay?' she asked, her voice full of concern.

'She's fine,' he snapped. 'Why the fuck do you care?'

'Because she's a nice girl, Nathan, and she loves you. Not that you deserve it.'

He laughed. They both knew she would pay for that slur. 'What did she tell you?' he asked her, his tone serious again.

'Nothing that I don't already know.'

He didn't respond. He made himself scarce and took his drink upstairs to the flat. It was only a short while later when Grace followed him up there.

'Has everyone gone?' he asked her.

She looked at him. Her jaw set defiantly. 'Yes, everyone's gone home.'

'Good.' He smiled and she knew she wouldn't be going home any time soon.

CHAPTER SEVENTY-FOUR

Nathan's body was drenched with sweat. The sheets stuck to his skin. He was breathless and his whole body shook. He heard screaming, and he wasn't sure if it was real or from his dream.

'Nathan, are you okay?' Grace asked him.

'No.' His voice was small and quiet in the darkness of the room. 'I had a nightmare. I haven't had one for ages.'

Lying beside her, he felt calmer just being near her. He placed his head on her chest and she stroked his hair, curling the strands around her forefinger. Her heartbeat thumped against his ear and its constant rhythm soothed him.

The ghosts began to fade into the shadows. He fell asleep eventually, with her arms wrapped around him.

Grace knew he wasn't talking about some regular bad dream, but one where he relived the horrors of his childhood. She remembered how they used to affect him. How he'd wake screaming and drenched in sweat.

It was then that she realized that he needed her to allow him to be there, that scared little boy inside needed to know that someone wanted him; to know that someone loved him.

And as she looked at him, she could still see that frightened little boy.

He lay his head on her stomach and she absent-mindedly stroked his hair, which was still damp with sweat. Looking down at his head, she could see his large frame, still trembling slightly, and wondered at the man who had brought her so much joy and so much heartache. The man who claimed to love her, yet most of the time, made her existence a living hell.

It could almost have been twenty years earlier – the two of them lying together like that. She remembered how often he would wake screaming, twisted in the covers, his face contorted in agony as his dream slipped away from him. Sometimes he'd make love to her, trying to erase the awful memories. Most times, he'd just lie with her, as he was now; seeking comfort; needing to feel loved. She remembered how much she'd wanted to take his pain away. How once she would have done anything to make him feel loved.

She wondered what drew them together; what continued to draw them together? She could have run away while he was inside, couldn't she? She could have taken Jake and emigrated. She certainly had the means to. But instead, she had stayed exactly where she was. Right where he could find her. Did some twisted part of her still want him too? God, surely not! Perhaps, they were some kind of perverse soulmates, destined to have their lives entwined for eternity. Maybe they were always destined to be in each other's lives. Their childhoods ran almost parallel, one different decision at any moment could have resulted in their paths crossing. As though fate was just biding its time, confident that one day they would meet – knowing that once they did, their worlds would never be the same.

For a very long time, she thought that one day Nathan would change; that she could change him; that she could save him. By the time she met him, the damage had already been done. She could see that he was entirely beyond redemption – wasn't he?

But if that was true, then surely she was too.

CHAPTER SEVENTY-FIVE

The sound of a dog barking nearby woke Nathan and for a moment he forgot where he was. He was tangled up in someone's arms and legs so he knew he wasn't alone. As he opened his eyes, he remembered he was with Grace. She was still sleeping soundly so he just looked at her. He wanted to wake her, to kiss her face and for her to kiss him back the way she used to. He wanted to kiss every inch of her body. He was hard just thinking about it. He knew if he tried then she'd let him, but probably out of fear, or even worse out of pity, and not because she wanted to.

She opened her eyes then and looked at him. 'Nathan?' she said, as though she'd forgotten he was there too.

He untangled himself until he was leaning over her, propped up on one elbow.

'Are you okay?' she asked him.

'Yes,' he answered, wanting to forget about the reason he was there. 'Thanks.'

She nodded and he knew he need not say anymore. It took all of his resolve to get out of that bed and leave her lying there, but she deserved that. He put on his shoes and kissed the top of her head before he left.

*   *   *

Nathan went home to shower and change before heading to The Blue Rooms. When he got there, John was waiting for him; pacing up and down Nathan's office with a face like a Rottweiler sucking a nettle. Nathan knew that his day was about to get interesting.

'What's the matter with your face?' Nathan asked.

'I was sure I had a lead on the Carter twins, but it was a dead end. I swear they've disappeared off the face of the fucking earth.'

Nathan shook his head. 'Did you speak to Joey the Grass, like I told you to.'

John nodded. ''Course I did, and he folded like a wet *Echo*. But he knows fuck all, mate.'

Nathan took a cigarette from his pocket and lit up. 'Well maybe they've fucked off somewhere never to return? Their arl fella's gone too. So, that's all fine by me.'

John stared at him. 'I'm surprised you're letting this go so easily. A few months ago, you were ready to wear their skins as a coat. Are you getting soft in your old age?' he laughed.

'Nah. I just have more important things to think about.' He shrugged.

'Well I'm not complaining, boss. I could do without the aggro myself to be honest.'

Nathan sat on his leather chair and pulled a bottle of Scotch from his desk drawer. 'Fancy one?' he asked.

'It's a bit early isn't it? Even for you?'

'I'm celebrating.' Nathan smiled.

'Go on then,' John conceded. 'What are we celebrating?'

Nathan poured them both a generous measure of Scotch. 'I've finally figured out what I want in life.'

'You didn't know before then?' John laughed.

Nathan shook his head. 'Nope. Thought I did. But I was wrong. Wrong about everything.'

'Fucking hell, mate,' John laughed. 'Have you been on the weed as well this morning?'

279

Taking a swig of his whisky, he smiled. 'Just because I've had an epiphany, John, doesn't mean you can take the piss.'

'I wouldn't dare. But I am worried you're getting a bit soft in your old age, mate.'

'I'm not fucking old. And yes, I might be getting a bit soft, but I still need a bit of action now and then. Speaking of action, you should see this new dancer who's started at the club. She can do things with her body that would make your eyes water.'

'You never change, do you?' John laughed.

'Nope.' Nathan smirked as he downed the rest of his whisky.

But it was all bravado. He had no interest at all in the new dancer at the club. There was only one woman who occupied his thoughts – and that was Grace.

CHAPTER SEVENTY-SIX

Eddie Redman lit himself a cigarette as he stood in the darkness of the alleyway facing the Rose and Crown pub. At nineteen, he appeared older than his years. His blonde hair was cropped close to his head and his blue eyes had no youthful spark about them. His skin was pale from lack of sunlight. Despite his six-foot stature, he was good at fading into the background, hiding in the shadows, which was exactly how he'd managed to follow Nathan Conlon around for the past eight weeks, without anyone noticing.

Eddie knew Nathan's routine well. It was stupid, a man of Nathan's standing and reputation, to be so predictable. Eddie was able to keep tabs on him easily. He only ever seemed to be in one of four places, his flat, The Blue Rooms, the Rose and Crown, or Grace Sumner's house. Eddie knew Grace Sumner. She and his mum were friends. She was okay. A bit stuck-up, but his mum seemed to like her. That Jake though, her son, he was another story. Never had to work for anything in his life. Always in designer clothes. Went to fancy private schools. Anything Eddie had ever wanted in life, he'd had to work for. If he wanted designer clothes, he had to steal them. If he wanted money, he had to get out there and earn it – or take it from someone who had.

His mum had never had any money when he was growing up,

not for any luxuries anyway. Why did people like Jake Conlon get to grow up wanting for nothing, while people like Eddie had to struggle for everything? It wasn't fair, and Eddie was fed up of it. He was sick of being treated like a nobody. It was time people realized just who Eddie Redman was, and what he was capable of.

Eddie flicked the end of his cigarette into the gutter as he watched the doors of the Rose and Crown swing open. Nathan Conlon strolled out, full of swagger and confidence, as usual. His girlfriend, Kayleigh, hung off his arm, and Jake followed behind. Eddie wondered how Nathan could have fathered a son like Jake. They looked alike but were as different as two men could be. Eddie knew that Nathan had come from nothing, just like him. It must have disappointed him to have such an entitled, idle ponce like Jake for a son.

Eddie watched as the three of them climbed into the waiting BMW. He felt the familiar tightening in his chest and his stomach lurched. A mixture of anger and anticipation. He knew that sometime very soon, his time would come. But not there, and not then. It was no use going in half-cocked. The timing had to be just right. He was good at being patient. All he had to do was wait. The perfect opportunity would present itself soon enough.

CHAPTER SEVENTY-SEVEN

Grace was listening to the radio in the flat above the pub when Nathan arrived. He must have gone to her house first; it was where she usually was on a Monday. But that night, she'd decided to work instead, though only for a few hours. She was unable to suppress her smile when he walked into the flat above the pub just before ten o'clock, demanding to know why she hadn't been at home. He glared at her and she was certain he was thinking she would pay for that at some point.

'So why weren't you at home?' he asked her again and she couldn't tell if he was grinning or snarling.

'I fancied working.' She shrugged. Fearing he was about to lose his temper at any moment, she poured him a large whisky.

'Here take this,' she said soothingly. 'It'll warm you up.'

He took the glass from her and downed it in one huge gulp. She poured him another as he took a seat on the sofa. She kept filling up his glass every time he took a drink.

'I know what you're playing at, Grace,' he said, and she froze.

'What?' she asked, as innocently as she could muster.

'Trying to get me drunk,' he replied, his words already starting to slur. 'To take advantage of me.' He winked. 'Or trying to butter me up for something.'

He smiled, that menacing smile of his. The one that said he was in the mood for inflicting some pain. But for the time being, he seemed content to drink his whisky, and make her wait. The terror implicit in the anticipation of what was to come, was always part of his game plan.

They sat in silence in what had once been their living room. He must have been suddenly hit with a wave of nostalgia as he said, in all sincerity, 'You've always been the best part of me, Grace.'

She laughed.

'I love you more than anything or anyone in the whole world.'

She almost choked on the glass of water she'd just taken a sip of. 'Are you kidding me?' she said to him, her voice raised but not quite shouting. 'You've never really loved me, Nathan. You don't know what real love is. You wanted to own me. To control me. Because that is all you understand about love. You know nothing of the sacrifice that comes with loving someone. Doing anything in your power to protect them. To want them to be happy even if it costs you your own happiness. That is love.'

He seemed confused. 'Of course, I love you, Grace. I always have, and I always will.'

He genuinely seemed to believe what he was saying. And she realized that, to Nathan, that was love. But he had to understand that it wasn't.

'The way you treat me is nothing to do with love. It certainly doesn't feel like love. In fact, it feels like hatred. Pure hatred. I don't know what I ever did to you to deserve your contempt.'

He shook his head and had the audacity to laugh at her. 'You don't understand.'

'Explain it to me then!' she said. 'Tell me, Nathan. Tell me why!' Suddenly, she needed to know. Because this was it, their last hurrah. If her plan succeeded, she'd never get the chance to ask him again.

'You know why, Grace. You already know, babe,' he slurred.

'Because I'd never been loved by anyone until I met you and I don't know how to deal with that. And then you went and you made me fall in love with you, didn't you? Me! Nathan Conlon, who swore he'd never love anyone ever again. I promised myself I'd never let anyone have that sort of power over me. But you, with your big brown eyes and your soft skin and your …' he trailed off then and his head dropped for a moment. After a few seconds his head snapped back up and he went on. 'And then you went and gave me our son, our precious boy. How dare you do that to me. So, I wanted to hate you, and I wanted you to hate me. It was easier to hate you if I treated you like you were nothing to me. But no matter what I did you always forgave me, you always wanted to see the best in me. And once I realized I couldn't bear it if I lost you, then I had to hold on to you the only way I knew how. To make you too scared to leave. I hated myself for what I'd become, and I took that out on you, because I could pretend it was all your fault. You were like a mirror, showing me who I could be if I could just shake these demons that I carry around with me. But I can never shake them, Grace. They are never satisfied.' He shook his head. 'And so I hated that feeling, that hopefulness you gave me, thinking one day I might just be … better. I hated it. But I couldn't let it go either, and so I could never let you go. I had to make sure that you were too scared to ever leave. I had to make you believe that living with me was the better alternative to what I'd do to you if you ever left. To make you believe that being with me is so much easier than being against me. But all that's about to change, Grace.'

He grinned at her inanely, and she knew that the vast amount of drugs she'd plied him with in his whisky had taken effect. Although his words did make her falter momentarily. Nathan had had such a traumatic and abusive childhood; there was no way that couldn't have affected him. He was never taught what love was, and so how could he have ever known how to love anyone. But then, she thought about Jake and as much as she felt

285

pity for Nathan, maybe still loved him in some twisted way, she loved Jake infinitely more, and she knew he could never be free while his father was alive.

She mentally chastised herself for allowing him to get into her head. To make her feel empathy for him, when he had ruined her life, had almost killed Patrick, and now threatened to ruin their son's life, too. Her resolve returned. She was strong, and capable. She'd gone back and forth so many times about what was about to happen. Everything had been in place for weeks but every time she went to take that final step, she lost her nerve. Because it wasn't just him she would be getting rid of, it was a part of her too. What would her life be without him in it? He seemed to have defined it for so long, she had no idea who she was without him. Then there was her pub. Her sanctuary. Her home. It broke her heart to think about what was about to become of it and it had taken her time to come to terms with what she was about to do.

But she'd visited her parents' grave that morning. She'd told them her plan and had made peace with the fact she was about to destroy their legacy. She knew that if they were still alive, they would understand that it was the only way she could be free. She had lived with a monster for over half of her life, and now she was ready to defeat him for good.

'You're right, Nathan,' she smiled. 'Everything is about to change.'

CHAPTER SEVENTY-EIGHT

Nathan smiled at Grace, his head lolling to one side slightly. She wondered how much of what she was about to say he would to be able to take in. She hoped he would hear every single word.

'After tonight, Nathan, you're never going to hurt me again. This is the end for you. You'll notice by now that you can't move. That's because I've given you some ketamine – well quite a lot actually. Enough to floor a rhino.'

His eyes narrowed as he stared at her and she was grateful he still understood what she was saying.

'What the fuck?' he slurred.

'Very soon, an unfortunate accidental fire is going to break out in here. You, being so wasted, will light a cigarette before falling asleep. That cigarette will then fall onto the pile of newspapers which are conveniently placed next to the sofa. Because of the bottle of whisky you've spilled on the floor, I imagine it will all go up pretty quickly.'

His eyes widened. 'What? Bitch!' he spat. 'You wouldn't dare. They'll know it was you.'

'Oh, I don't think they will. How could they prove anything? My prints will be all over the whisky bottle. All over this place. But of course they would be. This is my pub! And, I won't even

287

be here when the fire starts. Someone else will take care of that for me. He'll be wearing gloves though, he's not stupid. I'll be safely at home when the blaze takes hold of my beloved pub. And just in case there's any suspicion this is an insurance scam, I logged a call with police a few weeks ago to tell them someone had been coming into the flat and helping themselves to the whisky. I also called your probation officer, Rebecca. She seems nice. I told her how concerned I was about your drinking and drug-taking. And everyone's seen you these past few weeks. Almost permanently drunk or off your face on God knows what. Everything will point to you being a sad, alcoholic junkie, who burned himself to death.' She smiled.

'Fucking, fucking bitch.' His face was so red that for a moment she thought he may spontaneously combust and save her a job. He attempted to stand, but despite his efforts he was barely able to move more than an inch. 'You wouldn't,' he said again, as though he was trying to convince them both of that fact.

She laughed. 'Wouldn't I? You have no idea what I'm capable of. Who do you think tipped off the police about your lock-up, Nathan? Who do you think took the money you had squirrelled away in there?'

He looked at her with a mixture of anger and hatred. 'No,' he snapped and closed his eyes as if it might shield him from her words.

'That's not the worst of it though,' she laughed. 'The Carter twins tried to shoot you because they work for me. Stupid little bastards screwed up though, didn't they? So, that's why I decided to take care of you myself.'

He stared at her, his mouth hanging open.

'Yes, Nathan. It was all me. Stupid, little Grace. Are you proud of me? You should be. You taught me well. And while you're burning to death, I want you to remember that this is all your fault. This is payback for all of the horrible things you've done to me. For every time you've humiliated me, hurt me, raped me, threatened my son. I was happy for you to move on, but you would never let me go, would you? And this is the only way I can be free of you. The only way we can all be free of you.'

'All?' he slurred.

As if on cue there was a knock at the door to the flat.

'It's open,' she shouted. She knew who it was. She'd sent him a text twenty minutes ago to say everything was going according to plan.

'Grace,' Ben said as he kissed her cheek.

'Where's the gun?' she asked him anxiously.

'It's wiped clean and I've left it with your Aunt Helen.' He smiled.

'And has everyone gone?'

'Yes, the pub is all locked up. There's no one down there. It's time for you to go. Is everything sorted?'

'Yes. We're all set.'

'Then get going. I'll finish everything off here. I'll wait for an hour, give you time to get home.'

Taking hold of Ben's hand, she told him to be careful.

'You too, babe. And don't worry, everything will be fine.' And then he kissed her full on the lips. 'I'll see you tomorrow.'

Nathan was watching the exchange open-mouthed as Grace picked up her handbag to leave.

'Goodbye, Nathan,' she said to him and walked out of the door without looking back.

'What the fuck is he doing here?' Nathan demanded, although his speech was slow and thick. 'What are you playing at, Grace? Ben? What the fuck is going on?'

CHAPTER SEVENTY-NINE

Nathan could hardly move. He tried to stand up, but he couldn't. His brain was screaming at his legs to stand the fuck up, but they wouldn't co-operate. His head was swimming, his heart pounding. Blood screamed in his ears.

What the fuck had she done? That traitorous, evil fucking bitch. He felt like he was wading through treacle inside his head. The whole world had slowed down, and he felt like he was watching a scene being played out in slow motion. Oh, thank fuck, Ben was there. His Ben. His best mate. But why were he and Grace acting like they were best fucking buddies? In fact, like they were more than that?

'What the fuck is going on?' Nathan demanded, and he could hear that his own speech was slurred.

The words sounded perfect in his head, but when they came out they were slow and heavy. He didn't understand any of it. Now Grace was leaving; she said goodbye and Ben was kissing her, kissing his Grace. He wanted to jump off this sofa and rip Ben's fucking head off. With every fibre of his being he wanted to hurt them both, but he couldn't.

Grace was gone then and Ben, that traitorous bastard, sat on the coffee table just in front of him.

'So you want to know what's going on?' he asked Nathan with a smile on his face 'Well, I'll be happy to tell you.'

He told Nathan all about him and Grace. How they'd been seeing each other behind his back while he was inside. How Ben hoped they'd have a chance to be together once Nathan was out of the picture.

Jesus Christ, they really were going to fucking kill him! He had to get out of there. Nathan was filled with an all-consuming rage. His entire body shook. Even his brain rattled in his head. His body was on fire. He felt like he would quite literally explode if he didn't move soon. He wanted so desperately to smash Ben's face to a pulp. To break every bone in his former best mate's treacherous body; and then do the same to that slut of an ex-wife of his. But no matter how hard he tried, he could not fucking move.

'Do you think you can cross me and get away with it, you fucking bastard?' Nathan growled. 'I will end you and that slut. She'll be sorry she ever met you. Sorry she ever met me.'

Ben started to laugh then and shook his head. 'I think she's already sorry she met you, mate. I was happy to put a bullet in your head, but she wanted to make sure there was no comeback for either of us. I think she probably wanted you to suffer too. She asked me to help her pull this off and I was more than happy to. No one will ever know she was involved.'

Ben was still talking but Nathan was slipping in and out of consciousness, and he only heard some of what was being said. It seemed like he was underwater. It was as though he was swimming through a thick soup. He caught the odd word still, heard *accident* and *fire*, and then he heard nothing except the sound of his own heartbeat.

291

CHAPTER EIGHTY

Lying awake in the dark, Grace listened to the rain. She'd always loved the sound of the rain on the window, though it brought her no comfort tonight. She thought about her life, and she wasn't sure that she recognized the person she'd become. She had always tried to convince herself that despite any damage she might have done, any lives she may have ruined, she was nothing like him. She wasn't a monster.

Or was she?

Did it matter what her intentions were or what drove her to do the things she did? The outcome was still the same. She made choices based on what was best for Jake, always for him, regardless of who else may have been hurt in the process. And wasn't that what Nathan did? Isn't that what he taught her? She knew how to hurt people, even if she didn't intend to. She'd had a good teacher.

She was pulled from her thoughts by a knock at the front door. Although it was the knock she was expecting, she walked down the stairs slowly, holding onto the wooden bannister as she went. The sense of foreboding making her cautious, acutely aware of every movement she made.

She opened the door to a young policeman.

'Grace Sumner?'

'Yes,' she replied, although it was a struggle to force her mouth to form the word.

'I'm sorry, Ms Sumner. There's been an incident.'

She placed her hand to her mouth. 'What? Is it my son? Is he okay?'

'Can I come in?'

Once inside he started talking. Grace stood, her arms wrapped protectively around herself, clasping her upper arms tightly, fingernails digging into her skin. He said there had been a fire at the pub. But even worse they had found a body – someone's charred remains in the flat above. They hadn't been able to identify the poor sod yet, but there was a car parked outside, and they had checked who it was registered to.

'Would Mr Conlon have any reason to be there?'

'There's no reason, no. But I think he has a key. We used to be married and I think he's been staying there sometimes. I noticed some whisky going missing …'

The police officer told her they would be doing all they could to confirm the identity of the victim and would keep her informed.

They say that shock affects everyone differently. Grace dropped to the floor, her legs giving way beneath her as though they no longer took orders from her brain, like a puppet whose strings had been snipped mid-stride. And then she wailed. Deep, body-wrenching sobs that shook the breath from her body.

She stayed up after the young police officer left. There was no getting to sleep for her after that anyway. Her reaction when she heard the news about Nathan had surprised even her. Maybe it was the sheer relief at finally being free of him? At everything going to plan. She had to admit it didn't hurt her case either. She looked like she was suitably grieving for him, and for her pub being burned to a ruin.

She thought about seeing Ben later. Could they could finally be together out in the open? The thought gave her butterflies in her stomach. She would have been lost without him these past years. But could they ever work? She wanted to move on from her past, and Ben was so entwined with it that she wasn't sure she could ever look at him and not think of Nathan, of the terrible thing they had done.

It was after Nathan told Patrick about Tommy's murder that Grace's plan started to take shape. She knew Ben would be able to find out where Nathan was keeping the gun Jake had handled. He was still one of the few people Nathan trusted and Ben had come through for her, as he always did. He told Grace he knew where the gun was and how he could get it when she needed him to. It wasn't too difficult to get Nathan exactly where she wanted him. He'd become quite predictable. Every Monday he'd turn up at her house for some sort of torture. She knew if she wasn't at the house, he'd come looking for her in the pub, which was exactly what he'd done the night before.

She already had the open bottle of Chivas Regal prepared. She made sure that it was only a quarter full, so he'd drink the entire contents quickly. She laced it with enough ketamine to topple a rhino. She hoped that after what happened last time he took it, he'd have a similar reaction, and fortunately for her, he did.

Once she knew it was working, she sent Ben an innocuous text message to signal he could make his way over. He was going to start the fire. She didn't want to be there for that. She couldn't trust herself to go through with burning down her beloved pub. And anyway, to divert any suspicion that it was a possible insurance scam, she needed to be far away from that place. She made sure she made a phone call to Jake from her landline as soon as she got home, to prove she was there when the fire started.

If all went as planned after she left, Ben should have poured another bottle of whisky onto the sofa around Nathan, just to make sure it went up in flames. All that was left to do then was to put the lit cigarette onto the pile of newspapers next to the sofa, and wait for it all to catch fire. Nathan didn't stand a chance; the place would be burned beyond repair.

Grace loved that pub more than anyone would ever know. But lately it had become like a weight around her neck. It was no longer the place her dad raised her, or where she'd raised Jake. The happy memories she had there had been expunged by memories of Nathan. Now that Jake had moved on to university, she no longer felt tied to Liverpool in the same way she always had.

It was time for a new start. A new life. A new Grace? Nathan was gone. She would never have to see his smug face again. Never have to fend off his wandering hands, or feel the sting of a slap across her cheek. In a few weeks, she and Ben would move to her new house in the country. It was a huge, sprawling place, with gardens that went on for ever, and stables, where they planned to keep horses.

Grace pictured the happy times they might have there. Her and Ben having breakfast in the garden. Jake visiting for the weekend and bringing his new uni friends to stay in one of the many spare bedrooms, or throwing huge parties while she and Ben holidayed in the Costa del Sol. Maybe even one day, there would be grandchildren running around the place? Whatever happened, she knew they would be happy.

CHAPTER EIGHTY-ONE

Eddie had watched as Nathan parked his car in the small, private car park behind the Rose and Crown. He'd waited around for a while; he'd had nowhere more important to be. But it was raining, and cold, and after a couple of hours he'd decided he could find something better to do with his time. Nathan usually spent the night with Grace on a Monday and it was looking unlikely that either of them would be leaving soon. Eddie stuffed his hands into his coat pockets, preparing to emerge from the relative cover of the closed shop doorway for the walk to the nearest bus stop. Or if he was lucky, he'd come across a car that was ripe for the taking and drive home instead.

As he stepped out of the shadows, he noticed another car pull into the car park. It was the type of car Eddie always noticed. A sleek black Audi with tinted windows. The pub staff had all left; Eddie had watched them leave. Only Nathan and Grace were in there. So, who was this? He watched as a large man stepped out of the car and let himself into the back door of the pub; the entry that only people who were expected or who had a key to the place could use. Even in the darkness, Eddie recognized the man as Ben McKinley, Nathan's long-time friend and ally.

He waited there in the shadows. A few minutes later he watched as Grace emerged from the same door Ben had just used. She looked around, scanning the streets for any sign of life. As she opened her car door, she glanced around her again, before climbing in and driving off.

Something didn't feel right. The tiny hairs on the back of Eddie's neck stood to attention. He'd developed a sixth sense when it came to trouble. Deciding he didn't want to hang around outside any longer, he jogged over the road to the rear of the pub, sure that something was going on. And whatever it was, he was certain he could use the situation to his advantage. This was the opportunity he'd been waiting for. His chance to impress Nathan Conlon and prove to him that he was the just the type of man he needed by his side.

Nathan had been Eddie's hero since he was a teenager. Growing up on a rough housing estate, he'd been in awe of the men who worked for Mr Conlon, as he was known around those parts. He'd even done a bit of running for some of them. They always seemed to have an abundance of money, women, and fast cars. They reigned in Eddie's neighbourhood, and no one dared to mess with them, because Nathan Conlon wouldn't allow it. He looked after his lads. He made sure they were treated like kings.

Eddie would have done anything to be one of those lads, and it was becoming so close he could almost taste it. He'd been trying to infiltrate Nathan's inner circle for months. He'd even thought his mum's friendship with Grace could be a way in, but his mum had told him that Grace hated Nathan and there was no way she'd help him. Eddie didn't believe that. If it was true, then Grace spent a lot of time with a man she apparently hated, but Eddie kept his own counsel on that. He had learned that his mouth could get him into all kinds of trouble, but his ears never would. He held onto pieces of information like they were poker chips, ready to be used at the most appropriate opportunity.

Eddie made his way through the unlocked door which Ben and Grace had used earlier, and tentatively climbed the stairs. He heard a muffled voice. Pushing open the door to the flat, he walked inside, taking slow, deliberate steps to ensure he didn't alert anyone to his presence. The smell of burning hit him immediately. The rich smoky air filling his nose and lungs, he stifled a cough which threatened to expose him. He took a few steps down the short hallway until he was standing in the living room.

He saw Ben McKinley, or more precisely the back of him. He was standing over Nathan, who was slumped on the sofa, either unconscious or dead. Ben simply stood there, while a fire started to spread around the sofa, the flames dangerously close to Nathan's feet. If he wasn't dead already, he soon would be.

Eddie was adept at familiarizing himself with his surroundings, another thing he'd learned to survive on the estate where he grew up. He'd spotted the golf club leaning against the wall beside him as soon as he entered the room. Without much more thought about it, he picked it up and brought it crashing down over Ben's skull, sending him crumpling to the floor. Ever the opportunist, Eddie checked Ben's coat pocket and relieved him of the keys to his expensive Audi. He checked Nathan for a pulse. He still had one, a strong one that was racing almost as fast as Eddie's.

Despite his strong pulse and the fact that he was still breathing, Nathan was out of it and Eddie's attempts to rouse him were futile. Using every ounce of his strength, Eddie pulled him from the sofa and down the steps into the car park. Unlocking Ben's Audi, he bundled Nathan into the back seat before climbing in the driver's seat and starting the ignition. Despite the situation, Eddie took a moment to appreciate the soft leather seat as he slid into it, and the warmth of the leather steering wheel in his hands. This was the type of car he was born to drive.

Eddie smiled to himself as he drove Nathan home. He'd never been so happy in all his life. Nathan was unconscious but very much alive. And Eddie had just saved his life. Nathan Conlon was going to owe him – big time!

Eddie had a feeling his life was about to get a whole lot better.

CHAPTER EIGHTY-TWO

Nathan woke with a jolt. The smell of smoke and burning paper still in his nostrils. His throat was on fire and his head felt like it had been put through a meat grinder. He blinked as his eyes adjusted to his surroundings.

'Shush, baby. It's okay, you're home.' He heard a voice whisper. Soft hands caressed his face.

'Grace,' he croaked. She'd come back for him! But then the soft hands were gone in an instant, and he realized it was Kayleigh. He was at home, in their bed. 'Sorry, babe. What happened? Last thing I remember I was a goner.'

'Nathan, you scared the fuck out of me. I was just heading to bed when someone started banging on the front door. Some young bloke was standing there, with you practically in his arms. You were out of it.'

Nathan shook his head. He didn't remember any of that.

Noticing the puzzled expression on his face, Kayleigh went on. 'He told me he found you at the Rose and Crown. The place was on fire. You were unconscious, and someone was standing over you. This bloke hit him over the back of the head, and then he carried you out of there and brought you home.'

Nathan rubbed the back of his head absent-mindedly. 'Who was he? This bloke?'

Kayleigh frowned as she tried to recall his name. 'Eddie, I think he said. Eddie Redman. Yes, that was it. Because I thought it was like that actor's name who we saw in that film the other night.'

Nathan knew exactly who Eddie was, but he wondered if Eddie knew he was his father. Whatever Eddie knew, he'd saved Nathan from being burnt alive. Grace and Ben's plan to kill him had spectacularly backfired. He couldn't believe it. It all took a while to get his head around.

So, Ben was left there unconscious. Which meant he was most likely burned to a crisp. Pity, he would have liked to do that treacherous fucker in himself. Grace would have no idea he was alive then. She would assume he'd died in the fire. That murderous fucking bitch. Thinking she could try and kill him and get away with it. How fucking dare she! He couldn't believe the treachery of her. How she portrayed herself as some beacon of propriety. Yet for years, she'd been fucking his best mate behind his back. And if that wasn't bad enough, she'd been conspiring with that fucker all along; to get him sent down; to steal all his fucking money; to fucking kill him. Filled with adrenaline and rage, he jumped out of bed.

'Nathan! Where do you think you're going?' Kayleigh shrieked. 'You need to rest. You almost died.'

'But I didn't, did I? And now I am going to kill that fucking bitch.'

'Who?' Kayleigh shrieked, her eyes wide as she stared at him.

'Grace!' he spat. 'That fucking whore.'

He slammed the door behind him. He was well aware that he'd always been an angry bastard, that he had serious issues when it came to controlling his rage. But the rage he felt right then was indescribable. Every sinew, every nerve ending, every inch of him felt like it was on fire. Like he could quite literally explode. If he could see himself, he was sure he'd look like one

300

of those cartoon characters with steam coming out of their ears. He felt invincible. Fuck, he was invincible!

He jumped into Kayleigh's car, thinking of all the glorious ways he could torture his cheating whore of an ex-wife on the drive to her house. He wouldn't kill her quickly. That would be far too easy. Maybe he would drag it out for days? And to think he'd spent last night declaring how she was the only woman he'd ever loved. To think he was hoping that one day they might be able to put their differences aside and grow old together. And she repaid him by trying to fucking kill him. She would regret the day she ever laid her eyes on him. He would make sure of it.

CHAPTER EIGHTY-THREE

Grace was standing at the kitchen sink chopping some tomatoes for a salad. Ben was supposed to have been there half an hour ago. She'd tried phoning him, but his phone went straight to voicemail, and she was starting to worry. She heard the front door opening and heaved a sigh of relief. He'd arrived at last. She continued preparing lunch.

'You're late,' she shouted.

'Well, I got a bit caught up,' was the reply.

She froze.

That wasn't Ben's voice. It wasn't possible. Every hair on her body stood on end. The blood froze in her veins. She almost choked on her own breath. She dared not turn around, because if she did, her worst fears would be confirmed. But she knew that she must. She couldn't just stand there staring out of the kitchen window forever. She turned and saw him standing in the doorway, with a maniacal grin on his face.

'Expecting someone else, Grace? Oh, that's right. You were expecting Ben. You two were going to run off into the sunset together, weren't you?' He laughed. 'I'm afraid that won't be happening. You see he's burned to a crisp by now. A horrible way to go that, isn't it? To think of the pain he must have felt while the flames burned off his flesh. I'm so glad your little plan didn't go so smoothly.'

She knew this was it for her. There was no escaping him – no reasoning with him. She'd tried to burn him alive after all and even a saint couldn't forgive that. She tried to weigh up her options, but she had none. There was no running. No hiding. She would have to stay and face him, and she knew that only one of them would get out of there alive. She held out very little hope that it would be her.

Nathan moved across the kitchen in two quick strides, grabbing Grace by her hair and pulling her to her knees, making her cry out and drop the knife she was holding.

'You ungrateful, filthy whore,' he snarled and then he spat in her face. 'I'm going to make you pay for what you and that fucker have done. I'm going to make you feel pain like you have never felt in your life. You think you've seen me angry, Grace? You have no fucking idea!'

Dragging her into the living room, he threw her onto the floor. 'Of course you could always try and beg my forgiveness. Maybe I have a heart in here somewhere. Maybe there are ways you could persuade me to go a bit easier on you.' He laughed again.

It was a terrifying sound. She wanted to cry with the pain, and out of sheer terror, but she would not. Nothing would change what that monster was about to do to her, and she wouldn't give him the satisfaction of seeing her cry or beg. Never again.

Nathan took a seat on the armchair and she remained on the floor wondering what he planned on doing next.

'So tell me, Grace,' he started. 'Tell me all about you and Ben. How long have you been fucking him?'

She thought about her answer carefully. This was possibly the last conversation she would ever have in her life, so why shouldn't she tell the truth? Lying would only make Nathan feel better, and why would she want to do that? This was the only thing that was left in her control. The only thing she had left to hurt him with.

And maybe, if she made him angry enough, he would end it quickly.

'It started a long time ago, Nathan. A few months before you went to prison,' she told him honestly.

'What?' he shouted so loud she thought he was going to implode. She could tell that wasn't the answer he'd been expecting. 'While we were married? While we were still together?'

She nodded at him. Jumping up from his seated position, he slapped her across the face with the back of his hand. She tasted blood.

'Did you fuck him in our bed?' he snarled.

'Yes, Nathan. In our bed. On our sofa. On our kitchen table. He was good too, he knew how to really satisfy a woman,' she said defiantly.

'You filthy, fucking whore,' he spat.

She laughed. The sound surprised her, that she could find humour even in such a situation. 'I'm a whore?' She shouted back. 'I'm a whore? You screwed anything that moved, but I'm the whore? That really is something.'

'That was different, Grace. None of those women meant anything to me.'

'And you think that makes it okay, Nathan? You think that means I didn't feel like my heart had been ripped out every time you came home stinking of another woman?'

'But they were nothing to me,' he repeated, as though he was trying to convince himself as well as her. 'Did you love him?'

'Yes,' she whispered.

'More than me?' he demanded, ever the needy little boy.

'Of course not,' she told him truthfully, the words leaving her mouth almost involuntarily. She should have lied. She should have hurt him, told him that she never really loved him at all. But, how could she? Even thinking those words felt alien to her. Because she had loved him, the monster that he was, far too much, and for far too long. She had given him everything she had. Her heart and her soul, but it had never been enough. If she was the best of him then he was the worst of her.

'Do you still love me, Grace?'

When she didn't answer him, he really started. She felt the punches and the kicks raining down on her before she lost consciousness.

CHAPTER EIGHTY-FOUR

Grace woke up and tried to open her eyes. One was swollen closed but the other blinked in the bright light of her living room as she lay on the carpeted floor.

'Thought we'd lost you there for a minute, love,' Nathan said cheerily. He was sitting on the sofa eating a sandwich, as though he was visiting and was waiting for her to wake up from a nap. 'Can't have you missing out on the fun now, can we?'

Every part of her body screamed in pain. She could taste blood. Looking down at her body she could see she was almost naked; most of her clothes had been torn from her body. Who knew what that animal had done to her while she was passed out?

He stood up, wiping the crumbs from his hands. 'Ready for round two?' he smiled.

Please, for God's sake – just kill me, she wanted to beg. But she knew that wouldn't happen for a while. That would be too easy, too merciful for Nathan. Suddenly her mind was filled with thoughts of Jake – her beautiful, sweet boy. What would become of him if Nathan killed her? He would drag him into the gutter too. Maybe he would hurt him? Or God forbid even kill him.

The one thing in Grace's favour was that Nathan underestimated her; he always had, and he always would. She just had to think of something – anything.

Then she remembered what Ben had said about the gun. He'd left it with her Aunt Helen. This was her only chance. Grace jumped up and made a grab for the heavy vase beside her sofa. Just as she reached it, Nathan was on top of her, bringing her crashing to the ground and spilling the contents onto the floor in front of her. She fell so heavily that she bit her lip, tasting yet more blood. She heard Nathan laughing. No doubt he assumed she'd been intending to use the vase as a weapon.

Nathan stood up and loomed over her. He was chuckling.

'Don't cry, Grace. That was a good try. But when will you learn you'll never get rid of me? Why can't you accept that I own you? I control you. You will never escape me.'

Grace rolled onto her back and confronted the monster who had haunted her for most of her life. She smiled at him. Then, with a steady hand, she raised the Glock and pointed it at Nathan's chest. She desperately hoped there were bullets in that gun. Because if there weren't she was done for. Surely karma had to be on her side at least once where Nathan was concerned.

Nathan's face paled instantly as he stared down the barrel. Grace thought about how good it would be to savour the look of terror and confusion on his face. But she couldn't afford that luxury. As soon as he got over the initial shock, the adrenaline would kick in and he'd overpower her.

Squeezing the trigger, she heard the crack of the gunshot and watched Nathan's face as the pain tore through him like wildfire. Blood filled his throat. She could hear the choking noises emanating from his gullet as he dropped to the floor.

She stood over him, holding the smoking gun in her hand.

Grace was covered in blood. She looked around her living room. There was blood on the carpet, on the walls, on the furniture. It looked like a set from a horror film. She shook her head.

She had to think clearly. Using Nathan's motionless hand, she made sure that his and her prints were the only ones on the gun.

Grace's 'Aunt Helen', was in fact an alabaster vase. It was a huge, hideous thing, with the image of an old woman painted on it. But Helen had bought it for Grace as a gift shortly before she died.

She'd once told Ben it reminded her of her aunt and Ben had misunderstood and thought she'd meant the image looked like Helen. They'd laughed so much that ever since they'd referred to the vase as Aunt Helen. She kept it next to the sofa, where she could see it as a reminder of her beloved aunt. Even dead, Ben and Helen were looking out for her.

Picking up the telephone from the nearby table, Grace phoned the police.

'I've just shot my ex-husband,' she said calmly, before dropping the handset as the operator frantically tried to ask her questions and trace the call.

She dropped to her knees beside Nathan and the tears came like an avalanche from her body. Each sob like a convulsion. She cried for Nathan – for everything that bastard had ever done to her, and for the man he once was. And she cried for Ben, her wonderful Ben, who was dead simply because he'd loved her. But mostly, she cried for Jake. Her beautiful, sweet boy, and the possibility that he would never forgive her.

EPILOGUE

Seven Months Later

Grace walked out onto the decking in the garden, wrapping her shawl tighter around herself. She loved the crisp, cold mornings. Nothing but the sound of the crickets, the clucking of her chickens and the occasional disgruntled neigh from one of the horses, desperate to escape the confines of their stable and gallop free in the field instead. She knew how they felt and thought of the years she had been desperate to escape the bars of her prison. Sitting at the small table, she wrapped her hands around the hot mug of tea; the horses could wait a little while longer.

She found this time of the morning always led to some quiet reflection. She thought particularly that morning of how lucky she was to be there. She'd moved to her new house in the quiet village of Harewood shortly after Nathan's death. She wanted to be far away from her past life. Jake was still studying at Leeds University, so it meant she got to be close to him too.

She remembered the shock on the constable's faces when they arrived at her house on that awful day. It must have looked like a scene from a horror movie. Broken furniture. Blood everywhere. They took her clothes as evidence. Grace was sure that it was clear to them from the state she was in that she'd acted in self-defence.

She told the police Nathan had come to her house that afternoon and brought the gun with him, threatening to shoot her with it. She explained how he'd beaten her until she passed out and then, thinking she was still unconscious, he'd gone into the kitchen. She'd regained consciousness by this point and had taken the gun, which he'd carelessly left lying around, and tried to escape. He caught her though and lunged at her. So, she'd shot him – because it was either her or him. They believed her. They had no reason not to. Nathan's reputation as a violent psychopath was well known among the police too, and that only helped her case. This was confirmed when Grace's solicitor told her no charges would be brought against her.

She suffered a fractured eye socket, a broken jaw, two broken teeth and two broken ribs, as well as some internal bleeding. She was in hospital for three weeks.

Jake was at her side permanently for the first few days until she sent him packing back off to uni. She told him she was fine, and she really was. They talked a lot during those days though and it transpired that Grace hadn't protected him quite as well as she'd thought when he was little, and he'd witnessed a lot more than she'd realized. He knew Nathan was a violent bully, but he had genuinely thought, or at least hoped, that prison had changed him. He was a lot more mature than Grace had given him credit for.

The whole thing could be put to bed seeing as the inquest into the fire had finally been concluded and the insurance company had paid out in full. When Ben's post-mortem uncovered he'd been hit over the head, an investigation into his death started. It ended pretty quickly when Grace told the police that Nathan had just discovered she and Ben had recently started a relationship. That, and the fact that Nathan's car was left outside the pub, tied that up nicely. The logical conclusion was that he'd decided to finish Grace off the next day. She never found out who rescued Nathan and killed Ben but she supposed whoever it was didn't want to be implicated in Ben's murder so they kept their mouth shut.

She thought about Ben a lot and wondered whether he would have liked her new place. She felt as responsible for his death as she did Nathan's, but it was a guilt she could live with. She'd done so many things over the years that she wasn't proud of, she'd become adept at convincing herself she had no choice but to do the things she did.

Grace left Michael in charge of her former criminal empire. Now that Nathan was gone, she no longer felt the need to be a part of that world. Selling her share of the restaurants to Steph, Patrick and Sean, she had cut all ties with her former life. Patrick had eventually forgiven her for lying about Tommy's murder, and she made her peace with all of the Carter family. But after everything that had happened, the Carters were a reminder of a life she wanted to leave behind.

Grace had spent half of her adult life in fear, and the other half making decisions for other people. She was tired. At the grand old age of forty, she figured she deserved a rest.

Looking down at her swollen belly, she rubbed her growing bump as a tiny foot lodged itself under her ribcage. Now was the perfect time for a fresh start.

Grace Sumner was truly happy.

Grace Sumner was free at last.

ACKNOWLEDGEMENTS

Firstly, I'd like to thank Kimberley Young for taking a chance on me when I pitched *The Boss* to her at a book signing, and all of the Killer Reads/HarperCollins team who have helped bring this book to life. Special thanks to Emily Ruston, a great editor, for her invaluable advice and her belief in Grace's story. And of course to my wonderful editor, Charlotte Brabbin, for her ongoing advice, encouragement and support.

A big shout-out to the FG massive, the very best of women, whose friendships means more to me than they will ever know. To Mary Torjussen, my mentor and friend, who kept believing in me, even when I doubted myself. And to all my other friends whom I have bored with my journey to publication for the past two years.

Thank you to my family, with special mention to my in-laws for all the times you gave me the space to write. Extra special thanks and love to my wonderful mum and dad for everything they do for me. I appreciate and admire you both more than you will ever know.

A massive thank-you to my fantastic husband for his unwavering love and support. You truly are my rock. And finally, to my three incredible, amazing boys – you inspire me in so many ways, every single day.

KILLER READS

DISCOVER THE BEST
IN CRIME AND THRILLER

Follow us on social media to get to know the team behind the books, enter exclusive giveaways, learn about the latest competitions, hear from our authors, and lots more:

 /KillerReads   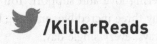 /KillerReads